I0563169

MERCENARIES OF DESTINY
BOOK 2: LEGACY

DANIEL CANO

Mercenaries of Destiny Book 2: Legacy

Copyright © 2025 Daniel Cano

Produced and printed by Stillwater River Publications.
All rights reserved. Written and produced in the
United States of America. This book may not be reproduced
or sold in any form without the expressed, written
permission of the author(s) and publisher.

Visit our website at
www.StillwaterPress.com
for more information.

First Stillwater River Publications Edition

ISBN: 978-1-958217-00-9

1 2 3 4 5 6 7 8 9 10
Written by Daniel Cano.
Cover & interior book design by Matthew St. Jean.
Published by Stillwater River Publications,
Pawtucket, RI, USA.

*The views and opinions expressed
in this book are solely those of the author(s)
and do not necessarily reflect the views
and opinions of the publisher.*

MERCENARIES OF DESTINY
BOOK 2: LEGACY

CHAPTER 1

As the sun shone over the ocean, the gentle waves splashed against the white beaches of the islands in the Southern Kingdom. The larger islands had various sailing ships leaving and entering port, catching the fresh summer breeze in their sails. Perched on lantern posts, seagulls squawked and ruffled their feathers as they prepared to dive into the water and catch their breakfast. Old men in woven straw hats smoked from their wooden pipes as they waited for their fishing rods to bend and alert them of any unlucky fish. Away from the tranquil port, the island town bustled happily as its inhabitants basked underneath the midday sun. They wore breathable, colored clothing and elaborate jewelry such as rings and earrings that reflected the sunlight. Women sat in the shade of their white clay houses as they called out to playing children, telling them to stay safe.

Further away from the town, a dirt path with beach grass along its sides gave way to a beautiful pearly white castle that sat on top of a grassy, yellow hill. Blue flags with a simple yellow sun sewn in the middle flapped in the wind as guards walked along the wall-walks, holding their pikes as they kept a lookout. The peaceful seaside sounds seemed to sing silently over the island as the cloudless sky smiled over it all.

Suddenly, a scream came from inside the castle, alerting the guards. Immediately, a swarm of them huddled together and charged through the halls towards the castle's solar. The metal plates of their armor clattered against each other as their shields bumped into one another, creating a cacophony of banging metal. As they reached the castle's solar, two of them charged forward and busted open the doors.

"Prince Olius! Are you all right?" shouted the leading guard.

All the guards saw was Hector and Darvell arguing with each other. Darvell was wildly gesturing while Hector stared him down with his arms crossed. Darvell was about to finish his sentence before he turned to the other guards and smiled, his sharp teeth making some of them unsettled.

"At ease gentlemen, I'm just settling a dispute with Hector here," Darvell assured as he gestured at Hector.

"Settling a dispute my ass! You burned some of Aurelina's hair off!" Hector accused him as he smacked Darvell's hand away.

The guards looked past the two and saw Aurelina sitting in a chair, combing a burned piece of golden hair. She had a distant look in her eyes as she stared at the floor.

"I worked so hard on fixing my hair. It took me all morning to get it smooth and silky," Aurelina mumbled to herself, rocking back and forth.

"It's not a big deal; we're going to be heading into jungles and deserts anyway. Why the hell do you want to look pretty?" Darvell said as he reached for a cigar.

"Darvell, she can look beautiful if she wants to!" Hector retorted fiercely.

"Oh right, you just want her to look pretty so you can have something to look at," Darvell mocked as he lit the cigar with his fingers.

Hector blushed angrily as the guards groaned, dispersing to get back to their posts. As they left, Olius squeezed between them, apologizing as he made his way to the front. He looked at Aurelina and sighed, walking towards her as he took the charred piece of hair and inspected it. He uttered a few arcane words as he attached the hair to Aurelina's head. She felt her hair reattach to her head as she took the comb and finished straightening it.

"Thank you so much Olius! I thought I was going to have to have my hair like that for most of our trip," Aurelina thanked as she grabbed Olius's hands and shook them.

"It's alright Aurelina, all you needed was a mending spell," Olius explained before he turned to face Darvell and Hector. "Does someone want to tell me what happened here?"

"Well Olius," Darvell said as he glared at Hector, "I didn't burn her hair on purpose, just so you know. I was just arguing with Hector about who took my last piece of jerky. I suspect it was him because he's the only one I let know that I have a secret stash. When I went to get the jerky for the trip, it was gone! When I went to confront Hector, Aurelina tried to calm me down but she got too close to me and her hair burned up."

"He hasn't said sorry about it!" Hector asserted as he glared back at Darvell. "I'm expecting an apology from him."

"All this over a piece of jerky?" Olius groaned as he rubbed his temples. "Darvell, you do know that this castle has boxes full of jerky?"

"It's the action of stealing that I'm angry about," Darvell argued as he turned to Hector. "Did you take my jerky?"

"No, I didn't. You probably ate it and forgot you did," Hector gibed. "Just because you told me you had a spare jerky stash doesn't mean I know where it is."

Darvell scratched his chin and thought about it. He stroked his beard and groaned as he abruptly took a seat in a chair.

"Fine, I believe you. Sorry for burning your hair Aurelina," Darvell apologized glumly.

"It's okay Darvell," Aurelina said as she felt the new strands of hair. "Hector, you apologize as well."

"Why? Wasn't I arguing for you?"

"Yes you were, but I don't want you to be angry with each other. This is going to be a long and dangerous trip and we need to be on good terms with each other," Aurelina explained as she pointed to Darvell. "So go apologize as well."

Hector turned around as Darvell looked back at him. Hector furrowed his eyebrows in anger as Darvell stuck out his tongue. Aurelina sighed as she took Hector by the shoulders and turned him around to face her. She gestured towards Darvell with her hand. Hector shook his head no as he crossed his arms and tried to walk away. Aurelina grabbed him by the shoulder and pecked him the cheek with a quick kiss. He blushed at first before turning towards Darvell, his face souring a bit. He stuck out his hand in front of Darvell with reluctance.

"I'm sorry," Hector mumbled under his breath.

Darvell looked at Hector's hand and narrowed his eyes. He let out a hearty laugh before he stood up from the chair and grabbed Hector, crushing him with a hug as he lifted him from the floor. Olius and Aurelina chuckled as Hector, gasping for air, tried to free himself from Darvell's grasp. As soon as he let go of him, Hector dropped to the floor and took a long breath.

"Well now that we've made amends, I'd like to know when we're leaving," Hector declared as he got up from the floor.

"We'll be leaving today I believe. Regibus just has to get the ship ready for the trip ahead of us," Olius responded as he searched through his bag.

"What are you looking for?" Aurelina asked curiously as she tried to get a better look.

"I made these pamphlets for everyone to read." Olius beamed as he held up a couple of papers.

"Read?" Darvell protested. "Why the hell do we need to read? We're going to be too busy killing stuff!"

"I spent most of my free time making these papers to help us prepare for the challenges ahead. The land we're about to explore isn't like the kingdoms. There are immense levels of magic that have terraformed the land. One moment we could be in a humid jungle and then we could be in a dry and barren desert," Olius explained.

"Well it's just a couple of different regions, what's the worst that could come our way?" Darvell argued.

"Darvell, these biomes are home to monsters we have never faced before. At most, explorers and adventurers have recorded their encounters but after barely escaping alive. This isn't some romp through some civilized kingdoms where the worst we have to worry about is cultists, pirates, or an evil tree," Olius cautioned as he handed everyone a pamphlet. "The least you could do for the group is read the pamphlet."

Darvell held the pamphlet in his hand, almost dropping it after misjudging its weight. He opened the first page and tried to make out the words and pictures written in black ink against the pasty yellow background. There were letters written in ancient languages, words in the margins written in a different colored ink, strange sketches of creatures and scenery with even more notes written next to the images. Darvell's eyes darted left and right, then right to left trying to make sense of any of the text. Words seemed to move on their own, making it impossible to understand anything.

"Uh...Olius?" Darvell meekly said as he tried to fold the pamphlet. "There's something I have to tell you."

"What is it?" Olius asked as he handed Aurelina a pamphlet.

"I don't know how to read that well."

Olius, Hector, and Aurelina stared at Darvell with blank expressions as Darvell nervously smiled. Hector coughed into his hand as Aurelina turned towards Olius, who stared at him. Darvell laughed to himself, causing Olius to rub his temples and groan loudly before taking in a deep breath to calm himself.

"You can't read?" Olius sullenly asked. "You're not joking are you?"

"Hear me out, I can read a small amount of simple text but nothing like this!" Darvell complained as he gestured to the pamphlet. "It's busy being a mercenary so reading never was my top priority to be honest," Darvell apologized as he accidentally tore a piece of the pamphlet, cursing under his breath.

"So you can't read or write?" Aurelina asked.

"I can't read but I can write," Darvell countered before he quickly faced Olius and began to whisper, "I actually can't, is that bad?"

"Yes, that makes it worse..." Olius groaned. "I'm already so busy planning the journey..."

"What's going on Olius?" Jade asked as she walked in. "I ran into a bunch of guards as I came to get all of you."

"It's nothing now," Olius explained as he watched Darvell try to sound out some of the words to Aurelina and Hector. "Actually, could you do something for me? Apparently, Darvell can't read or write and I need him to understand the pamphlet."

"Don't worry Olius, I'll read it to him and teach him to read," Jade interrupted. "I have some more experience with magical creatures so I can make sure he understands it."

"Thanks Jade, I don't want him running blindly into a fight without knowing anything," Olius thanked her as he handed Jade a pamphlet.

"Oh no, I'll read it to him. The real problem is if he'll remember what he heard during the fight." Jade laughed as she walked past Olius. "Anyway, Regibus says the ship is ready to sail and that we can all come to the pier."

"Well let's make our way then," Hector said as he picked up his things.

Everyone made their way out of the solar and went to the port to regroup with everyone else. As they made their way down the castle road, nearby people praised and congratulated them. Darvell eagerly waved back to the islanders as everyone calmly waved instead.

"Don't let the flattery and praise get to your head yet Darvell," Hector warned as they walked down the street.

"There's nothing wrong with being a beacon of hope, Hector. Also, I'm not the type of person to let this kind of stuff get to my head." Darvell concluded with an enthusiastic wave to the people around him.

Hector looked at Aurelina as she gave a quick shrug and a smirk. After walking into town, they stopped at the pier and walked down the dock. Numerous boats were tied to wooden poles as fishermen unloaded crates full of fish, crabs, lobsters, and foreign exports from the other kingdoms. At the end of the dock, Theia and Chantal were standing by the boat as Theia angrily yelled at one of the dockworkers.

"What do you mean we can't stay parked here any longer?" Theia harshly asked as she stepped closer to the dockworker.

"Please miss, the dock is full and we need this spot for the import ship." The dockworker stammered nervously. "Please try to understand me I mean no—"

The man flinched as Theia took another step forward. Darvell jogged up and stood between Theia and the dockworker, extending his wings.

"Theia, leave the poor man alone," Darvell ordered.

Theia looked at Darvell and scoffed before boarding *Poseidon's Glory*. After the dockworker thanked Darvell and promptly left, he turned to Chantal for a response to Theia's sour mood. Chantal just shrugged and shook her head no.

"I'm surprised you don't know. You're always by her side," joked Darvell.

Chantal punched Darvell on the arm extremely hard before crossing her arms.

"Fine, you aren't breathing down her neck all the time then." Darvell groaned as he rubbed his arm. "How about you go comfort her then, and see what's the problem?"

Chantal confirmed the idea with a nod. She walked up the

boarding plank and went to go find Theia. Darvell breathed a sigh of relief and looked towards the ocean. He watched the waves move back and forth as the bright sun shined down on him.

Beautiful view isn't it?

Darvell looked to his left and saw a little version of himself floating right beside him. Unlike Darvell's usual getup, this version of him was dressed in more formal half-plate armor with an amber glow and a glittering orange toga wrapped around everything.

"Scales, I like the new look," complimented Darvell. "Where have you been lately?"

I've mostly been busy with the affairs of other gods and such. I came to say that I'll be busy for a few months trying to settle some disputes. So don't get angry when you contact me and I don't respond, okay?

"What kind of disputes?"

Oh you know, the kind that gods always get into. "He took some followers from me" or "I haven't been worshipped in a few millennia, I want to be worshipped."

"Sheesh," Darvell remarked. "I hope you don't get bored then."

I appreciate it. By the way, you still know how that ring works right?

"Yeah I do, just turn the ring towards your palm and just start killing," Darvell responded as he put out his hand and observed the ring.

Good. I wish you the best on your travels.

With that, Scales disappeared into a smoky *poof!* and Darvell was left alone on the wooden dock. He then heard someone calling his name from the ship.

"Darvell!" Regibus yelled as he waved a new black tricorn hat to get his attention. "Come on, we're heading out soon!"

"I'm on my way!" Darvell yelled back as he began to board the ship.

The people waved goodbye as the group sailed further out to sea. The cheers and acclaim grew faint as the ship sailed out of their view. The calling of seagulls and splashing of waves resounded in the salty air as *Poseidon's Glory* sailed on the bright blue waters.

Although the departure was full of life, traveling on sea proved to be very boring after a few days. Darvell was busy devouring a brand new box of salted jerky. Aurelina and Hector slept on the balcony near the mast, cuddled up and quietly snoring under the sun. Chantal practiced her fighting by softly hitting the sides of the mainmast as if it were a wooden dummy. Theia yawned loudly and lazily, observing the sky above. She pulled out an arrow to shoot at a passing group of birds. She picked one, pulled back on her bow and successfully impaled it in the gut, causing it to fly down towards the sea. As it fell, Theia made a mocking whooshing sound and a small explosion as soon as the bird hit the water. Jade, up above in the crow's nest, polished her rifle and looked down its barrel to spot any imperfections. Regibus whistled a sea shanty as he tuned his guitar, gently plucking the strings to make sure the sounds were crisp and clear. Olius sat impatiently in a wicker chair, reading his book, before he abruptly closed it.

"This is quite depressing, look at us! Here we are lying about with nothing to do."

"The sea isn't as exciting as one would think," Regibus explained with an amused chuckle. He plucked the guitar strings, their sounds melting into each other. "Most of the action happens on land."

"If you're so bored, how about you explain to us what we're

going to be facing once we get to the action?" Theia playfully remarked.

"Not a bad idea! Get everyone rounded up and I'll give a lecture to all of you." Olius beamed as he went inside the ship to gather some materials.

Darvell looked over to Theia and gave her an angry look.

"Oh please," Theia defended. "I heard you can't even read the pamphlet."

Hector took a seat between Aurelina and Darvell as they waited for Olius to give his lecture. Olius nervously flipped through his book while moving his hands, causing a chalkboard to appear behind him. The board startled Olius, causing a couple of pages to fall out of his book. He scrambled to get his papers and mumbled nervously. Darvell picked his ear and burned the wax off by lighting his finger on fire. Chantal looked at Theia, who only gave her a shrug. Olius quickly got up and blushed, turning around to calm himself down. He turned back around and smiled.

"Sorry, I'm kind of nervous," Olius stated with an eager smile. "I've always wanted to be a teacher, you know? Preparing lessons, writing magic curriculums, teaching arcane lore and all that fun stuff."

"That sounds bor—" Darvell grunted as Theia smacked him in the stomach.

"I'm sure you would be a great teacher," Theia reassured. "How about you tell us more about where we're going?"

"Well, we'll be heading to a piece of land that goes by many different names: Valley of Monsters, the Forgotten Garden, the Garden of the Gods and many more. But Valley of the Monsters is the most common of them."

"How about Forgotten Garden?" Hector chided. "Valley of Monsters sounds a bit too scary and ominous."

"Call it whatever you want, what it's known for is the nine different regions as shown on the board," Olius explained as he waved his hand over the board, nine individual rings forming on the blackboard. "The exact size of this area is unknown and how it's able to house so many kinds of biomes is beyond me. All I can say is that over centuries it has been magically terraformed. The first ring should give us no problem since it is only a rather large beach. It was at first a landing site used to initiate explorations into the Valley of Monsters but stopped after the funding ceased. With all the buildings already built, many of the older folk who led the project decided to turn it into a beachside town for them to live in."

"So what, a retirement home for the kickass?" Darvell laughed.

"Well you're not wrong. Most of them stayed on the island to keep themselves busy with adventures. After that, the next ring is a dense jungle filled with dangerous flora and fauna. It's extremely dense from what the book has told me and is filled to the brim with these so-called 'Guardians' who protect the jungle. The third ring transitions into a circular gorge. Nothing else about the gorge itself, no history of geographic importance to the rest of the continent," Olius explained as he looked through his notes.

"Is there a bridge we can cross?" Jade asked as she looked at the chalkboard. "Or are you just going to teleport us across?"

"Well it says here that there is a bridge but I have no idea what state it could be in or how it's designed. I'd rather just use some magic to get us all across instead. However..." Olius said as he slowly looked up at Darvell.

"What?" Darvell asked.

"Please don't do anything to break the bridge. It could be a historical landmark and it would be terrible if you happened to destroy it."

"I'm not going to break the bridge," Darvell sternly defended.

Everyone turned towards Darvell, who furrowed his brows and sighed.

"Well, not on purpose anyway," Darvell grumbled.

"Continue Olius, what's the fourth ring?" Hector asked as he turned back around.

"Ah yes, the fourth ring is actually an intricate circle of caves and caverns. The combinations of turns, dead-ends and pathways almost makes the entire thing a deadly maze. When we get out of there, we are onto the fifth ring: a ginormous area full of mountains and evergreen forests caught in an eternal wintery landscape."

"Sounds like home," Theia remarked as she hugged Chantal.

"Moving on, the sixth ring is actually the reason why there are fourteen seas rather than thirteen. This sea, however, is rather deadly since most of the sea life are giant sea monsters that could topple and destroy ships. I'm still puzzled on how such an area can contain an entire sea but that's for me to figure out later."

"I'm sure it's nothing *Poseidon's Glory* can't handle," Regibus boasted as he patted the ship.

"Once we get past the fourteenth sea, we enter the seventh ring which is an open field of grass and hills. The book records it as being rather peaceful but I suggest caution if we do run into anything. The eighth and ninth rings consist of a giant desert. The only difference between them is that the eighth ring has some semblance of life; the ninth is completely barren and dead. That explains what we're up against, how did I do?"

"Well Hector's scared half to death and Darvell looks pumped and ready to get there. So I say you did a pretty good job of explaining," Aurelina said as she comforted Hector.

"Well this is only the tip of the iceberg. I could go on forever on the variety of magical creatures, monsters and history. But

I'll spare you the details because most of the information is in the pamphlets I gave you all."

"How much longer do we have to stay at sea! I want to start adventuring!" Darvell yelled as he quickly rose from the floor.

"We'll reach land in about a week. The waves are too calm to get any real distance and we've been meagerly sailing with the few gusts of wind that have blown by," Regibus explained as he looked at the sails.

"Ugh! This is taking too long! Can't you magic up some spell to get this ship going, Olius?" Darvell complained.

"Darvell, don't be so inconsiderate. Last time Olius 'magicked up' this ship, he looked half-dead. Just be patient and find something else to do," Theia badgered.

"Fine, I'll find something else to do," Darvell growled.

"How about you learn to read?" Olius suggested.

Darvell gave Olius a blank look as if he didn't comprehend the suggestion. Olius sighed and started to clean the board.

"If you want something to do, Darvell, you could fish with me. Nothing better keeps me occupied at sea than fishing," Regibus said as he got up from the floor.

"Well it's better than nothing." Darvell sighed as he looked towards the water, hoping to see the first sign of land.

CHAPTER 2

The evening sun was beginning to set as the orchestra of purples and oranges blended together, reflecting off the darkening blue waters. The stars in the sky began to twinkle as the sun started to kiss the horizon below. Seagulls let out the occasional cry as they flew overhead, flapping their wings to catch any stray winds. Sitting on some wooden stools, Darvell and Regibus looked over the ship's railing.

"This is boring," Darvell groaned. "We've been here all day and haven't caught a thing and the sun is already falling down."

Darvell and Regibus sat on the side of the boat holding fishing poles, with a bucket of giant worms right between them. Regibus took a drink from his beer and looked at the empty bucket where their fish would have been.

"Okay then, I guess fishing isn't for everyone." Regibus laughed weakly. "How about we have a chat then?"

"What's on your mind?" Darvell asked as he pulled out a cigar.

"I'd like to know how Jade's doing. She hardly speaks to me and when she does, it's a short bombardment of questions to tell her what my deal was with Cutthroat," Regibus explained as he took a sip from his beer.

"Why don't you tell her? We both know that when she finds out she still can't exorcise you unless you and Cutthroat agree to it. I don't see the problem with telling her."

"But if I tell her, she'll find some loophole and get him exorcised and our deal will be broken. I can't have that happen at any cost," Regibus said as he looked towards the water.

"What the hell is so important that you have to keep it from her?" Darvell asked as he felt a tug on the fishing rod.

"I can't just tell you. Jade will just pry it out of you or you'll casually just say it and not know you did."

"I wouldn't dare! I promise I can keep a secret." Darvell grunted as he tried to pull up the fishing pole.

"Uh, are you good?" Regibus asked. "Do you need help pulling that thing up?"

"No, I can do—"

Darvell was pulled forward towards the wall as he started to dangle over the blue sea. He looked back at Regibus and nervously smiled.

"I'll take that help right now actually." Darvell grunted as he gripped the fishing pole.

Regibus grabbed the fishing rod and they pulled on it together. The both of them grunted as they pulled back on the fishing pole. The pole began to bend even further as the two of them took a step back. Suddenly, they fell to the floor as the fish flew up into the air and landed on the deck with a heavy thud. Regibus and Darvell slowly got up and looked at the fish, their eyes wide open. It was slender and had long white whiskers protruding gracefully from its face with scales that sparkled in the sun's rays, alternating between silver and bright gold. The fish was a few inches bigger than Darvell and just as wide as him. It flopped on the deck for a few minutes before it stopped.

"Well I'll be damned! That's some fish!" Regibus exclaimed as he inspected it.

"Ugh, nothing to it." Darvell groaned as he tried to stand up straight.

As the two of them continued to look at the fish, coming up with ways to cook it, Theia walked out of the kitchen to see the fish sprawled across the deck.

"Jeez, this is one huge fish! We're going to be eating well for a while," Theia exclaimed. "Anyway, I came out here to ask for Darvell's assistance for something."

"Can't it wait 'til later? I think I pulled something trying to haul this overgrown fish out of the water," Darvell mumbled as he tried to crack his back.

"No it can't," Theia replied rudely. "We need you in the kitchen right now."

"Ugh, fine."

Theia hurried into the kitchen as Darvell shuffled behind her. As Darvell entered the room, he could see that it was dark, all except for a few lit candles on the table. Darvell slowly reached for his revolver and lifted the window blinds.

"Surprise!"

Darvell abruptly turned around and saw everyone jump out from their hiding places. He quickly put away his revolver before any of them noticed. He saw that the candles were actually placed on top of a cake covered in brass-colored frosting with red sprinkles along the top. There was a slice already cut, which revealed three layers of chocolate with strawberry jam between them. Beside the table, there was a crate of red wine and a bag full of fresh, high quality jerky tied with a brass-colored bow. On top of the cake was a small, plasticine figurine that looked like Darvell with his tail wrapped around his feet.

"Oh wait, hold on a minute," Hector said as he pulled out a match.

Hector walked over and lit the tail's end with the match. Darvell stood there amongst everyone with a blank expression.

They looked at each other as Darvell nervously stood there, not knowing what to do or say.

"What's wrong Darvell?" Olius asked. "It's free food, you should be happy."

"I uh…oh wow. I've never really had anyone do this for me," Darvell stammered as he approached the table.

"Come on Darvell," Jade demurred. "Everyone has at least one birthday celebrated."

"I forgot today was my birthday, how the hell did you guys know this?" Darvell asked.

"While we were at the castle, I happened to come across a few documents relating to the soldiers who served. There was a document about each individual soldier and any family members, and your birthday showed up with the information. I told everyone else and we decided to throw you a party while we were out at sea," Theia explained.

"I even baked the cake," Hector said proudly.

Darvell winced at the idea of Hector cooking the cake. However, everyone but Hector chuckled.

"Don't worry Darvell, I helped and we used regular ingredients," Aurelina assured as she reached for a glass of wine.

"Well in that case…" Darvell cheered as he grabbed the first slice, "let's celebrate!"

Everyone cheered and reached for a piece of the cake and a glass of wine. They laughed and sang songs through the night. As the candles around them began to burn the last of their wicks, they decided to call it a night. As everyone went to sleep, Darvell walked out to the deck and sat down to look at the stars. They twinkled in the night as they danced in the sky, keeping him company as the waves quietly slapped against the boat. He reached for a cigar and touched the tip, setting it ablaze. He breathed in the new cigar's flavored smoke and blew out a ring before shooting a plume of smoke through it. He sat down on the deck against the mainmast of the ship, and began to rest his eyes. After a few minutes, he suddenly heard footsteps approaching him from behind. He opened his eyes and saw Jade take a seat next to him.

"I can't sleep for some reason. I saw that you were up so I decided to give you some company," Jade said as she admired the constellations above them.

"Thanks. It gets awfully lonely around this hour," Darvell said longingly, memories creeping into his mind of days spent in cold stables with Atilla.

"Why are you out here anyway? You're a heavy sleeper, aren't you?"

"I usually am," Darvell replied as he blew out another smoke cloud. "I've been thinking a lot about the party you and the others threw for me."

"What about it? It was just a party." Jade quietly laughed.

"For you maybe, but it was my first one in a long time. I've never celebrated with anyone before. From what I can recall, when I knew it was my birthday I just sat at a bar and just silently drank until morning. The bartenders even gave me a piece of pie on the house because they assumed it was my birthday," Darvell explained as he put out his cigar to smoke later. "Soon after, the date just slipped out of my mind."

"That's no way to live. Even Regibus threw me a party when he was home," Jade said as she moved a bit closer to Darvell.

"Well that's because you had him. I've never traveled in a group until I met all of you. It still feels strange to me, traveling with a bunch of people."

"But you look so happy when you're with us," Jade mentioned.

"I never said I wasn't. Although it's strange for me, I'm still happy being with all of you. It's a good kind of strange." Darvell chuckled.

Jade blushed and looked out at the sea. Darvell yawned as the two sat in silence, looking out at sea watching the waves splash against the ocean.

"Darvell, I have something to tell you that I've been thinking about for a while."

"Yeah, what is it?" Darvell yawned as he smacked his lips.

"I...I just want to say. I just want to say that I—"

Darvell snored quietly as Jade sat against him with a flustered face. She turned around to look at him and saw that he was fast asleep. She sighed and took off her cloak and laid it around Darvell and herself.

"I was right about you. You aren't the guy they said you were when they gave me the contract," Jade whispered as she closed her eyes. "I promise I'll do my best to protect you."

Jade gently kissed Darvell on the cheek and they both went to sleep under the starry night sky. The sound of the waves and the rocking of the ship eased their sleep as the moon looked down at them, shining its dull light on them.

CHAPTER 3

The ship reached land after two weeks as the group cheered at the first sign of land. As the ship docked, Darvell jumped from the deck and landed on the wooden pier. He began to kiss the ground and cry tears of joy. Everyone else got off and walked around the beach.

They looked at the seaport and saw that it wasn't like the busy ones back at the kingdoms. Most of the shops were small and rural with straw roofs and wooden sticks holding up planks to act as the porch's roof. The thing that stuck out the most were the people themselves. They were all significantly old but acted as if they still had their youth. Some of the old men were carrying piles of logs while the women had huge wicker baskets stuffed with fruit and vegetables on their backs. As they walked around the sandy streets, they looked for a place to restock. As they tried to ask the old people, they were only met with shunning and disapproval. Darvell sat down and grunted in annoyance.

"How the hell do you respect elders if they don't give you any respect back?" Darvell complained, speaking louder for the locals to hear.

"Come on Darvell it's not a big deal," Hector said as he was walking away from an old couple. "Let's just keep asking."

"No! I don't want to keep getting shunned by old people!" Darvell roared.

Darvell jumped on a soapbox and started to rant. The old people began to gather towards Darvell as the others decided it would be best to move away from him.

"Hey you geezers! Yeah, all of you! Get the wax out of your ears and listen up! My group and I are on a mission to kick Zlo's ass and get him off his high horse! While you were probably burning your skins under the sun, we went ahead and freed the Four Kingdoms from his rule. If you could ever so kindly tell us where we could get some supplies we'd appreciate it, unless you're too busy cleaning the dirt from your wrinkles!" Darvell yelled.

The old folks looked up at Darvell with furious eyes and seething, toothless mouths. The other old folks looked at the others as they pulled out their old guns and rifles and aimed at him. Darvell opened his eyes wide as he stared down their barrels.

"Well damn," Darvell mumbled.

One of the old folks shuffled to Darvell, leaving cane tracks in the sandy beach. The old man walked up and pointed his finger at him. He then pointed his finger at the ground and Darvell got off the soapbox. He grabbed Darvell's face and studied his features, moving his head side to side. The old man let go and blew on his fingers to cool the small burns. He looked at Darvell and smacked his gums. He began to chuckle quietly and then he burst into laughter and tears of joy as he smacked his knees.

"It really is you!" the old man cheered in his raspy voice.

"What are you talking about old man?" Darvell asked.

"I would recognize that fiery attitude from only one person. Marius, you came back! You haven't aged one bit."

Darvell stood there nervously looking at the happy faces of the old people as they lowered their weapons to cheer. Darvell scratched the back of his head and sighed.

"Well, you're half right." Darvell chuckled uncomfortably.

"So you're telling me that Marius actually did die and sent his son to kill Zlo," the old man said as he sat down in a cool and sunlit room. "Sorry that my men gave you a cold shoulder. We've been waiting here in hope that Marius would come back and lead us to victory again. We all grew old yet the spirit of adventure wouldn't die down," the old man proudly said.

"But who are you guys? I thought this part of the Valley of Monsters was home to adventurers. All of you are just so...old," Theia disappointedly stated.

The old man stood up and went to the back of the room. He stood by a tattered green banner with a black falcon in the middle acting as its insignia. The falcon grasped two crossed swords with its sharp claws. The old man turned around with a triumphant face as he held his hand on his heart and spoke in a proud and booming voice.

"We are the saviors of the people! The men and women who have soared high and fought back the force of evil that is Zlo's tyranny, we are the legendary Falcon Faction!" the old man recited, running out of air near the end. "We were your father's squadron, Darvell. We served with him until that fateful day."

"Not only do we have you Darvell, but now we have your dad's army!" Theia exclaimed.

"Who might you be, young lady?"

"My name is Theia Morwan."

The old man looked at Theia and clapped his hands in joy. Theia narrowed her eyes in concern as the old man finished clapping.

"Then you must want to see your father! He's gone through so much, I'm sure he'd love it if you paid him a visit."

"I don't want to see that son of a bitch at all!"

The room grew silent as everyone stared at Theia. Suddenly there came the creaking of a wooden door opening as everyone directed their attention to a man walking into the room. He had a wooden peg leg and wore shabby clothes that went well with the unkempt beard and face he had. His hair, although he wasn't balding yet, was full of long white strands streaking down to his shoulders. His eyes were sullen and tired with a simple rich dirt brown coloration to them. He walked with an awkward shuffle as the wooden peg leg shifted back and forth.

"Hey Charles, I wanted to give you your hammer back...I didn't know we had guests. Well, my name is Wilhelm Morwan and you already met Charles Ponlate," Wilhelm said, his voice deep and smooth despite his age.

"Wilhelm, right now is not the best time for this," Charles whispered.

"Well why not?"

Theia walked up to Wilhelm and gave him a hard slap across the face. She stormed out the door and walked back onto the boat with a face full of tears. Wilhelm rubbed his face and looked at the ground as if he had a long dead spectre sent back to haunt him. He stood there as Darvell walked up to him and tried to console him by patting his shoulder.

"Was that who I think it was?" Wilhelm asked shakily.

"You bet man," Darvell said as he took a drink of water. "She is really pissed just to let you know."

Wilhelm and Darvell walked outside towards the ship and stopped before getting on to look for Theia. Wilhelm turned towards Darvell and smiled weakly as he put his hand on his shoulder.

"I appreciate that you came with me to talk to my daughter. I don't really think I could do this alone. Having a Letholdus always eases my tension," Wilhelm thanked as he looked towards the ship.

"Well anything for a friend of my dad's. Let's just hope that Theia's in the mood to listen," Darvell said as he stroked his beard.

Wilhelm sighed and walked up the boarding plank. They walked to the door and Wilhelm stood by the door to knock on it. He hesitated for a moment and looked over at Darvell. He gave him a reassuring nod as Wilhelm knocked on the door three times.

"Honey, it's me. Can we talk?" Wilhelm said.

"Go away! I don't want to talk to you or even look at you!" Theia yelled through the door.

Wilhelm sighed and walked towards the dock. Darvell looked over the balcony and yelled for his attention. Wilhelm looked up at Darvell, his face tired but not shaken.

"Is that it? You're going to give up so easily?" Darvell chastised as he grabbed him by the shoulder.

"It's the only thing I'm good at," Wilhelm lamented.

"Why is that?"

"Let's get back to the hut so I can tell you. I don't want to have her hear it."

Darvell and Wilhelm walked towards the far end of the village. Along the sandy shores was a small, worn-down hut. Wilhelm opened the faded white door and walked in. Darvell followed suit and went inside. He looked around and could see the remnants of a long-forgotten past littered inside the hut. He saw faded scrolls spread across tables as dirty stone cups filled the clay wash bin.

Darvell looked to the main wall and saw a small painting of Wilhelm and his dad posing awkwardly for a picture, a slight smile forming on his face. Darvell looked at the picture for a few moments before letting out a warm smile. He walked towards the painting and could see that the ridge below it had little photographs of Wilhelm and Marius laughing and having a good time. Darvell picked up the photo and suspected it was the work of some magic that created it.

He took a seat on a worn-out wicker chair and looked around some more. Hanging on a frame near the back wall was a rifle, much like Jade's, but worn out from either use or poor maintenance. The day was coming to an end and the dusk's bright orange light crept in through the window slits of the walls. The others were scattered across the village, either getting to know the people or running errands.

Wilhelm walked by another chair and took a seat. He handed Darvell a cup of whiskey and took a long sip from his.

"What did my daughter tell you about me?"

"Well, she said that she wanted to join Hector and I on our quest. She was dead set on finding you until we actually met you," Darvell said as he downed the cup in one drink.

"Did something happen to her recently?" Wilhelm asked as he refilled Darvell's cup.

"As a matter of fact, when we were going to leave the castle she was rather angry. I don't know why though."

"The castle? You mean the castle that belongs to the royal family?" Wilhelm asked, his voice getting more concerned.

"Yeah, what about it?"

Wilhelm groaned as he rubbed his face in desperation. Darvell looked at him and continued to drink, albeit a bit slower to not upset the mood.

"She must have read the royal documents. Theia probably got curious and read about my history serving to get a clue on where I was."

"She got more than a clue?" Davell asked as he wiped his mouth.

"You could say she got the answer for my long departure. As I was stationed with your father on the pass between the Western Kingdom and Northern Kingdom, we were attacked by Zlo's army. We all fought bravely and fiercely. Well..."

Darvell looked at Wilhelm and gave him a questioning look. Wilhelm paused for a long time and looked down at the floor.

"Well what?"

"Everyone fought except me. I escaped the battle and fled to the safest part of the country. When I went home to retrieve my stuff, I was grabbed by some passing guards and they dragged me to the king. He asked me why I was away from my post. I tried to lie to him to save my sorry ass but he could see right through me. He took away my ranks and exiled me here. Months passed and small wooden boats began to land upon the shore. I ran up to them and saw that it was the rest of the Falcon legion. They were spared by Zlo and were sent to live out the rest of their lives here. I guess he didn't see them as a threat so he didn't kill them, probably so he wouldn't spark any fires of rebellion in their relatives. None of them spoke to me except Charles. I thought it couldn't get any worse until Theia showed up," Wilhelm lamented as he placed his face in his hands to hide it from Darvell.

"Well I'm sorry, but how were we supposed to know you were a horrible coward? What doesn't add up is why you stayed in the army for so long," Darvell said as he put the whiskey cup down.

"Can you not say coward? Anyway, to answer your question, it was because of your father. He was an inspiration to all of us and especially to me. He gave us what no other leader we had could during such dark times: hope and inspiration. He made me his second in command and told me everything, well, except that he was a dragon. Then the day came when he told me that he wasn't going to make it during our last battle. We had been through thick and thin, the harshest weather and fought the most dangerous soldiers. But when he told me he was going to die that day, I couldn't bear to see him fall. So all I could think of was leaving," Wilhelm said as he held back his tears, remembering the past that pervaded his mind.

"You just left? You could have saved him!"

"You don't think I wanted to! You're not the only one who misses him!" Wilhelm snapped as he slammed his hand on the table. The tears finally revealed themselves as Wilhelm sobbed. "Everyone on this godforsaken beach misses him! He told me it was inevitable and that we wouldn't be able to stop it from happening. We lost our leader and we have no way to avenge him! We're all too old and dull from the lack of fighting. Some of us are missing teeth, have broken bones, poor senses and everything in between!"

Wilhelm clutched his chest and slowly sat back in his chair. Darvell reached over to help him but Wilhelm moved his hand to tell him he was okay.

"Even if some of us didn't have these ills, we have one that has no cure. We're all on the brink of fading away and letting the stories of old tell what we did," Wilhelm mumbled.

Wilhelm and Darvell sat in silence. The orange light from the dusk sun shone its last bit of illumination and made way for the cold blue glow of the moon. Darvell took a long swig of whiskey and sighed. The sound of crickets chirped in the night as the quiet splashing of waves could be heard outside. Darvell put down his cup and stood up and walked to the door. Wilhelm looked at him and sniffled.

"Are you leaving?" Wilhelm asked.

"No," Darvell replied as he looked out the door.

Wilhelm raised a questioning eyebrow.

"I'm not going to stand by and let this happen. I know deep down that Theia still loves you. We've been through some tough situations and she could have just quit. However, she wanted to find you with every inch of her being and that got her through everything. Now that we're here, I don't want that hard work to go to waste. I have a plan to help you get back her respect," Darvell said as he stared at the smiling moon.

"Really!" Wilhelm gasped as he scrambled to his feet, almost tripping as he got up. "How are you going to do that?"

"I'm going to make you look like a hero. I'm going to make it look like she's in danger and then you go and save her. It'll be a surefire plan!" Darvell smiled as he turned to Wilhelm.

Wilhelm looked at Darvell with a concerned look as he scratched his chin.

"That doesn't sound like the best plan. I mean anything could go wrong and I'll lose my daughter," Wilhelm worried as he looked at the floor.

Darvell groaned as he grabbed Wilhelm's shoulders, causing him to jump as Darvell pulled him closer to stare at the moon with him.

"Listen, do you want your daughter back or not?" Darvell asked.

"Of course I do," asserted Wilhelm.

"Then we go with this plan and that's it! I'm not leaving until we get you back with Theia and that's final!"

Wilhelm nodded and Darvell smiled. They exchanged handshakes and Darvell made his way out to prepare for tomorrow. Wilhelm drank his whiskey and walked over to the picture of Marius and him. He picked it up and began to chuckle to himself.

He's just like you, isn't he Marius. I just hope he can make it through this without losing too much.

CHAPTER 4

Darvell strolled up the ship's boarding plank. When he got onto the deck he came face-to-face with Theia, whose face was red from crying. Darvell could see she was holding an empty bottle of whiskey.

"Where were you?" Theia asked bitterly, her words slurring here and there.

"I was...uh...I was taking a stroll and then grabbed a drink," Darvell said as he tried to come up with an excuse.

"For an entire hour! I don't believe you!" Theia accused as she pointed her finger at him menacingly, her stance wobbling as she took a step forward.

"Theia, strolls usually take about thirty minutes and I'm a heavy drinker. Of course I'd be gone for an entire hour," jested Darvell as he crossed his arms.

Theia put her judgmental hand down and began to sniffle. Darvell panicked at the idea of her crying more, knowing that Chantal was probably near.

"I didn't mean anything by it," Darvell pleaded.

"I'm sorry Darvell," Theia mumbled as she threw the bottle to the side. "I've just been having a rough day."

"Well there's no need to cry, how about you tell me about it?" Darvell suggested.

"Sounds good. How about we go inside, it's getting chilly out here."

Theia sat down by the kitchen table as Darvell poured two cups of coffee. Darvell brought the cups over and sat across from Theia. She grabbed a cup and took a few sips before slumping over with a sad expression across her face.

"What's wrong?" Darvell asked.

Theia mumbled something and closed her eyes. Darvell furrowed his brows and shook Theia to get her attention.

"I want to help, but you have to tell me. So, what's wrong?"

"I spent my entire childhood thinking that my dad was some great war hero that I could save," Theia began as she slowly lifted her head. "Then I find out he's nothing more than a fraud and we just so happen to land on the same exact beach he's on. It's a real punch to the gut knowing I had come on this trip just to see the shell of a man. I wasted my time trying to find him."

"Well that's a punch in the gut for me," chided Darvell as he put his coffee down.

"Why?"

"Because you just wanted to go and see your dad! We let you come with us because we thought you were going to be with us the entire trip. So I guess you're going to just leave us on the next ship home, huh?"

"No not at all. I didn't—"

"What about Chantal? Did you stay for her or was it still your selfish nature that made you stay?" Darvell accused.

"Don't bring her into this!" Theia yelled as she jumped from her chair.

"Why not? Is it true?" Darvell instigated as he got up from his chair.

"It can't be any farther from the truth! I love her and I stayed with you guys to be with her and with all of you! You guys are my family and I want to make sure we all see this to the end. I forgot that I was looking for my dad because I had her and the rest of you!" Theia yelled as she scowled at Darvell.

Theia seethed as Darvell looked at her with a judgmental stare. She slowly stopped and realized what she said. Darvell cracked a smile and began to laugh. He slammed his hand on the table and continued to laugh as Theia watched him.

"Looks like you finally came to your senses," Darvell said proudly. "I'm glad that I could help."

Theia sat down and began to murmur. Darvell looked over and groaned as he turned to face Theia.

"What's wrong this time?"

"Every time we have an argument you always end up making me feel better even though you won. Every time I start doubting myself I just have to look at you going blindly, yet bravely, into a fight to get my confidence back," Theia confided.

"Has it ever occurred to you that you aren't so different from your dad, Theia? You must have read when he was kicked out of the army right? When was it?" Darvell asked as he finished his coffee.

"It was when he was with your dad at the Western Kingdom trying to stop Zlo. What does that have to do with anything?"

"Up until that point, he was by my dad's side no matter the problem. Look at you; you were in the Northern Kingdom your whole life until I came around with Hector. You must have seen something in me that Wilhelm saw in my dad to have the spirit to keep fighting on. What if you didn't see me charging into a battle? Would you hesitate to fight?"

"I...I think I would," Theia stammered.

"Exactly. By the way, don't think for a second I just charge into a fight blindly. I'm not just fighting for myself; I'm fighting for all of you. You guys mean the world to me and I don't know what I would do if I lost any of you," Darvell said, a few tears trying to escape with his words.

"Well, most of this is easy for you to say. You already met your father and he wasn't a coward," Theia muttered.

"Well he's dead!" Darvell retorted. "I only got to see him once and it was just for a few minutes. Meanwhile here you are groveling at the idea that your dad is alive and well, missing you with every inch of his being."

Darvell sat down and stared at the ground. Theia looked into the distance and sighed. The moon was still smiling as its bright moonlight put Theia under the spotlight. Darvell got up and began to walk out of the kitchen.

"Where are you going?" Theia asked.

"Somewhere that isn't here, Theia. Before I leave, just know one thing: you may hate him now, but the moment he's gone you'll wish you still had him around," Darvell said as he stopped by the door.

Darvell walked out and left Theia in the cold kitchen, alone with her thoughts. She reached over for a tissue and began to cry quietly among the lifeless wooden boards.

CHAPTER 5

The sun was rising over the watery horizon as the bustle of the beach port came to life. Olius and Darvell were conversing as they walked through the town. Olius walked around the stands, buying ingredients for his potions and spells. Darvell was explaining his plan as Olius winced and sighed at the mention of the worst parts. Olius began to become irritated until he broke and put his staff in front of Darvell, abruptly ending his explanation.

"Listen Darvell, your heart's in the right place but I can't condone this," Olius interrupted as he turned to face him.

"Why not?" Darvell asked as he pushed the staff away from his face.

"For one, you are a monstrous force of fire and flames. Second, you want a frail old man to fight you? What happens if I lose control of you, that being if I can even control you in the first place?" Olius explained.

"I don't see your point."

Olius groaned and drew pictures in the sand. Darvell watched as Olius moved his staff through the sand and created a stick figure.

"Look down here. This little figure represents you here,"

Olius said as he began to draw more symbols in the sand. "These lines I'm drawing around you—"

"They look like stink lines," Darvell said as he pointed to them judgmentally.

"I can assure you they aren't. They represent the raw energy you emit, something that's really hard to control. If it were anyone else, I would be able to control them but with you it's an entirely different thing. What you're asking me to do is like loading a cannon with small iron balls then putting a cover over the opening with a small hole in it, expecting the little balls to fly one by one out of it. It just can't be done."

"Actually, didn't my sister control Darvell?" Aurelina mentioned.

Olius and Darvell looked up to see Aurelina floating above them. She looked at the two and smiled.

"While we were at the base, Lilith took control of Darvell. Hector and I took him down and, well, we blasted Lilith's eyes out."

"Aurelina, you make a good point," Olius pondered. "Could you control Darvell for his plan? I'm sure divine magic would be way easier to use than regular magic."

"Well not really. You see, her scythe is the whole reason she could control him. She made an almost perfect replica of our father's scythe. I could help you make a temporary spell to carry out his plan," Aurelina said as she softly touched the ground.

"Why not a permanent one? We could really use that kind of magic," Olius suggested.

"Temporary is better. Your control over magic is good but not good enough for such a high level spell. Either you learn it on your own or you sell your soul to some otherworldly being so they can give it to you, " Aurelina explained.

"I think I'd rather wait," Olius groaned disappointedly.

"Then come with me because I'm going to need help. Darvell, you can go on with your day," Aurelina said.

"Why can't I help?" Darvell offered.

"I think it would be better if Aurelina and I just work on this. How about you go get Wilhelm ready?" Olius quickly countered.

"Fine," Darvell responded grumpily.

He walked away from them as the two sighed in relief. Darvell headed down the beach and entered Wilhelm's hut. He looked inside and could see him frantically packing up his stuff in a large leather bag. Wilhelm looked up at Darvell and smiled nervously.

"It's not what you think," Wilhelm said as he moved his hands away from the suitcase.

"Sure it isn't. Listen, all you have to do is fire a couple shots into me and you'll look like a hero! How hard can it be?" Darvell sang.

"I'm a fragile old man with a creaky, wooden peg leg who hasn't fired from his rifle in fifteen years and you want me to fight you, a young and spry half-dragon who could easily rip my spine in half?" Wilhelm nervously explained as he paced his room.

"Well if you put it like that, then yeah it's hard," Darvell acknowledged. "But that shouldn't stop you! Just come down by the beach in a few and we'll get this show on the road."

"That is easier said than done," Wilhelm muttered.

"Then do it for Theia," Darvell reminded him. "You miss her don't you?"

Wilhelm nodded and sighed as he unpacked. Darvell patted Wilhelm on his back and made his way down the beach. As he walked along the beach, he was hit in the back of the head by a large rock and knocked to the ground. He spat out the sand and dusted himself off. He looked around to see if anyone was in throwing distance. The only things around him were the bright blue ocean splashing against the hot white sand and rocky plains separating the beach from the deep jungle a few miles away.

He looked down and saw a strange looking amulet at his feet. It had a dark purple glow with an etching of an eye on it. As

Darvell bent down to pick up the amulet, he could hear whispers in the back of his head.

Pick up the amulet. Put on the amulet.

"Well it does look cool. But Olius told me not to take strange and cursed objects of immense power from strangers," Darvell said out loud.

Forget about the prince. Pick up the amulet. Put on the amulet.

"I'm pretty sure this thing is cursed," Darvell noted as he began to walk away from it.

Put the amulet on!

Darvell shook his head and stopped hearing the voices. The appeal of the amulet grew stronger as Darvell reached over and grabbed it. He felt it latch onto his hand and dig into his skin. The amulet dug in deeper and Darvell frantically tried to pry it out of his hand, but to no avail. He then felt his hand move towards his neck as he wrapped the amulet's chain around his neck. The amulet released itself from Darvell's hand and latched onto his chest. He felt the amulet dig deep into him as he felt his energy fade out of him.

CHAPTER 6

"Have any of you seen Darvell? I've been looking for him all day and I can't find him," Jade asked as she walked up to Chantal, Hector, and Regibus, who were sitting down at the kitchen table inside *Poseidon's Glory*.

"Last time I saw him he was with Olius and Aurelina," Hector said as he reached over for his drink.

"I can come with you and help you look for him," Regibus suggested with a smile.

Jade glared at him and made her way out. Regibus's smile faded as Chantal reached over and comforted him with a pat on the back. Jade walked through the moderately busy streets looking around for Olius's bright blue robe or Aurelina's grey wings among the old people. Suddenly, she heard screams coming from the far side of the village. She pulled out her rifle and ran towards the cry for help. She stopped in her tracks to see Darvell burning down a couple of huts as people ran away in terror.

"Darvell! What the hell are you doing?!" Jade yelled.

Darvell turned around and snarled, his razor sharp teeth gleaming in the sun. His eyes were bloodshot and hidden under the shadow his forehead cast. His claws were longer and sharper as his stance was more hunched and animal-like. Jade narrowed her eyes, raised her rifle, and looked down the sights.

"You're not Darvell," Jade whispered.

She fired a bullet into Darvell's chest, aiming to slow down his destructive wrath. Darvell winced at the pain and growled. Jade watched a heavy plume of smoke exit his nostrils as he stared her down. Suddenly, Darvell bit down on his teeth as fire flew out the cracks and crawled upwards across his face. He grabbed his greatsword and charged towards Jade, the fire continuing to fly out of the sides of his mouth.

I did not think this through, Jade thought as a bead of sweat fell off the side of her head.

Darvell charged towards Jade and raised his greatsword in the air, the light of the sun shining off the blade. As he took the swing, she rolled out of the way and reloaded her rifle. Jade fired one more shot, this time into Darvell's back. The bullet flew into the air but fell short of its target as Darvell turned around for the backswing.

Jade closed her eyes as she heard the sound of metal clanging against something. She looked up and saw a small blue barrier humming around her as Darvell continued to slam the greatsword at her. Almost instantly, she saw a knife stab Darvell in the face and explode upon impact. She looked back and saw Olius pointing his staff at the shield and Aurelina dashing towards her. Aurelina slipped through the shield and grabbed Jade, yanking her back to safety.

"What the hell happened? Why is Darvell going crazy?" Jade said as she dusted the sand off her cloak.

"Hell should I know! We just saw smoke coming from the village and we came running," Olius responded as he moved his staff away from the shield, causing it to disappear.

"We didn't take control of Darvell yet, maybe it's something else that's making him go crazy," Aurelina said as she pulled out another knife and tossed it at Darvell to keep him at bay.

As the knife exploded, shrapnel launched itself everywhere over Darvell's body and face. He roared and began to breathe a stream of fire at the trio. Olius raised his staff and the sand in front of them flew into the air to form a wall. The fire dispersed across the wall and flew out from the sides, scorching the sand. Once the fire stopped, the front of the wall was now made of raw, cloudy glass.

"Why the hell were you guys planning to take control of him?" Jade questioned as she peeked over the corner of the blazing sand wall. She took a couple of shots at Darvell's legs to prevent his movement.

"He wanted to get Wilhelm to look like a hero so Theia would forgive him. I was expecting the plan to backfire but not so soon," Olius answered before his eyes began to glow.

Olius tightened the grip on his staff, causing the sand beneath Darvell's feet to grab him and drag him down into the ground. Darvell squirmed and gnashed his teeth as he tried to find a way out. He roared and jerked his head back and forth before giving up. The three walked over and looked over Darvell, who stared at them in anger.

"How the hell are we going to cure him now? We don't even know what it is this time," Aurelina stated as she ruffled her feathers.

"What's going on here?"

They looked back to see Wilhelm dressed in a faded soldier's uniform. It was a dark green cloak that flapped in the wind. On the back was the silhouette of a falcon grasping a rifle and an olive branch in its talons as the wings hugged Wilhelm's shoulders. He wore black leather armor over a white tunic as a single bullet hung from a copper chain. His new peg leg was made of black iron with a studded brass ring attaching it to his leg stump. He held in his hand his rifle, now polished and cleaned.

"Well Darvell has gone crazy and we're trying to cure him," Aurelina explained.

"Well wasn't this the plan? He was supposed to act crazy so we could have Theia forgive me."

"Why would I forgive you?" Theia barked.

Wilhelm and the other turned around to see Theia standing behind them. She looked furious as she walked over to Darvell's head.

"Let me guess, his plan was to make you look like a hero so I would forgive you?" Theia asked.

Wilhelm reluctantly nodded in agreement.

"Do you think I'm dumb?" Theia asked as she turned around. "I'm a grown woman! Why the hell would I fall for this?"

"Okay Theia, that's enough. He wanted to go through this for you," Jade scolded, trying to calm her down.

"You don't get a say in this! You're trying to save this idiot's ass for coming up with this stupid plan," Theia bitterly responded as she pointed her finger at Darvell.

"Don't you dare talk to him like that! At least he's a lot more forgiving than you," Jade retorted.

"Let's not start fighting now you guys, we still have to cure Darvell," Olius said as he walked between the two.

"And you! I can't believe you and Olius went with his crazy plan!"

"Why the hell are you putting the blame on us?!" Aurelina yelled. "We didn't even start the plan!"

"What the hell is going on here? Theia, why the hell are you accusing Aurelina?" Hector asked angrily.

Hector, Chantal, and Regibus ran towards the others. Hector stopped in front of Theia as Regibus and Chantal walked over to examine Darvell, who looked like he was moving a little bit more.

"Your girlfriend and Olius somehow turned Darvell evil and now don't know how to cure him."

"We didn't turn him evil, the spell wasn't close to being ready and we saw smoke coming from the village," Olius explained.

"Then it's not their fault. Theia, why are you being so mean?" Hector instigated.

"I'm not being mean! I'm being reasonable! I'm possibly the only reasonable person in this group!" Theia exploded.

Chantal looked back and glared at Theia. She looked at Chantal and frantically tried to come up with something to say.

"Okay, well Chantal is an exception," Theia stammered. "She hasn't said anything stupid."

"That's because she can't speak," Aurelina rudely reminded her.

"I know she can't speak! Uh! Let's just let this go and—"

A large explosion of sand sent everyone flying in different directions. As the cloud of sand cleared, Darvell could be seen climbing out of the hole and resuming his path of destruction.

"Damn it! I lost my concentration on Darvell from paying attention to Theia's ranting," Olius said as he looked through his book, looking for another spell to use.

"Oh so it's my fault?" Theia shot as she got up from the ground.

"Will you shut up?!" Olius shot back as he reached for his staff. "I never said it was your fault! Let's just focus on Darvell now and—wait."

"What is it, Olius?" Hector said as he helped Aurelina from the ground.

"Where's Wilhelm?" Aurelina worriedly asked as she looked around.

"I see him," Theia quietly said, her voice trembling.

She pointed towards Darvell and they saw that Wilhelm was standing right in front of him, staring right down the eyes of death.

"I know you're in there Darvell," Wilhelm sputtered nervously. "I don't want to do anything drastic."

Darvell growled as he dragged his tail through the sand. Wilhelm quietly gulped as he watched Darvell lick his teeth, his nostrils flaring as small bursts of flame jutted outward. Wilhelm could see Darvell raise his greatsword. Wilhelm raised his rifle, anxiously aiming down the sight. Suddenly, an arrow flew through the air as Theia ran in front of Wilhelm. Darvell roared as the arrow pierced the side of his neck, causing him to drop his greatsword. Darvell then grabbed Theia by the throat as he began to breathe out a burst of fire.

"Let her go!" Wilhelm roared as he aimed his rifle.

Wilhelm fired a shot that pierced Darvell's forearm. He roared in pain as he dropped Theia, her body hitting the sand with a thud. Wilhelm pulled out a short sword and ran towards Darvell. He slashed him across the mouth and chest before he pulled back and thrust it into Darvell's gut. Darvell hissed painfully as blood burst forth, and he smacked Wilhelm into a nearby wall. Wilhelm flew and collided with the wall as a large crack formed behind him. As Darvell staggered for a bit, everyone else tried to reach Theia and bring her to safety. Davell's radiant heat, however, was too much to bear.

Wilhelm dusted himself off, his vision growing blurry as he looked up. As he looked at the blotchy colors that made up Darvell, he could see a purple glow on his body. Wilhelm weakly got up and ran towards Darvell, almost tripping over his iron peg leg, eventually leaping up into the air and landing on Darvell's back. The heat began to singe Wilhelm's body as it burned through his armor. His teeth pressed against each other as the smell of burning flesh entered his nose. He took his shortsword and sliced a bit of flesh off Darvell, opening up his muscle to reveal the purple amulet. Darvell roared as he grabbed Wilhelm by his throat, crushing his windpipe before throwing him to the side. Olius narrowed his gaze and pointed to the now visible amulet.

"It's that purple thing! We have to destroy it!" Olius yelled.

"Easier said than done, Olius. We can't get near him or Theia without melting our faces off," Regibus said as he fired a bullet at Darvell.

"I have an idea," Olius said as he looked at Jade. "But I'm going to need Cutthroat."

"Oh no! We are not calling him out," Jade retaliated.

"Do you want to save Darvell or not?" Hector barked as he fired at Darvell.

Jade scowled and groaned but eventually shook her head in reluctant agreement. Regibus nodded back and closed his eyes. The water around them began to move faster as a stream of it began to slither towards Regibus, wrapping him up like a cocoon. Enveloped in the water, his clothes began to morph back into those of Cutthroat's. Regibus's skin began to dilute and melt away to reveal a familiar skull. As Regibus's eyes melted away, two bluish-green fires burst out of the sockets as they looked around excitedly. Cutthroat began to laugh as the water jumped off him and splashed onto everyone else.

"Well, look, you needed my help after all," Cutthroat said as he looked at Jade.

"We reluctantly needed your help," Jade corrected as she wiped the water from her face. "Olius, just get on with your plan."

Olius opened his book and placed it in the air. The pages started to flutter back and forth as the knob of his staff began to glow blue.

"Bene Aqua!"

The ground near Darvell began to spurt out water as the sand began to solidify. Eventually Darvell was surrounded by water on all sides. He tried to move away from it, but the water seemed to follow him. The water that touched him immediately began to evaporate and cloud up his vision.

"Okay Cutthroat, I've made Darvell's position a source of water. Where he goes, the water will circle around him. It'll give you an advantage over him while you try to break the amulet on his chest. Don't kill him, just break the amulet," Olius explained.

"I wouldn't think of killing the dragon child, he's my ticket to getting back at Ronson," Cutthroat growled as he walked towards Darvell.

Cutthroat pulled out his cutlass and took a step into the water. His body began to absorb the water as a thin layer formed around him. He could feel his bones harden as a sense of strength overcame him. Cutthroat smiled, dashed towards Darvell, and took a swing towards his shoulder. The wounds that Darvell already had on him slowed him down as he blocked the violent swings Cutthroat delivered. Jade bit her nails at every clash of metal, keeping her hand on her rifle.

"Can't you be more careful?!" Jade yelled.

"Let me have this! I lost to him once and I won't lose again!" Cutthroat roared happily as he swung downward.

"What!"

Cutthroat laughed as he pushed Darvell to the ground and placed his foot on his chest. Darvell was being drowned as the water covered his face. Cutthroat chuckled as he pulled out his flintlock pistol. The pistol was made out of black iron with golden waves dancing across its barrel. The plate and all of its components were made of a diamond-like material that glistened under the sun. Before he fired the bullet, Cutthroat narrowed the lights in his eyes as he saw the skull of Ronson inside the amulet.

"Say yer prayers Ronson!" Cutthroat bellowed. "I'm coming for you."

Cutthroat pulled back on the trigger and the bullet pierced the amulet, causing it to shatter and jump out of Darvell. The heat Darvell was emitting slowly died down as he closed his eyes. The water sank into the ground as Darvell breathed in before passing out. Theia got up and looked around the beach worriedly.

"Where...where is he?" Theia weakly mumbled.

Theia then set her gaze on the smoking body a few feet away. She ran towards it and flipped it on its back, staring at the burned body of Wilhelm with a heavy heart. His body was scarred and burned all down the front, some sections charred so far they revealed sections of bones. Despite the gruesome image, Wilhelm had a smile on his face that looked relaxed, almost a state of pure peace. Theia began to quietly sob as the tears fell into the wounds. Aurelina walked over and knelt down, comforting Theia by putting her hand on her shoulder.

"I can bring him back, you know?" Aurelina consoled.

"You would do that?" Theia sobbed. "After I yelled at you?"

"I almost lost my father once, I know how it feels."

Theia reached over and hugged Aurelina, who was caught off guard for a moment, but smiled as she returned the embrace. Theia moved back and watched as Aurelina put her hands over Wilhelm, her eyes glowing a vibrant golden yellow. Her halo slowly formed around her head as lines of light coursed through Wilhelm's body. Skin, tissue, and muscle began to slowly reform until his body was good as new. Theia hugged his body, gripping it tightly as she felt a weak embrace envelop her. Theia burst into tears as she heard his first words after coming to life.

"Your mother said hello."

CHAPTER 7

As Regibus and Hector guided the wagon out of the ship, Theia and Wilhelm walked along the beach. The sun was high in the sky while the waves splashed along the shores. The salty air entered their noses to the sound of tropical trees swaying in the breeze. The air was warm and enjoyable, something that the two hadn't experienced before meeting each other.

"So you and your friends will be leaving soon?" Wilhelm asked.

"I'll come back, I promise," Theia said.

"No, you don't have to promise me anything," Wilhelm interrupted.

"What are you talking about?"

"The Falcon Faction has promised you and your friends that they will help in the war. They were inspired by your group's bravery and thought it was high time that they moved out of their huts and back into the limelight of war. Of course, I'm not part of the Falcon Faction anymore."

"So then what?"

"Well, Charles and a few others have asked me to lead a new faction. I believe it was called the Dragon's Legion." Wilhelm beamed.

"They asked you? I don't mean any offense but why you?"

"We had this rule in the old faction that anyone who could take on a dragon was more than capable of leading. Of course Marius was the leader and no one was willing to take on a dragon just to lead..."

"Until now I suppose?"

"Exactly. They saw that I took on Darvell and I was returned not only to my previous rank, but as I said before, I get the chance to lead everyone into battle. This time, I won't be running away," Wilhelm promised as he tightened his fist.

"Thank you, Dad." Theia smiled.

"Thank you for looking for me. I believe it's time for you and your group to head on out. One question before you leave."

"What's your question?"

"Between you and Darvell, who's the leader?" Wilhem asked.

Theia stood there and pondered. She looked at her father and saw herself in his eyes. She saw his dirt brown eyes and remembered her own. She cracked a smile and gave Wilhelm a hug.

"To be honest, I guess it runs in the family to inspire people," Theia responded.

Wilhelm chuckled and gave Theia a kiss on the forehead as he handed her a wooden box. It was made of a simple tropical wood, held together with a grey bow. She untied the bow and gasped at its contents. A platinum-colored cloak lay neatly folded inside the box. As Theia took it out, she could see that there was an upright falcon stitched into the back of the cloak with black thread. Two golden disks, one with a moon and one with a sun, adorned the neck section of the hood. Alongside the cloak was a platinum-colored eye patch with the symbol of a standing falcon.

"It's something I made while I was on the beach. It was going to be your eighteenth birthday present if we ever crossed paths again." Wilhelm smiled.

"I love it." Theia beamed as she put on her new attire.

They walked back to town and met up with everyone else at the wagon. Darvell was attaching the reins to Attila as the others started packing up the essentials. Darvell's face was tired and almost dead. His eyes were sullen and dark bags could be seen under them. His hair was all over the place, unable to settle in any specific style.

"Darvell, are you okay?" Theia asked as she and Wilhelm walked up behind him.

"Huh? Oh I'm fine. The amulet took a lot out of me and I'm not really up to anything right now. Olius said he would make up some potion or something to wake me up. Coffee hasn't been working lately."

"Well, before you leave Darvell I would like you to know that I don't want you to feel bad about burning me to death," Wilhelm said as he carefully patted Darvell's shoulder.

"I'm really sorry about that. I'm not usually manipulated like that."

"It's quite alright. Just do me a favor and take care of Theia for me as you make your way through the valley."

Darvell yawned and nodded his head weakly with a smile on his face. Wilhelm sighed and gave Theia one final hug. As the others finished up the packing, Darvell wearily made his way up to the coach seat. Before he could sit down, Hector tapped on his shoulder.

"How about you let me drive for now? I think Olius has that potion ready."

"Thanks Hector," Darvell said as he hugged him.

Hector jumped up on the coach as soon as Darvell got off. Attila reared up and began to trot down the road. The old soldiers began to wave goodbye as the wagon trotted out of sight. They slowly made their way down the road towards the jungle. Inside the wagon, Darvell was slumped over a table as the others chatted near the fire pit. Olius walked over and placed a white mug in front of Darvell. He looked up and studied the black and steaming liquid.

"This is just coffee," Darvell remarked disappointedly.

"This is black coffee, Darvell. You kept putting cream and sugar in the other cups. You need this to wake up."

"I thought you were going to make a cool elixir or something," Darvell complained as he watched the bubbles of the black coffee swirl in the cup.

"You're just tired. It would be really unnecessary to make an entire potion with the same qualities of coffee when we have coffee."

Darvell sighed and downed the cup of coffee in one go. When he finished, he looked up at Olius with the same tired eyes. Olius inspected his face and rubbed his chin.

"Did it work?" Olius asked.

"I don't—"

Darvell's head slammed on to the table and he began to snore loudly. Olius groaned and went to his room to make a potion. While Darvell snoozed away, Aurelina made her way to the coach seat and sat up next to Hector.

"So Hector, you seem pretty calm about riding up front."

"Why wouldn't I be? It's not like we'll be driving through cold snow or blazing heat. It's just a little bit of jungle mist and some plants."

"True, but don't forget the ferocious animals and monsters that could be lurking out here. I looked into Olius's pamphlet and I read that some of the monsters here are probably twenty feet tall and are unbelievably ferocious," Aurelina warned.

Hector laughed as he frantically reached for his shotgun. Aurelina laughed and hugged him.

"Don't worry; I'll stay here with you."

"I'd appreciate it," Hector said as he looked at the jungle in the distance, gulping nervously.

The wagon reached the jungle, its trees looming over them like giants as the leaves nearly covered the entire sky above. The hot jungle mist was awfully thick and humid, even without entering the jungle itself. Hector's armor began to grow humid on the inside as they got closer. He started to sweat underneath his armor and slowly faded in and out of fainting. Hector had to stop the wagon before going any further. He fell from the coach seat and began to take off his armor, gasping for air as each piece came off. Regibus jumped out of the wagon and went to see what the problem was. Suddenly the spell of jungle mist came over him and he was hit with an unbearable heat. Regibus felt his skin boil as he fell to the floor. Darvell came out drinking a bottle of green juice to examine the problem. He looked rejuvenated as he threw the bottle to the side.

"What's wrong with these two?" Darvell asked.

"I think it's the jungle heat. I don't think Hector has ever experienced humidity like this in *Woodhurst,* but I have no idea why Regibus is fainting," Aurelina worried as she tried to comfort Hector.

"He's only ever experienced humidity in the ocean," Jade said as she jumped out and walked over to the others. "The way this humidity feels, it's either extreme or magically created."

"Great, we haven't even started the journey and we're already fainting," Aurelina grumbled.

"How come you aren't sweating?" Darvell asked.

"Well I'm an angel, we don't perspire," Aurelina boasted. "How about you, Jade? You look pretty warm under that armor."

"I've trained near geysers and pools of water heated up by magma, I don't think humidity is going to kill me," Jade said as she crossed her arms.

"But I'm not sure that the rest of the group will be able to handle it," Aurelina said.

Aurelina gestured to Theia and Chantal, who upon walking out of the wagon, fainted from the humidity. Olius, on the other hand, walked out without a problem.

"Olius, you're wearing heavy robes. How come you aren't fainting?" Jade asked.

"I never really had a problem with heat and humidity but I had a tailor make me a new set of linen clothing just in case. I also enchanted it to keep me at an optimal temperature so it wouldn't disrupt my spell casting. I'm sure the rest aren't going to make it inside the jungle if they're gasping for air right now."

"We...can still...hear you," Hector wheezed between his gasps of air.

"I'll make something; for now, let's just get them inside," Olius said as he made his way back to the wagon.

Olius poured a few cups of cold water into a cauldron and threw in a few dashes of frozen mint, along with drops of a mysterious blue liquid. He began to mix it up with an iron stick and dipped four colored bandannas into the liquid. He pulled out his book and spoke an incantation.

"Frigius Magicae."

The blue liquid began to glow and emit a cold mist. Olius pulled the bandannas out and walked over to place them on their foreheads. As he finished tying them on, Hector was the first to come back, shaking his head as the feeling of humidity faded away. Soon after, everyone else started to come to. Theia tried to pull off her bandanna, but Olius reached over with his staff and pulled her hand away.

"I suggest you all keep it on. The deeper we go into this

jungle, the more humid it will become," Olius said as he pulled back his staff.

"Well now that we fixed this, what about Attila?" Darvell asked.

Olius looked back and gave Darvell a worried look.

"I don't have any bandannas her size and any other clothes wouldn't work," Olius replied.

"I'm not making her walk in this humidity, she'll die halfway through! I have no idea what's in this jungle either."

"Then what do you suggest we do? Who's going to pull the wagon?"

Darvell rubbed his chin as he thought of a plan, a childish smile curling around his lips.

The wagon gently rolled through the humid and damp jungle as cracks of sunlight peered through the leafy rooftops. Thick, green vines and dried-up leaves covered the jungle floor. The flapping of wings filled the air as exotic birds glided from branch to branch. The large jungle trees loomed over the wagon as water trickled down their bark, dripping onto the colorful flowers that wrapped themselves around the trunks. The cascading of a distant waterfall could be heard as the occasional creaking of the wagon along the jungle path interrupted the hot but still air. Hector wiped his brow as he leaned over the coach seat.

"How are you doing, Darvell?"

Darvell continued to trudge through the jungle floor as he dragged the wagon. He started to exhale and inhale heavily as he made his way through the forest. He looked back and gave Hector a sarcastic grin.

"I think I have an idea of how you guys feel about my plans now," Darvell groaned.

"Well, at least you know now."

Darvell rolled his eyes and continued to walk through the jungle. After a few hours of trudging through humid jungle heat, Hector and Darvell heard a noise beside them. Darvell stopped the wagon and removed the reins from his shoulders. As he pulled out his revolvers, Hector jumped down from the coach seat and pulled out his shotgun. Suddenly, the rustling of a nearby bush caught their attention. Hector nervously aimed his shotgun as Darvell walked towards the bush. The rustling of the bush stopped as a black rooster waddled out towards them. It looked up at Darvell and Hector and just wiggled its head. It then sat down and puffed out its feathers as it let out a single cluck. Darvell put his guns down as Hector breathed a sigh of relief.

"It's just a rooster," Hector said as he put away his shotgun. "He looks friendly enough."

The rooster strutted toward them, clucking quietly as it stopped by Hector's feet and began to peck at his foot. Hector picked it up and showed it to Darvell. The rooster nested in Hector's arms as Darvell scratched its head.

"This little fella is neat." Darvell laughed before looking around the jungle. "Wonder what he's doing here all by himself?"

"Hey, why did we stop?" Theia asked as she jumped from the back of the wagon. "Did Darvell already get tired?"

"No, we found this rooster," Hector explained as Theia approached them. "If this is one of the monsters Olius was talking about then this trip is going to be a breeze."

The earth suddenly began to rumble as everyone tried to keep their balance. The tree branches creaked and shook the leaves above, accompanying the sound of scared birds flying away. The three of them looked around nervously as the others in the wagon climbed out.

"What happened?!" Olius yelled as he quickly looked around. "We felt the earth shake from inside the wagon, did you guys do something?"

"Besides finding Nugget, no not really," Darvell said.

"I don't think we should go any further until we've scouted the area," Jade said as she armed her rifle. "That earthquake could have been the movement of a nearby monster preparing an ambush for us."

"Agreed," Theia said as she moved her eye patch off her magical eye. "We should go in pairs and cover as much ground as possible."

As the others prepared themselves, Chantal looked beyond the jungle trees. She felt a small pang of pain in her head that caused her to rub her temples. She rushed over to Theia and tugged on her arm, urging her to follow her. As the two of them ran into the forest, Olius caught a glimpse of them leaving.

"Well, those two are already gone."

CHAPTER 8

In a distant part of the jungle, Olius and Regibus walked together along the shore of a jungle river. Animals could be seen taking drinks along the river's shore as the colorful fish dashed through the water. Regibus walked through the shallow part of the water as Olius walked beside him on the dirt shore.

"Hopefully whatever caused that earthquake is long gone. We're on a tight schedule here and we shouldn't be splitting the party like this," Olius grumpily stated as he looked around.

"Are we? We already forced Zlo out of the kingdoms and I'm sure he's not going to try and take over again with Darvell around," Regibus replied as he soaked in the cool water. "I think we can breathe easy and relax for a bit."

"Easy for you to say," Olius countered. "You don't really have much at stake back home."

Regibus flicked his finger at Olius and a small stream of water splashed him in the face. Olius spat out the water and looked at Regibus, who gave him a stern look.

"Of course I have stuff to lose if we don't stop Zlo. I won't have a world where I know Jade can be safe. I'll also have Cutthroat constantly taking over my body just to get more treasure."

"What does Cutthroat have to do with any of this?"

Suddenly, a trickle of water started to crawl out of the river.

Regibus held Olius back and pulled out his flintlock. Olius sighed as he walked past Regibus and pointed his staff at the stream of water.

"It's just water Regibus," Olius said.

"I'm far more than just some water, wizard boy."

The water began to take the shape of a small man. The finer details came through, and Regibus and Olius could see that it was only Cutthroat in a boisterous pose. They looked at him with annoyance they kept trudging through the jungle. Cutthroat scoffed and reappeared on Regibus's shoulder.

"You know wizard boy, I could always tell you about our little deal," Cutthroat instigated.

"I don't trust you," Olius replied. "I'd rather hear the truth from Regibus."

"How rude, I am trustworthy. Just ask him." Cutthroat laughed as he pointed to a newly materialized version of himself. "Come on grandson, tell him."

"Cutthroat, could you leave?" Regibus said sternly.

Cutthroat scoffed again and disappeared in a white puff of mist. Olius shook his head and shrugged as he continued to walk. As they walked, Regibus sighed as he stopped Olius.

"Listen, to keep this short, I made a deal with him that he would keep Jade safe. With Zlo running about I can never stay at ease knowing that she could get killed out there. Cutthroat isn't the best option but he was the only one that would get the job done."

"But Regibus, she's not a little girl anymore," Olius explained. "I'm sure she can take care of herself."

Regibus sighed and scratched his chin.

"You're right about one thing, Olius. She isn't a little girl anymore. I'm just sad that I wasn't able to be with her when she needed me."

Olius reached over and awkwardly patted Regibus on the shoulder. Regibus looked over and saw Olius blush.

"Looks like you need one of those cooling bandannas too."

Jade slashed vines with her metallic arm as she walked through the thick underbrush. As she peeled off the vine residue, Aurelina flew slightly above her, watching as she picked branches and leaves out of her hair.

"You know we could've just taken a different path," Aurelina said as she flew closer to her.

"I don't know why you're complaining, you're three feet above everything."

"Well you can't blame me. I was born with wings so I might as well use them."

"Well the least you could do while you're up there is to see if there are any monsters around that could have caused that earthquake," Jade ordered as she continued to survey the area.

Aurelina nodded and flew up into the highest reaches of the treetops. She landed on a thick, protruding branch and looked around. Out in the distance, she could only see thicker bushes and hanging vines; nothing, except the flora around her. She flew back down and shook her head at Jade.

"Nothing around here. I'm pretty sure we're just wasting our time here."

"How do you know that? It's not like you've been here before, have you?"

"I've been here multiple times. It's called the Garden of the Gods for a reason," Aurelina argued. "I've come here to visit the other gods that don't like to hang around the mortal realm. However, I haven't been here in a while so I'm not sure what monsters are actually here. I helped Olius with the pamphlets by giving him any information I could."

"Alright then," Jade said as she looked around.

"How about we change the subject? There was a reason I insisted on going with you. How are things between you and Darvell?"

"What the hell are you talking about?" Jade questioned as she began to walk faster.

"Don't deny it. It's getting pretty obvious," Aurelina stated as she flew in front of Jade. "Well, to me at least."

"I can assure you there isn't anything between us," Jade quickly replied, trying to avoid eye contact.

"No, you're probably right. From the looks of it, it's more of a one-sided relationship," Aurelina jested as she placed her elbows on Jade's head, continuing to fly above her.

Jade pushed Aurelina off her head and looked at her angrily. Aurelina laughed as she pointed to Jade, causing her to suddenly blush.

"Ha! I got you. You do have a thing for him. Now why is the real reason?" Aurelina asked herself.

"You haven't proven anything!" Jade countered, trying her best not to blush. "I don't have feelings for him whatsoever!"

"I doubt that. But my question still stands: what do you see in him? He's not like my sweet Hector; he's caring, sweet, and oh so cute when he's scared. Darvell is, well...he's Darvell," Aurelina faltered as her voice trailed off.

"What are you trying to say?" Jade instigated, visibly getting angry.

"Well, that he's a bit loose in the head. He may be the world's hero but he can be a real loudmouth," Aurelina concluded.

"Well, Hector isn't much to look at either. Not only is he a cannibal but he sucks at being one! Coming back to that thing about him being scared, he's scared often. Sure, he can take on a few people but honestly, he takes down five people while most of us have already fought about twenty." Jade scoffed as she looked around the jungle.

"Are you saying that just because he doesn't have any magic abilities he's useless?" Aurelina gritted through her teeth as her feathers began to ruffle up.

"Exactly! Most of us are going to have to save his sorry ass during this trip. I'm glad you came to realize that," Jade teased as a ruffling sound entered her ears.

Aurelina turned around and flipped her off. Jade pulled out her rifle and pointed it at Aurelina.

"Listen Jade," Aurelina stammered, "a rifle may be a little—"

"I'm not aiming at you. Something is watching us right now," Jade whispered.

Aurelina looked around and could hear a rustling in the thick underbrush. She pulled out her mace and gripped it tight, swinging it by the handle.

"When we finish with this, we're going to finish that conversation," Aurelina ordered.

"Sounds delightful," Jade groaned.

"Hey Hector, how do you think the girls are doing?" Darvell asked as he whacked the bushes with his greatsword. With each whack, the bushes parted in front of him. Hector followed, as he held Nugget in his arms.

"I'm not sure, but I know they're having a swell time like us! Isn't that right Nugget?" Hector asked.

Nugget shook his head in agreement. After a while, they came upon a spot where the underbrush stopped growing as large rocks stood against the giant trees. Darvell sat down and took a breath as Hector put down Nugget and looked around. Suddenly, a very loud whistling could be heard around them. Hector frowned and turned to Darvell to tell him to stop, only to find him playing with Nugget.

"Uh...Darvell, do you hear that whistling sound?" Hector asked.

"Yeah, I thought it was you," Darvell responded.

"Well neither of us are whistling and it's still going, pretty loudly at that."

Darvell put Nugget to the side and pulled out his revolvers. He looked around for the source of the whistling sound but didn't see anyone. The whistling slowly grew more distant until it could barely be heard. Darvell smiled as he sheathed his revolvers.

"I think it's gone now—"

Darvell flew backwards as he crashed into a boulder. He felt the pain travel across his body, instantly knocking him out as he slid off the rock. Hector turned around and stared at the monster that was attacking them. Its shadow covered Hector as he shook in fear.

Theia and Chantal ran across the mossy jungle ground as Chantal led the way. She would occasionally stop running, look around and shake her head as if she didn't find what she was looking for.

"Chantal, we haven't found anything running around like this!" Theia exclaimed. "Whatever caused that earthquake must be long gone by now."

Chantal stopped running and quickly turned towards Theia. She signaled with her hands that she had felt a familiar sensation when she walked out of the wagon. Theia rubbed her chin and thought for a few moments while Chantal, impatiently running in place, urged her to keep following her.

"Look, if you did feel something then it would be best to have everyone with us in case it was a trick. We don't know what this jungle is capable of," Theia said as she pointed back in the direction they came from. "We'll see what it is once we can be sure we can take it on."

Chantal sighed before accepting Theia's wish. The two of them began to walk back, suddenly realizing that the trees they were walking past seemed to look too similar to each other. Theia put her hand in front of Chantal and motioned for her to stay put. She then walked forward for a few minutes until she suddenly saw Chantal in front of her. She quickly rushed to her, longbow in her hand, and startled Chantal.

"It seems that something is messing with us. We haven't moved at all."

Chantal nervously signed concern about what they should do next.

"I'm not sure; neither of us knows what's causing this to happen."

"Then allow me to explain," a voice whispered through the air.

Theia and Chantal turned behind them and saw a tall woman appear from behind a tree. She towered over them even when she knelt down to get closer. Her skin was a beautiful bronze color, almost glistening in the sunlight that fell from above. Her long, blonde hair was covered in patches of moss with flowers woven into her braids. She wore a thin, white toga that flapped gently in the breeze. Her eyes were like molten gold that shined like two suns.

"Hello children, it seems that I have found some of the disturbances in my beautiful jungle."

"Disturbances? You have to believe us we haven't touched anything," Theia pleaded.

"I know dear, you two are quite alright. There are some others who have harmed my jungle and I plan to show them punishment," the woman said as she rose up. "You two are free to leave as long as you do not try to rescue them."

They watched as the woman walked away, slowly dissolving into rose petals that floated away in the wind. Theia quickly turned to Chantal and grabbed her by the shoulders.

"We need to find the others and get out of here."

CHAPTER 9

Nugget ran frantically amidst the fighting as Hector fired a couple of shots into the creature. Darvell slowly got up and dusted off the rubble from his clothing. He shook his head to clear his blurry vision and could finally see what had decided to attack them.

A lanky ogre stood there, staring the three of them down. The putrid and lacerated skin of the ogre was a sickly grey, akin to that of a bloated and rotting corpse. On top of his head was a wide, hole-filled straw hat that shadowed what could possibly be the most disfigured face Darvell, Hector, and Nugget had ever laid eyes on. Its jaw wasn't hinged to its head so it swung back and forth with its movements. The ogre lacked a nose bridge, forcing it to breathe with a disgusting nasally sound, and occasionally spurted out black mucus that trickled down its face. The face was also covered in boils and blisters that poked through the rough, elephant-like skin.

All it wore besides the straw hat was a cloth in a makeshift design of overalls. The material of the ogre's clothing looked like that of a crocodile skin stitched together and poorly dyed blue. With his right hand, he carried a large, brown cloth bag on his back. With his left, he slowly twirled a large machete, blade rusty and aged from use.

"That has to be the ugliest thing I've seen," Darvell groaned as the pain in his body died down.

"Stop talking to yourself and help me!" Hector yelled.

Darvell pulled out his revolvers but then saw Nugget run towards him. He was frantically flapping his wings in fear as he ran behind Darvell. He crouched to the floor and patted Nugget's head.

"Nugget, stay here and try not to get hurt, please?" Darvell pleaded as he moved Nugget beside the rock.

Nugget wiggled his head in nervous confirmation. Darvell ran towards the ogre, unloading a barrage of flaming bullets into its gut. The bullets passed through the ogre, flying out his back. The monster turned away from Hector and looked towards Darvell. Although its mouth didn't move, out came a spine-chilling wail as a deathly grey mist and black phlegm exited its mouth. It took one large and slow step towards Darvell and tried to smash him with its bag. Darvell dove between the ogre's legs and shot it in the back again. That only seemed to bother the monster, causing it to swing the bag again, successfully pinning Darvell beneath it. The monster gave out a confused groan as he saw smoke billow beneath the bag. Suddenly, the bag exploded and Darvell stood up and regained his stance as piles of burning bones fell on top of him.

"Ew! Why were there bones in that bag?!"

The monster roared furiously and hinged its jaw to its skull, leaving a large flap of skin dangling below, and blew into his free hand. To Darvell and Hector's surprise, the whistle sounded distant, almost if it wasn't coming from the monster.

From deep within the jungle, Hector and Darvell could see a black horse ride from out of the trees. It raised its hooves in the air and smashed them into the ground, causing a small tremor around them. On top of the horse was a man dressed in a fine black cloth and wearing a black, large brimmed hat. Hiding his body was a dirty black poncho that gently flapped as the horse rider came closer. No matter what angle Hector or Darvell tried to look at the rider, the hat seemed to obscure the face of the creature. Two black and ravenous dogs rose out of the shadows and stood beside the horse rider. He pulled out a large rifle and pointed it at Hector and Darvell as the dogs began to violently bark louder. As Hector regained his balance and Darvell picked up Nugget to save him, they looked at each other.

"You think we can handle these two?" Hector said as he reloaded his shotgun.

"Of course! Just shoot and stab, how hard can it be?" Darvell joked, breathing in heavily to regain his stamina.

"Right, shoot and stab," Hector worriedly repeated as he raised his shotgun.

Nugget ran in front of Hector and clucked wildly. Suddenly, they watched him grow to the size of a donkey. As he grew, Nugget's body became thinner than before as his neck stretched out and black frills emerged from it. His wings were longer and sharper as they folded onto his body. Nugget's clucking began to sound more raptor-like as he approached Hector. He dove between his legs and propped him on to his back. Hector held on for dear life as Nugget raced towards the fight, screaming wildly and frantically. Darvell quickly picked up his greatsword and went to chase after them only to be stopped by the roaring of the ogre.

"Damn it! I should have at least tried to look at that stupid pamphlet!"

Jade and Aurelina looked around for the source of the rustling as the jungle grew quiet. Suddenly, a horde of little gremlins poured out of the bushes, screaming as they ran towards the two girls. Their feet faced backward and they only wore their long, ragged hair on their bodies as clothing. Their green faces were flat and broad as their ears stuck out backward.

Jade fired a couple of shots at the gremlins' heads, causing their bodies to fall to the floor and release a putrid odor. Aurelina quickly summoned her halo and grabbed it. She shook it around and heard it begin to buzz loudly. She leaped forwards and threw it like a frisbee. The buzzing halo flew downwards and sliced into a line of the gremlins, splitting them into two and fading away in a flash of light. However, the ones that lived continued their pursuit. Aurelina and Jade ran away from them as they weaved through the jungle underbrush.

"Aurelina! Do you have any idea what the hell these things are?" Jade asked as she jumped over a bush.

"Not in the slightest! This is the first time I've seen these little bastards," Aurelina responded as she threw a couple of knives. "Looks like Marimonda's been busy making new monsters."

"You know who's doing this?" Jade asked as she fired some shots behind her.

"Well naturally, Marimonda is the goddess of jungles, the spirit of nature and..." Aurelina said her voice trailing off, reluctant to say anything else.

"What else is she?"

"She's also my aunt, sort of," Aurelina groaned. "My mother, the Oracle, left my father because he believed that evil must persist in the world while she believed good should. She always hated my father and even stood trial against him. She promised my mother that she'd be nice to my siblings and I." Aurelina growled as she threw her halo. It flew through a couple of them, slicing them in half, before it returned to her hand. "But so much for that."

As the gremlins got closer, they became increasingly ferocious, driving Jade against a tree. They slowly walked towards her, licking their lips and making high-pitched squeaks. Aurelina tried to draw their attention away from Jade, but only managed to get some of them chasing her. She hovered in the air as they pathetically tried to jump up to reach her. Jade smacked and kicked the gremlins off her to no avail. She transformed both her feet into iron and impaled them into the tree behind her. She reached the top and perched herself on top of one of the branches. Aurelina flew upwards and perched herself beside Jade.

"Well, no one said this was going to be easy, right?" Aurelina chuckled.

Jade looked at her and shook her head disapprovingly. Aurelina scoffed and looked down to see the little gremlins try to climb up the tree. They hardly reached halfway up the tree before they fell off and shattered their stiff legs. Jade looked closer and could see that their legs didn't bend at all.

"Hey Aurelina, why don't they have knees?" Jade asked as she looked down.

"Oh hey, you're right. I guess Marimonda was running out of ideas and just got sloppy making these things," Aurelina responded as she looked down as well.

"She made all of this?"

"Well not completely. Vita, the god of life, doesn't make any more things, he says he's too old now, so the gods were left to make their own once they asked him how he made everything. She made them to keep people out, or in our case eat them alive. Speaking of which, we can't lead them back to the wagon," Aurelina explained.

"Good point. Let's just lose them in the treetops, we can just head back when they stop following us."

As they tried to jump to the nearest tree branch, they started to smell a foul vapor in the air. Aurelina and Jade started to gag and covered their noses. They looked down to see the gremlins vomiting on the trees, burning the wood as the vomit trickled down the trunk. Aurelina gagged at the sight while Jade gave out a little snort. Aurelina looked back and started to badger her.

"What's so funny?" Aurelina asked.

"Oh nothing, it just reminded me of someone." Jade smirked, Aurelina giving her a mean glare. "We need to get out of here. I have no idea how this could get any—"

"Don't say that! You know bad shit happens when people say that," Aurelina warned as she covered Jade's mouth.

Off in the distance, the two girls heard the crackling of fire. Wisps of fire began to appear in the air as a flaming woman jumped out of thin air. Her long hair was floating in the air and burned a bright orange. She had no visible feet but had long slender arms with patches showing off her ghostly silver bones. She wore a loose white rag that covered her ethereal body.

"Okay, she put effort into this one," Aurelina marveled.

Olius and Regibus continued to walk until they came across Chantal and Theia along the riverbed. They saw the two run out and then run towards them, out of breath and panting heavily.

"Did you guys find anything?" Olius asked before narrowing his eyes. "Why were you guys running so fast?"

"We just made enemies with a vengeful spirit or goddess Olius," Theia said as she breathed in heavily. "We need to find the others and get out of here."

"Damn it," Regibus cursed. "We have to find the others."

"None of you shall take another step."

They turned towards the river and saw that Marimonda was rising out of it. She had a furious look on her face as she stared them down with an icy glare. They tried to reach for their weapons, but their bodies stiffened mid-reach. The sensation of wind began to push their bodies together, as if a strong gale were blowing against them.

"I offer you my mercy and you turn on it!" fumed Marimonda. "Well, you will pay the consequences of betraying my hospitality. I will have the entire jungle and its creatures rip you limb from limb. Starting with this!"

The woman snapped her fingers and cackled. The four of them felt the wind push them to the ground and quickly blow away. The sound of bubbling water filled their ears as they looked up at the river. Rising from the murky water were the scaly heads of crocodiles, quickly moving towards them.

"Crocodiles? You got to try better than that, I've wrestled a gator or two...in my...life," Regibus said, his voice trailing off.

The crocodile heads began to rise out of the water to reveal their dark green humanoid bodies. Their soft, pale green underbellies were wrapped in soaking brown togas. They started to hiss and bellow, slowly opening and quickly snapping their snouts as they raised their swords. Theia pulled out her bow as Regibus quickly changed into Cutthroat. He looked around and saw Marimonda hovering over the water. His eyes widened as he took a step back, the other three watching it with surprise.

"Is that old Mari? Haha! How have you been?" Cutthroat stammered nervously, his skeletal hands shaking quickly.

"Cutthroat? Why are you with these mortals?" Marimonda asked, her brows furrowing with anger.

"Part of the deal I made with the Saint. How have you been?" Cutthroat nervously asked.

Marimonda snorted rudely and she stuck her nose up in the air. Cutthroat tucked in his head, realizing he had asked a sore question. The others sucked their teeth once they realized he had made the situation worse.

"You are a sore sight for my eyes. Just having to hear the dreadful name fills me with the desire to see the one who uttered it hanging from a tree branch," Marimonda threatened with a vicious glare.

"Now don't get any ideas, we can just talk this out," Cutthroat offered, his voice quavering as he spoke.

"Wow, never seen Cutthroat talk like this before," Theia whispered to Chantal.

"That's because she's a goddess. We're all mortal here kids, she could kill us in a heartbeat," Cutthroat whispered as he turned around to face them. Despite being a skeleton and a ghost, he was sweating profusely.

"I intend to," Marimonda creepily intoned as she appeared behind Cutthroat.

Out of pure instinct, Cutthroat punched her in the jaw and sent her flying back into the river. They all stood there with vacant expressions and looked at Cutthroat, who began to sweat even more after realizing what he had done. His jaw hung wide open while the sea green glow in his eyes flickered in and out, as if he were rapidly blinking.

"We are royally screwed," Olius said as he turned to Cutthroat.

"You think?" Cutthroat replied, the fear choking his words.

The crocodile people began hissing and bellowing as everyone pulled out their weapons. They slowly walked backwards as the creatures glared at them.

"Do you think they can run?" Theia asked out loud.

The crocodile people set foot on land and showed off their stubby legs. Their heavy bodies left deep prints in the mud as they waddled towards them.

"Probably not," Olius said. "I say we book it for the hills and find everyone else and get the hell out of here."

"Sounds like a plan," Cutthroat said as he felt his foot hit against a tree. "On the count of three then? One."

The crocodile people raised their sabers and began to waddle faster as more of them waded out of the river.

"Two."

They started to bellow louder until they eventually broke into a sprint, running towards the group.

"Three!"

They ran into the jungle as the crocodile people chased after them. Despite their stubby legs, they managed to keep a steady pace as they trailed behind them. The group weaved through the trees as the crocodile people bumped into each other, snarling and barking as they waved their swords wildly.

"Damn, I thought they would fall over or something," Theia said as she turned around and fired an arrow.

The arrow whizzed through the air and exploded as it struck the leading crocodile. The explosion knocked down some nearby trees and blocked the path. Despite the blockade, some of the monsters managed to slip through and continue the chase. They sheathed their swords, got onto all fours, and broke into a much faster sprint.

"Cutthroat, aren't you some all-powerful ghost pirate? Do something!" Olius yelled as he flung a large bottle of acid behind him, the splash of the acid burning a couple of the crocodile people.

"Let's get one thing straight: I'm not even demigod powerful, let alone all powerful. These things could probably bite my bloody face off if I faced them all," Cutthroat explained as he fired two shots into the crocodile horde.

"Well we'll fight them together!" Theia effused proudly.

Chantal raised her hand victoriously as Olius nodded in confirmation.

"That's nice that all of you think we could take these things on together," Cutthroat deadpanned. "But if they could bite my face off, then they would mutilate all of you. Wizard boy, can't you magic up some kind of escape for us?"

"I might have something, let me check."

Olius almost tripped as he pulled out his book. Once he recovered his balance, Olius frantically flipped through his spell book. As he flipped through the pages, the crocodile people began to gain on them. Cutthroat continued to fire his guns while Theia fired exploding arrows. Olius flipped the pages and yelled in anger. He flipped to a blank page in the book and drew a circle before ripping out the page.

"What are you doing Olius?" Theia asked, running out of breath.

"Sometimes the simple solution is the most effective," Olius quickly responded as he pulled out a silver feather from his robe pocket.

Within the circle he inscribed a few crudely written words as he stopped running. Everyone else looked back and saw him throw the paper on the ground and stab the center of the paper with the bottom end of his staff. A bright blue glow began to emanate around Olius as the others ran back towards him. Once they ran up to him, they could see the crocodile men had already caught up. The ones in the front jumped in the air to dive at them. They closed their eyes and waited for a scaly death. However, they only heard the faint sound of claws tapping on glass. Everyone opened their eyes to see that the crocodile people were held back by a clear blue barrier that Olius had created. Cutthroat fell to the floor and began to laugh. Chantal walked up to the glass and knocked on it. The crocodile man outside hissed and tried to gnaw on the barrier.

"Wizard boy, why didn't you do this sooner?" Cutthroat asked as he lay down on the floor.

"It didn't occur to me earlier. I guess it just popped into my head during the chase," Olius responded as he started to read through his book.

"But these things were created by a god," Cutthroat stated as he stared outside. "If you could create a barrier to hold them back..."

"Let's not think about fighting these things yet. We need to find the others," Theia said as she adjusted her bow's string.

"These things have caught our scent, girl. They will stop at nothing to find and murder us," Cutthroat explained. "I suggest that us three hold off these feral river beasts while the wizard finds the others. Apparently, these things aren't as strong as I thought they would be."

"It does seem like a plan," Olius concurred. "I could find that teleportation spell and rework it. I can have them teleport to us rather than the other way around."

"Then let's get to it! Ready yourselves now ladies; it's time to take on these ugly brutes," Cutthroat said as he pulled out his cutlass.

"Aurelina, this jungle is pissing me off!" Jade yelled as she maneuvered through the tree branches, dodging the skulls of fire being thrown by the spirit chasing them.

"Trust me, I feel the same way. I'm not fond of my aunt for reasons like this," Aurelina responded as she cast beams of light at the ghost.

The ghost dodged the beams of light, howling and moaning loudly as it gained on them. Jade and Aurelina watched as it let out a deafening, ethereal howl as it continued to throw the skulls. The gremlins below continued to chase them, sometimes falling over and getting trampled on by the ones behind them as they snarled and barked.

As they traveled through the trees, Jade extended her hand forward and clenched her fist. Her hand began to morph between different types of metals and gems until it became black like onyx. Jade opened her hand and formed a bullet before loading it into her rifle. She jumped forward and quickly turned around, aiming at the chest of the ghost as she fired. As the bullet pierced the ghost, her deafening wail was cut short as she staggered in the air. Unfortunately, the ghost recovered and continued its pursuit.

"What the hell did you shoot?"

"During my travels and studies, some stones and gems can

harm ghosts and other ethereal beings on a more physical level," Jade explained as she reloaded her rifle. "If I could get a better shot, I could do more damage."

"Then let's do that!" Aurelina cheered.

"What? Hold—"

Before Jade could retaliate, Aurelina grabbed her and flung her high into the air. As her hood came off, Jade tried to get her bearings. Aurelina had thrown her into the air with such force that she barely grazed the leafy treetops above her. She looked down and could see that below her was the ghost, flying towards her with spiteful fire in her eyes. Jade frantically aimed her rifle at the ghost's head. She felt the world around her slow down for a bit as her heavy breath briefly filled her ears. As she pulled back on the trigger, she saw the onyx black bullet fly down the sight of her rifle. The bullet pierced the head and caused the ghost to explode into red goo.

"Ha ha!" Jade exclaimed.

The goo started to fly towards her and she was covered in the ghostly sludge. Jade wiped it from her eyes to see that she was falling back to the gremlin infested ground. Jade tried to reach for a branch to grab onto, but was falling too fast to react. She braced for impact, clutching her rifle. Suddenly, Jade felt her entire body stop immediately but felt no solid earth or the slashing of little gremlins on her. She opened her eyes and saw Aurelina holding her by the scruff of her cloak.

"Good work Jade, that's one less thing we have to worry about," Aurelina congratulated, grunting as she tried to hold up Jade.

"What about the gremlins? We said we can't lead them back to the wagon."

"If the two of us try to take them head-on we'll be overwhelmed. We can just have Darvell or Olius burn them all."

"Fair enough. By the way, could you put me down?" Jade asked. "You don't have to carry me."

"Good, you were starting to hurt my arms." Aurelina groaned as she flew towards a nearby branch.

Darvell fought the ogre as they exchanged wounding blows at each other. Although the monster's swings were slow, his long arms covered a large area as he did his best to duck under each swing. Darvell managed to land some swings and deliver some damage, but the monster's wounds slowly closed up as they continued to fight. Darvell breathed heavily, sweat dripping off his forehead as he looked at the monster, trying to find any exploitable weakness.

Meanwhile, Hector and Nugget dashed across the field as they fended off the demonic horse rider. The man raised his hand and pointed a bony finger at Hector. At the tip, a black orb of light began to form as a loud humming sound entered Hector's ears. Instinctively, he put up his shield and braced for the blast. The magic ricocheted against the shield as the monster snarled, his ghostly growl crawling into Hector's ears.

The sound of barking alerted Hector as he looked down to see the two dogs running up against him. Up close, their snouts were boney and their eyes burned like dull coals. They drooled a slimy grey spit that emitted an awful smelling vapor. Hector reached for his shotgun as the horse rider continued to fire black beams at him. He fired one shell into the dog to his left and then another into the one on his right. The bullets penetrated right through the skulls of the dogs and forced them to stop in their tracks. The dogs howled as they stopped running, slumping over and turning into fine black dust. The horse began to neigh, exhaling a thick grey vapor that trailed behind it like a steam train. The gas began to crawl into Hector and Nugget's noses, forcing them to cough horribly.

Nugget dashed away from the horse as Hector reloaded and

fired twice at the rider. The bullets only managed to tip off the hat of the monster, revealing a disfigured and bone chilling face. Although not completely bone, there was hardly any skin. A greasy and poorly maintained mustache and eyebrows visibly contrasted the rotting red flesh of the man as his decayed, putrid, hole-filled teeth were shown with his permanent hellish smile. The horse rider pulled down the hat and guided the charging horse towards Hector and Nugget. The two riders dashed past Darvell and the ogre as they continued to throw swings at each other.

"I had just about enough of you!" Darvell barked through his teeth, fire flaring out of his nose.

Darvell breathed in deeply as the monster raised its machete. A small ball of brass-colored light formed inside Darvell's mouth and he breathed outward, a blazing wall of fire consuming the creature. It screamed in agony as the fire enveloped it and tried to back away from Darvell. When the last burst of fire stopped, Darvell could see that his fire only scorched the monster. Most of its clothing was still on him, despite being slightly on fire. The only significant difference the monster showed was that its grey and moldy skin looked crunchy and burnt. Darvell rolled out of the way as the monster smacked his machete into the ground. He continued to breathe fire, hoping that enough of it would finish the monster off. The constant barrage of flames only infuriated the monster further as it tried to cleave Darvell in half.

As the ogre swung downward, Darvell swiftly moved his greatsword to block the swipe. The force of the monster's attack knocked Darvell's greatsword out of his hand and impaled it into the ground. The machete met with Darvell's flesh, digging deep into his shoulder. A bright flare of brass light burst in Darvell's eyes as he extended his wings, roaring so loudly that the ogre's ears began to bleed. Darvell yanked the machete out his shoulder and punched the ogre in the stomach. The force of the punch pushed it back, knocking it to its knees. Darvell felt thick sweat pour into his beard as a heavy pain in his muscles began to pulse harder.

"How are you holding up Hector?" Darvell yelled as he watched the ogre slowly get back up.

"We're doing just great!" Hector yelled back.

The horse rider let out a deathly moan as the horse coughed out more gray smoke. Hector held his breath as Nugget did the same. As they approached, Hector jumped off Nugget and onto the horse, knocking the rider off his mount. Hector took his shotgun and blasted the horse in the back of the head. The beast exploded into a cloud of black smoke that dissipated in the wind. Hector braced for impact with the ground, rolling for a few seconds. He slowly got up, shaking the grass and dirt from his armor, and walked to the rider. He pulled out his spear and impaled the horseman in the chest with one quick downward thrust, twisting it deeper until he reached the ground. It let out a pained groan, the red flesh melting away as the earth absorbed the corpse of the monster. Hector dropped to his knees and breathed heavily, whooping weakly as he smiled.

The ogre turned around to see his fallen ally and groaned furiously. He smacked Darvell to the side and charged towards Hector, raising his machete in the air. Hector put up his shield, feeling the brunt force of the ogre knock him to the ground. The ogre swung left and right, each swing pushing back against the shield with such incredible force that Hector began to feel his bones crack under the pressure. Suddenly, he felt the monster pick him up by the shield and dangle him in the air before he was grabbed by the ogre's other hand. The ogre began to crush Hector, grunting as it shook him.

"Darvell!" Hector screamed between his gasps for air. "Help!"

Darvell turned towards the ogre and growled, his sharp teeth pressing down on each other as he clutched his greatsword. Moving through the pain, Darvell slowly made his way over to the ogre. Hector felt his bones crack under the pressure and was beginning to faint. Before completely blacking out, Hector could suddenly breathe again and felt the grip of the ogre loosening. He saw Darvell's greatsword pop out of the ogre's chest as he fell to the ground.

Behind the ogre, Darvell tensed his body as he lifted his greatsword, still impaled in the ogre's chest, as steaming black blood poured out of the wound. He flung the ogre behind him as he turned around, a heavy grunt escaping his mouth as he threw the monster. The ogre landed on the ground with a thud, shaking the earth below them as Darvell's wings and muscles twitched. Darvell slowly cracked his fingers as he watched the ogre rise from the ground once more, cracking its neck in a mocking fashion. Darvell tasted the blood in his mouth as he stood up straight and glared at the ogre, his pained smile enraging the monster.

The ogre charged as Darvell narrowed his gaze, taking in heavy and slow breaths. The air around him began to thin as the familiar sensation of heat formed in his mouth, black smoke billowing out as the fire in him burned harder. Once the ogre was right in front of him, Darvell roared one last time as a jet of hot fire spewed forth. The stream pierced through the ogre's chest, exiting out the other side. Darvell moved the stream down the monster and slowly began to cut it in half. Once he stopped, the two pieces fell apart and hit the ground before they turned to black smoke. Darvell laughed quietly as he put his greatsword back into its sheath. He could feel a blazing pain in his body with every movement. He turned around and extended his hand to help Hector up.

"This jungle ain't so tough Hector!" Darvell exclaimed with pride, wincing as he pulled Hector up from the ground.

"You got that right," Hector affirmed. "But let's try and get out of here soon, there could be more monsters like these."

"Well, mount up on Nugget and let's go find the others."

CHAPTER 10

As the shield opened up, Cutthroat jumped out and began shooting wildly into the crowd of crocodile men. As he pulled the trigger on his flintlock, he laughed like a madman. Chantal and Theia ran out to help fight off the creatures. Chantal punched and kicked as Theia pulled back on her bow and sent a volley of arrows through the air. As they fought the creatures, a heavy rumbling could be felt through the jungle. The scaly beasts stopped fighting and began to flee from the fight, headed back in the direction they came from. Cutthroat chased after them, wildly shooting his gun and insulting them as they fled his sight.

"Where ya going you yellow-bellied lizards! Come back and fight!" Cutthroat insulted as he fired a few more bullets into the air.

"Cutthroat, something scared them off. Something that's probably bigger and scarier," Theia worried as she looked around.

"There's nothing to fear, archer. Marimonda's magic is weak right now. We can rest easy knowing that...oh."

Cutthroat stopped midsentence and looked above Theia and Chantal. A large shadow began to loom over everyone as the girls turned around to see what it was. As they slowly turned around, they could see what had taken an interest in them. A gigantic snake, larger than any of the imperial ships they faced out at sea, slithered slowly towards them. As it slithered, the snake brushed up against the trees, uprooting them from the earth. It had four large white horns framing its head, two on its nose and two under its bottom lip. Its eyes were glossy and white as it glared at them. It looked down and began to hiss, flicking its forked tongue in and out. Its hiss was deep and caused the leaves and branches to shake, creating a disorganized symphony which sounded like the humming of beetles.

"Chantal, you have a snake spirit, right?" Theia quietly asked as she reached for an arrow. "See if you can try and calm it down."

Chantal signed quickly before she put up her fists and readied herself with a stance.

"Okay, so you can't talk to it," Theia announced, huffing worriedly. "I guess we're going to have to fight it."

"Aye lass," Cutthroat laughed as he walked closer to the snake. "This snake is probably just as weak as—"

The snake darted its tail at Cutthroat and flung him in the air and ate him. The snake swallowed and shook its body, causing the scales to emit a rattling sound. It began to flick its tongue out more as it reacted to the salty taste Cutthroat left in its mouth. Theia and Chantal looked up in horror and disgust as the snake looked back down at them, letting out a deep bellow as it began to slither towards them.

"Olius! How much longer on that spell?" Theia yelled as she aimed her arrow.

"I still need a few minutes," Olius said as he peered out of the shield. "Why do you—is that a giant snake!"

The snake screeched and darted toward Olius, its mouth open with its fangs pointed forward. Olius went back into the shield, causing the snake to collide with the barrier at full force. The snake lashed out in anger and smacked its body against the shield. Olius looked up at the creature and frantically looked through his book.

"Help me!" Olius yelled, his voice muffled from the barrier.

Theia pulled back an arrow and fired it at the snake's giant white eye. The arrow found its mark and exploded upon contact. The snake stood upright and roared loudly in pain, showing its large white fangs that dripped slick green poison. It turned its attention towards Theia and Chantal and started to slither towards them. Chantal cracked her knuckles as they became imbued with vibrant green and orange light. She dashed towards the snake and leaped into the air. She landed on the snake's underbelly and started to climb towards the head. When she was about halfway up, she flung herself up toward the head and landed on the middle of the snake. Theia continued to fire arrows at the snake to draw its attention away from Chantal. The snake's tail darted rapidly at Theia to impale her. She rolled out of the way, scoffed, and pulled out a purple arrow. She pulled back on the bow and watched it lodge itself in the tail. The arrow began to melt into the tail, excreting a purple liquid that solidified around it. The snake struggled to keep its tail in the air and it fell to the earth with a thud.

"Take that you overgrown garden snake!" Theia exulted as she pulled out another arrow.

The snake furrowed its brows and dashed towards Theia, causing Chantal to lose her balance and fall on her back. Theia dodged the snake's charge and tried to head towards Olius's shield. The snake threw itself in front of her and blocked her path. Theia jumped away and fell on her back, cursing as she tried to get up quickly. Chantal regained her balance and began to punch the snake's head. Vicious cracking of scales and bone could be heard as the snake threw its head back in the air, flailing around to get Chantal off. She grabbed on to the snake's scales and held on for dear life. When the snake stopped shaking its head, it began to slither around, abruptly moving its body to shake Chantal off again. Theia pulled out an arrow and tried to aim at the snake, unable to find the right time to let go of the bowstring.

"What do I do?!" Theia panicked.

"Maybe we can be of some assistance?" Aurelina yelled from up above.

Theia turned around and saw Aurelina flying through the air as Jade jumped from branch to branch. Jade jumped down from the branches and landed on the snake's head. She put out her arm and put her fingers together, watching them fuse. They turned into iron and formed a spike. She then jabbed her hand into the snake's skin and grabbed Chantal. They held on as the snake lashed out violently, bellowing and hissing in pain. Aurelina dove down, picked up Theia, and dropped her on top of the raging snake.

"What are you doing? This is possibly the most dangerous place to be!" Theia yelled as she took out her large dagger and jabbed into the snake.

"Well you would be right if it weren't for those things," Aurelina said as she pointed down below.

Theia looked back and saw an outpouring of little gremlins come from the underbrush. They began to surround the snake and fed on its scales. Some of the gremlins surrounded Olius's shield and started to pound on it furiously.

"Wait?" Jade questioned. "Where's Regibus?"

"Don't freak out but this snake swallowed him."

"Swallowed! We have to get him out of there!"

Suddenly, a large saber appeared out of the snake's upper body. It began to cut through the snake's body until it did a complete rotation. The white eyes of the snake grew opaque as the head fell to the ground, followed by the rest of the body. Everyone on top of the snake's head held on and felt the force of the thud as the head hit the ground. They watched Cutthroat climb out of the snake, covered in a thick and foul-smelling gunk. He took a few steps before falling to his knees.

"What did I miss?" Cutthroat slurred, the saliva dripping between his boney jaws.

He then collapsed and dissipated into a puddle of water, leaving only Regibus's limp body on the ground. The gremlins turned their attention away from the others and began to dash towards Regibus. Olius looked up and gasped as he slammed his staff on the ground, causing the shield to attach itself to the top of his staff. He dashed through the gremlins, knocking them over, and covered Regibus with the shield. Olius closed his eyes and whispered some words as Regibus began to levitate up towards the others. Jade and Chantal moved Regibus onto the snake's head as Aurelina and Theia helped Olius up. The shield shattered as Olius moved out of it and shuffled towards Regibus. He put his ear on his chest and felt the slow rhythmic beat of his heart.

"He's just exhausted!" Olius exclaimed.

"Aurelina can heal him while we try and figure out what to do about these gremlins," Theia said as she looked down at the ground.

They both looked down to see that the gremlins were trying to climb up the snake. Once they reached the midway point of the corpse, they didn't have enough strength to hold on. They dropped back to the floor, crushing those beneath them.

"Apparently this has been the work of some malevolent and horrible goddess," Olius growled as he got up. He looked down and flicked his finger, sending a small bolt of magical energy through one of the heads of the gremlins.

"That goddess would be my aunt, Olius," Aurelina reluctantly explained.

"Oh. I'm sorry I didn't mean anything—"

"No, I'm with you, I don't like her and she probably doesn't like me. If she did, then these monsters wouldn't be attacking us."

"Can we cut the chitchat and actually do something about these things?" Jade urged.

Everyone looked back down and saw that the gremlins stopped trying to climb the giant snake. Instead, they just lay on the floor with annoyed expressions on their faces. They made small grunting sounds as they looked at each other and snarled. Olius looked down and an idea popped into his head.

"Since they gave up, we can use this time to teleport out of here. Everybody huddle up and we can—"

"Haha! We found you guys!"

Everyone looked in front of them to see Darvell shuffling towards them while Hector rode on Nugget. The gremlins got up and charged towards them, snarling and barking while they bared their teeth.

"What are these things?" Darvell asked as he squinted his eyes. "They look stupid."

Darvell took his revolvers and began to shoot at them while Hector did the same with his shotgun. As the first shots were fired, the gremlins barked in fear as they scurried away from Darvell and Hector. The others hopped off the corpse of the snake as Darvell and Hector walked up to them.

"For once in my life, I'm glad I don't have to fight anything," Darvell mentioned as he holstered his revolvers. "I'm too tired and sore to move."

"Glad you guys could join us," Theia exclaimed. "We need to get out of here and fast."

Jade walked over to Darvell, who was leaning against the corpse of the snake. He was breathing heavily as he rubbed his muscles, trying to soothe them.

"You look hurt," Jade pointed out as she stood beside him.

"Just a little tussle with some ugly monster." Darvell laughed weakly. "I'll be alright."

"I suggest you have this then," Jade offered as she pulled out a clear bottle. Its contents glowed a vibrant blue and green as it sloshed around. "It'll help ease the pain."

Darvell smiled as he received the bottle and drank from it. Darvell's posture straightened out as he flexed his wings. Jade took a step back as Darvell extended his arms forward, the sound of his bones cracking following soon after.

"I feel brand new!" Darvell exclaimed as he went to hug Jade. "I guess it's time to leave then."

"None of you will be going anywhere!"

A violent wind of red petals appeared out of the air as Marimonda appeared in front of them. Marimonda raised her hand and closed her fist, the earth spitting out multiple vines that latched onto everyone. The vines curled around them like snakes, constricting tighter as they tried to move. Darvell tried to burn his way out but the vines grew as fast as he burned them off.

"There are consequences to angering gods, mortals," Marimonda threatened, her eyes glowing a pale white. "Prepare to die."

"Uh...Marimonda," Aurelina grunted, grinding her teeth to bear the pain.

Marimonda turned to Aurelina and gave her a puzzled look.

"Honey, what are you doing here? Are they holding you hostage?" Marimonda asked as she tightened her fist.

Aurelina dropped to the floor as the vines holding onto her let go. The vines restraining everyone else, however, began to tighten. The vines grabbing onto Hector reached his neck and began to wrap around. Hector looked down in fear as he began to hyperventilate, his pale skin turning a faint shade of blue.

"No, they're not taking me hostage," Aurelina fretted as she ran to Hector and tried to loosen the vines. "We were just passing through your jungle."

"Is that all? All of this could have been solved peacefully if any of you said you knew my beloved niece," Marimonda cheerfully said as she loosened her fist.

The vines retracted back into the earth and everyone dropped to the ground. Regibus landed with a thud as he fell on his head. He slowly opened his eyes and looked around.

"Ugh, where am I?"

"Don't worry about it, Regibus. Looks like we can leave without any problems," Olius said as he helped him up.

"To be honest, I find this hard to believe," Darvell questioned. "I remember Aurelina telling us that you aren't the forgiving type."

"Darvell!" Aurelina whispered harshly. "I don't think now's the time to start remembering stuff like that."

"No, he's right. I was kidding that this could be solved with peace after all of you have killed so much of my jungle. I only let you go to see all of you struggle to live after I'm done with you. As for you Aurelina, your mother would be devastated if anything happened to you. So when I'm done mutilating your friends, I'm sending you right to her."

Marimonda laughed wickedly as she sunk into the ground, Aurelina falling to her knees. Suddenly, a deep rumbling could be felt in the ground beneath them as everyone drew their attention to the giant snake corpse. The two pieces began to wriggle violently as dark green slime burst out from its flesh. Two new snakes, a bit smaller than the original, slithered around as they looked down at the group.

"You think they remember us?" Regibus asked as he summoned his cutlass from thin air.

The snakes roared and dove down at them. They all jumped out of the way as they watched the two snakes dig into the earth, leaving a large hole in their wake. Theia slowly got up and pulled out her bow.

"I think they might have a small grudge against us," Theia sarcastically declared.

The two snakes rose from the ground and began to knock down trees in an effort to crush them. As Jade ran, she tripped and fell to the ground. She looked up to see a tree falling down towards her. She closed her eyes and then felt a warm presence around her. She turned to see Darvell catch the falling tree. He was breathing heavily as he looked down at Jade and smiled, his teeth clenched against each other.

"You mind moving?" Darvell grunted as he dug his claws into the tree bark. "I don't think I can hold this tree any longer."

"Oh! Sorry."

Darvell looked at the two giant snakes and furrowed his brow. He dug his claws deeper into the trunk and lifted the entire tree above his head. Darvell began to sink slowly into the ground as he held his breath. He threw his arms forward and launched the tree at the two snakes, letting out a pained groan upon releasing his burden. One of them managed to slither away, but the other was pinned to the ground. It let out a pained screech as it tried to move from under the tree trunk. The snake that managed to get away started to slither around the area and smashed more trees to the ground.

"This fight seems counterintuitive, don't you think?" Aurelina said as she took Hector into her arms and flew upwards.

"How so?"

"Well, she wanted to stop us from destroying her jungle and here we are now, fighting two giant snakes who did more damage than us in the span of a few minutes."

"Now that you say it out loud, you do make a good point. By the way, I need you to drop me," Hector asked.

"What! Why?"

"We're right above that pinned snake. I'm going to see if I can impale it."

"Hector, sweetie, I'm sure you think you could impale this thing but this is a snake created by the gods. All you would do is anger it even more."

Hector looked down and gulped. He took out his spear and

looked back at Aurelina. She could see in his eyes a reluctant confidence.

"You really want to go through with this do you?"

"I took on a haunted horseman earlier. I think I can manage a giant snake," Hector chuckled nervously.

Aurelina bit her lip and closed her eyes as she let go of Hector. He pointed his spear downwards as he spiraled towards the snake's head. When he reached impact, the spear penetrated halfway through the snake's skull. Its eyes burst forward in pain as the snake, using the adrenaline the impact caused, moved the log pinning it to the ground off its body. The snake began to slither around violently, throwing its body across the jungle floor as it tried to shake Hector off its head. Hector held onto the spear tightly as he screamed in fear. Aurelina yelped and dove down to go help Hector.

Meanwhile, Theia and Jade were in the trees firing shots at the snake below them. Darvell, Olius and Regibus were doing their best to kill the snake but their attacks only seemed to bother the beast rather than hurt it. Darvell reared back and breathed out a plume of fire. The flames only managed to spread across the snake's scales upon impact. Darvell stopped breathing fire when he saw that it wasn't doing anything and pulled out his greatsword, channeling the fire into his blade. He extended his wings and took flight as a cloud of dust formed from the takeoff. Darvell flew towards the snake's mouth with his blade in front of him.

"Take this you scaly son of a bitch!"

The snake turned towards him and opened its mouth. Darvell, helpless to stop his momentum, was snapped up just like Cutthroat. Jade gasped and furrowed her brows in fury.

"Spit him out!"

Jade jumped from her tree branch and landed on the snake's head. She extended her arm outward as it morphed into a thick blade. She thrust it into the snake's skull like last time. She then pulled it back out and thrust it in again. Although it didn't go as far as Hector's spear, it left a large gash with every thrust. The snake, however, didn't flinch at the strikes and was unaware of her presence on its head. As the snake looked at the others, it began to wince and awkwardly curl parts of its body.

"Uh guys? Why is the snake making that sound?" Olius yelled as he finished firing another bolt of magic.

The snake began to snort out thick black clouds of smoke from its nostrils, coughing out fire. The fire burst through the tree Theia was on, cutting it in half. Theia put away the arrow in her hand and pulled out a new one. The arrow had a long rope merged into the shaft of the arrow. She pulled back on her bowstring and launched the arrow into a nearby tree. As the arrow flew and wrapped itself around a tree branch, Theia grabbed onto the rope and swung down from the falling tree. The snake thrashed around and knocked the rope Theia was clinging on, causing her to fall. Before Theia could crash into the ground, she was caught by Chantal who had run over to catch her.

"I'm glad you're on our side Chantal," Theia said before she kissed Chantal on the cheek.

Chantal blushed at the remark and placed Theia on her feet. Olius and Regibus ran towards them to regroup. They looked tired as beads of sweat trickled down their heads.

"These snakes are becoming a hassle," Regibus stated as he reloaded his flintlock. "We need to finish this now and get the hell out of here."

"Easier said than done. I'm pretty sure Marimonda enchanted these things to keep sprouting out new bodies if we cut them," Theia responded.

The snake bellowed as it slithered towards them. Regibus aimed his flintlock as Theia pulled back on her bow. The two of them fired and shot the eyes of the snake. The bullets and arrows pierced right through them, making the snake jolt up in pain and release another burst of fire into the air. Jade was jostled off and began to fall towards the ground. The snake's midsection was violently ripped open as Darvell, now drenched in stomach acid and ooze, flung himself out of the snake to catch Jade. Darvell caught her and held her tightly as he slid across the dirt floor. He wrapped himself in his wings as they collided with the ground, leaving a burned trail of dirt and grass in his wake. As he opened up his wings, Jade looked up to see Darvell staring up at the sky with an expressionless, stoic face.

"I can now say that was probably the most disgusting thing I have endured," Darvell shuddered.

Jade couldn't help but laugh as Darvell looked down and smiled. The momentary peace was interrupted by the sudden loud and disgusting gurgling from the dying snake. Everyone looked up to see that the snake tried to form a new body but couldn't due to the seared flesh Darvell left inside it. Bile and ooze poured out some of the burned wounds but nothing was able to come out fully. Suddenly, the body of the snake fell to the floor with a tremendous thud. Olius's eyes suddenly opened wide as he turned towards Darvell.

"Burnt flesh can't regenerate!" Olius informed as he pointed to the other snake. "Darvell, you have to burn the body!"

"You want me to burn it?" Darvell asked, a smile forming on his face. "I can do that."

Darvell got up and pulled out his greatsword as he ran towards the other snake. Hector looked down to see Darvell gesture to force the snake down. Hector nodded and jabbed his spear deeper into the snake's skull. The snake roared as it lowered its head to fling Hector off. Once low enough, Hector yanked the spear out, a surge of pain that made the snake faint and collapse to the ground. Darvell jumped in the air and lit his greatsword on fire as he cleaved right through the snake's body, the sound of scales snapping and flesh crisping entering his ears. The snake screeched in agony, writhing violently before succumbing to its death. Darvell lifted his greatsword and placed the blade on his shoulder as Hector jumped down from the snake's head.

"I guess we killed it," Darvell gloated, his body sore from moving all day. "These things weren't so tough."

"You think there are more of these things around here?" Hector asked as he placed his spear back on his back.

"We don't have to worry about that Hector," Aurelina said as she landed right beside him. "I'm sure we can walk out of this jungle soon."

"Good, I just don't want any more surprises. Come on Nugget! Let's get out of here."

Nugget ran up to Hector and morphed back into his rooster form. He jumped up into his arms and wiggled his head back and forth in an excited manner. Everyone made their way out of the area and headed back to the wagon. Deep within the bushes, however, was a beast heavily breathing as it darted its stare back at Darvell and Chantal. Although neither of them saw it, Chantal stopped in her tracks, clutching her head as the familiar sensation returned. The hidden stalker slithered back into its hiding spot, the quiet rustling of the underbrush masking its escape. Chantal looked back and peered into the underbrush, shaking her head in confusion as she ran back to the others.

CHAPTER 11

As the group looked around and found the wagon again, Darvell put on the reins and continued to drag it. The dense trees of the jungle began to clear as the sight of a crystal clear lake by the side of the road caught his attention. The lake smelled like a fresh mint that danced its way into Darvell's nose. The local flora around the lake added a lot to the view: moss covered stones, hanging vines blooming with different colored flowers, peaceful waterfowl that floated along the surface of the lake and faint rainbows floating above it all. Darvell smiled as he admired the sight, dragging the wagon past it as he made his way.

A few more minutes up the road, Darvell came to a small fork with multiple branching paths leading deeper into the jungle. Looking at the paths, Darvell decided to continue going straight. As he drove along the path he came across a crystal clear lake with a beautiful rainbow shimmering against the bright blue sky. Darvell scratched his chin and studied the lake, a feeling of déjà vu overcoming him.

I guess this place has more than one lake.

A few minutes passed and Darvell stopped at an eerily familiar fork in the road with branching paths. Darvell furrowed his eyebrows and decided to take one of the paths on his left. After an hour of dragging the wagon, he stopped at the same lake he had seen the other two times. Darvell unhitched himself from the wagon and rushed towards the edge of the lake. He dipped his hand in the water and felt it slide off his hand like regular water.

Darvell scratched his head and turned towards a nearby tree. He took his hand and singed its bark with some fire. He scratched a poorly drawn letter "D" on it. Once Darvell was back in the reins of the wagon, he walked a few more minutes and stopped at a fork in the road with branching paths. Darvell growled quietly as he looked at the paths before him.

This is starting to get annoying.

Darvell took a path to the right and walked for an hour or so until he came up to the same lake as before. Darvell was beginning to get flustered as he walked towards the same tree and saw the burn mark. Darvell punched the tree, leaving a big dent in the now burning wood.

"That's it! I'm pissed now!" Darvell roared as black smoke billowed out of his mouth.

Darvell pulled out one of his revolvers and began to fire into the lake, hoping it would do something or provoke someone to punch. Olius walked out of the wagon to see Darvell hollering and yelling at the lake.

"Let us leave! I don't want to be hauling this cart forever!" Darvell yelled to the sky.

"Darvell, what are you doing?" Olius asked.

"We're lost Olius," Darvell responded bitterly as he turned to face him. "I keep coming back to this stupid lake and I'm getting really pissed."

"Well you are driving the cart; of course we would be lost."

Darvell glared at Olius and gave him a sour look.

"Anyway, I'll just look at the compass and tell you where we have to go."

Olius pulled out the compass from one of the pockets in his robe. He pulled it out and furrowed his eyes at it. They both watched as the compass needle violently spun clockwise for a few seconds and then counterclockwise until it returned to spinning clockwise again. Olius put the compass away and stroked his beard.

"It seems some magical force is keeping us trapped here. It appears that Marimonda is running out of ways to attack us." Olius chuckled. "We can't leave until Marimonda lets us. So I guess we're stuck here until she gets bored or we figure out something, fast."

"Hopefully fast and soon, we have a world to save."

"Don't you think I know that? Let's just ask Aurelina, maybe she knows how to get us out."

"What do you mean there's no way out!" Olius exclaimed angrily as he slammed his fist on the table.

"Exactly, there is no way out," Aurelina repeated before she took a sip of tea from her cup. "Marimonda is very malicious when it comes to intruders. We had our chance to escape but once her guardians found out where we were, it was too late. What bothers me is that we didn't even do anything to alert them so why were they on patrol?"

"So, now what?" Hector said as he picked up Nugget and petted him.

"I say we show her what for and do a little more damage," Theia said as she pulled out an arrow from her quiver.

"I wouldn't recommend that. The only thing that would do is speed up our time before you all die," Aurelina said as she stirred some more sugar into her cup.

"Before we all die? What do you mean by that?" Jade questioned rudely.

"Yes, before you all die. Marimonda can't touch me or my mother would have her head."

"So I guess none of this concerns you then?" Jade harshly replied.

"I'll have you know, I do have my concerns. Besides getting Darvell through this jungle and killing Zlo, I have to make sure Hector gets out of here safely."

Hector couldn't help but blush and chuckle a little bit.

"My dad said he wanted to meet him and make sure he's good enough for me."

Hector's chuckling stopped and was replaced with a nervous gulp. Darvell walked over and patted him on the shoulder to comfort him.

"Then if you want to have any of those things happen, you have to help us get out of here," Jade reminded.

Aurelina looked down at her tea and furrowed her brows. She got up and walked out of the wagon. Hector looked at Jade and glared at her.

"Great, now you got her upset," Hector complained.

"Shut up," Jade barked back.

Aurelina walked back into the wagon with a devilish smile on her face. She turned to Olius and Regibus and gestured for them to follow her.

"I'm going to need you two. We're all going for a little swim."

As the others stood around, passing the time and waiting for the next step of the plan, Olius was busy flipping through his spell book until he stopped at a page and began to read its contents. Regibus stretched his arms and touched his toes as he prepared himself. Aurelina was busy inspecting the water as Theia walked up and knelt beside her.

"So what's down at the bottom of this lake?"

"Well Theia, at the bottom of this lake is a magical fish that Marimonda adores. This fish is magical and can influence the terrain around it. It seems that it has created an inescapable area around it so we have to capture it and neutralize its magic."

"A giant fish?" Theia questioned.

"Yes, it sounds weird but trust me," Aurelina sighed. "I've lived with her for a few hundred years; I know what I'm talking about. By the way, let's try not to kill this thing or we run the risk of turning this problem into something much worse."

Theia nodded and walked away. Aurelina turned towards Olius and Regibus, who were waiting to hear what the plan was.

"Okay, what I need from you, Regibus, is to push the water away from us while Olius here will create a slab of rock to guide us down to the deeper parts of the lake. The rest of us will fend off whatever tries to kill us. Once we get to the bottom, then we can have a water breathing spell put on us. Ready to go Regibus?"

Regibus nodded and walked to the edge of the lake. He put his hands together as if he were going to pray. He then slowly pointed his fingers towards the lake as he moved them forward. The water in front of him slowly began to bubble. He then slowly moved his hands apart as the water began to follow Regibus's hands. After a few minutes, the water was separated as Regibus's arms were fully outward, his palms facing away from him as if he were pushing against a wall. Olius briefly looked through a page in his book and closed it. He took his staff and slammed it into the earth below.

"Forma Petra!"

The earth slowly began to form a large stone slab near the ridge of the lakeshore. Olius stepped on it and began to poke it to check its sturdiness. Olius motioned to the others to come aboard as he placed his staff on the slab. As they all got on, Darvell put his hand through the wall of water and pulled it back out again.

"Can you not do that?" Regibus grunted. "This water is heavier for some reason and it's a pain to keep it at bay."

"My bad."

"The water here may feel like regular water but it is in fact designed to keep the more magical creatures in the lake. It isn't designed to suppress human magic but it can still be a pain to work against," Aurelina explained.

Olius moved his staff forward and the slab of stone slowly moved down. As the group delved deeper into the lake, the light from the surface began to fade until the lake above them covered them. Regibus continued to push the water away from them, creating an orb of air around them. Darvell grabbed his tail and lit it on fire, the light allowing everyone to see the beauty of the underwater life. Around them were large mountains of stones covered in coral of all shapes and colors. Some of them entwined with each other while others made complex arches. A large group of sea turtles swam above them as the deep moans of a far-off whale alerted the group. Suddenly, the beautiful glow of numerous jellyfish gently floated past them, their ever-changing colors mesmerizing the group.

"This place is like its very own ocean," Regibus admired. "I thought you said this was a lake?"

"Well it looks like a lake on the surface," Aurelina responded. "But the magic here creates this small realm for all of Marimonda's aquatic animals. All of this land that she owns is her little sanctuary for animals."

"Sanctuary?" Jade questioned. "How many animals does she have here then?"

"All of them. She's got every animal under the sun, in the water, and beneath the ground. She's very keen on keeping them safe."

"I kind of feel bad now," Darvell mentioned. "We were tearing the place up a few hours ago."

"Don't feel too bad, this place is magic. It repairs itself constantly," Aurelina consoled. "If the world were to ever end, the animals here could restart civilization."

Colorful fish swam past them, all kinds of colors on their scaly bodies. Slender fish darted past them as slow, lumbering ones just moved above Regibus's air bubble. One fish, however, darted right through the water and smacked Darvell in the face. He picked it up and frowned until an idea popped into his head. He took the fish and placed it in his palm and began to cook it. The smell of cooking fish began to fill the bubble as everyone began to gag.

"Darvell, can you not be hungry for once?" Theia said as she pinched her nose.

"Come on, I've got to have a snack before a big fight," Darvell replied as he took the cooked fish and took a bite.

Darvell slowly chewed the fish, his face going through a number of queasy displays. He looked down and gave a disgusted look at the fish in his hand, quietly gagging as he tried to swallow it. Hector walked over to Darvell and grabbed the fish.

"It's not good is it?" Hector asked.

Darvell shook his head and looked into the distance as he continued to reluctantly chew the fish in his mouth. He finally swallowed and gagged a little more before he threw the cooked fish back into the water. To everyone's amazement, the dead fish began to grow its head back as it swam away, leaving everyone dumbfounded. Darvell rubbed his stomach in disappointment as a loud growl resonated from it.

"I want to eat real food," Darvell grumbled.

The group continued to slink down into the lake as the fish swimming around them became scarce as time went by. Regibus's arms were starting to give in as he weakly tried to push the water away from everyone. Olius tapped his staff and two thin pillars perched themselves under Regibus's arms, helping them stay up.

"We're only in the second ring, Regibus. I don't think drowning is the most heroic death," Olius chuckled.

Regibus smiled as he positioned himself and continued to

push the water. A few more minutes passed and the white gleam of sand could be seen in the distance. As the stone slab reached the floor, Olius moved his staff to guide the stone forward.

"Okay Aurelina, where do we go from here?" Olius asked.

"Well, all we would have to do is go straight from here. The fish is in the middle of the lake."

"This is taking forever!" Darvell whined. "I bet I could just swim there."

"Darvell, be patient," Aurelina scolded. "This isn't just some fish, it's—"

A loud splash could be seen as Darvell began to swim towards the center of the lake. Everyone else was left in the dark until Olius pulled out a crystal and shook it. The crystal emitted a bright alternating light of white and blue.

"A giant one."

"We better go after him before he goes too far," Jade said to Olius.

"Good idea, I just realized that he forgot to stay for the water breathing spell."

Darvell swam through the dark waters as he held his breath, searching for the giant fish. He stopped mid-swim and realized he was running out of air. He grasped his mouth as bubbles began to come out rapidly. Darvell reached for the ring but stopped himself.

I turn this thing on and everyone will boil to death.

Darvell frantically looked around for a place to breathe, his head darting through the water. Suddenly, he laid his eyes on the entrance of a large cave. As he swam towards the cave, he could see around him the ruins of an ancient temple. Pillars of black quartz with archaic and jagged symbols inscribed on them were scattered about. Hidden within the sand were all kinds of weapons and shields, damaged and rusted from the water. Darvell scrambled inside and found a pocket of air near the roof of the cave. As he swam towards it, he could feel his lungs beginning to collapse as water poured into his nose. The sound of coughing and deep breathing ensued as Darvell rose out of the water. All around him was darkness and stone. The musty smell in the air bothered his nose as he prepared himself for another deep dive.

"Darvell! Hold on!"

Darvell looked down and could see the bright glow of Aurelina's halo enter the cave. He breathed in and dove down once more. As he descended, he could see a thin bubble on Aurelina's shoulders. Darvell gestured to the bubble.

"This thing? Since Regibus can already breathe underwater, Olius gave the rest of us these things to breathe with. If you waited, Olius could have given one to you."

Darvell rolled his eyes as Olius and the others appeared at the mouth of the cave. Darvell pointed to his head asking for a bubble. Olius shook his head and crossed his arms.

"You should really be more patient," Olius reprimanded.

Darvell pointed to his head again, this time with an angry look on his face. Olius smacked Darvell in the stomach, all of his air escaping his mouth, and swished the bubbles around Darvell's head. A similar bubble formed around Darvell's head as a small glow of magic emanated from it before disappearing. Darvell breathed heavily as he felt the fresh air enter him.

"What was that for?!" Darvell yelled, his voice slightly echoing in the bubble.

"Stop charging into the unknown, idiot! Most of us don't even know what's in these waters," Olius explained.

"Did you have to smack me in the gut?"

"No I didn't. But I wanted to." Olius devilishly smirked. "C'mon, if this is the cave, then let's get this over with."

Olius slowly swam in as the rest of the group entered the

cave. The entire cave began to rumble, causing the stalactites above to crack and sink downwards, impaling the soft sand and clay floor below. A horrible growl echoed through the water of the cave. As the growling subsided, Olius looked back at Aurelina for some reassurance.

"It's probably the giant fish that we're looking for," Aurelina said as she looked around. "He could be waking up right now."

"Great," Hector angrily complained. "As if it couldn't get any harder."

"We need to move now. The longer we stay in here the greater the chance we might get trapped here," Jade said as she pulled out her rifle.

The group walked deeper into the cave, looking around rocks and at the ceiling for any unwanted monsters. Surprisingly, the cave was devoid of any life other than the rocks around them. As they traversed farther, the water began to grow thin until they walked onto a cay. The bubbles around everyone's heads popped once they got out of the water. Jade took a knee and inspected the sand, rubbing it between her fingers.

"This isn't sand, this is...this entire piece of land is made of bones," Jade informed, her voice slightly quivering. "It's all ground-up bones."

The air around them smelled fresh and clean, as the lapping of small waves crashed against the white bone sand. Olius raised his staff and cast a bright blue light. The cave around them was large and spacious with other tunnels below the water. The murky water splashed along the bone sand of the cay as the others looked around. Darvell took a seat on the ground and scooped up some bone dust. He lit his hands on fire and watched as a thick plume of black smoke flew into the air. He threw the remaining dust into the water and groaned.

"There's nothing here!"

"It would seem so," Aurelina remarked. "Last time I was here it was swimming around."

Suddenly, a deathly howl escaped from the murky depths. Everyone clutched their ears and fell on their knees as the howl pounded against their heads. An eruption of water came from below as a giant pink creature emerged. Its belly flopped onto the beach as it let out another ear-shattering cry from its slender mouth. On top of its head was a hole that occasionally spurted out water. Its long flippers extended outward, almost reaching the two ends of the small cay. The lake monster moved its eyes around and observed the group. It stopped at Regibus and furrowed its eyes.

"Oh no," Regibus mumbled.

The creature charged right through the group and dove back into the water. It had left a large ditch in the middle of the small island. Water began to seep through, splitting the cay in half.

"Why the hell am I getting attacked all the time?!" Regibus said as he pulled out his flintlock.

"It's not you Regibus; almost every living creature here can sense Cutthroat's presence now that Marimonda knows he's here."

The beast rose out of the water again and screeched, slamming its body onto the cay once more. The land was almost gone as the pink creature sank back into the water. Everyone looked around frantically as they tried to find a place to put their feet on.

"It's trying to get us in the water!" Jade yelled as she felt the ground beneath her slowly dissipate.

"You're right," Olius worried as he thrust his hand upwards. "It's trying to make sure we can't fight back."

One large stone platform extended out of the wall as Olius initiated a quick muttering of arcane words. Everyone jumped onto it as the remaining bone dust sank into the water. The creature began to swim towards the platform as they watched it sink back into the water. Everyone slowly caught their breath as Olius finished the incantation.

"This thing is pissing me off!" Darvell growled. "How about I just boil the hell out of it?"

"Darvell, we need the fish alive!" Aurelina scolded as she wrung out her clothing. "You scorch an inch of its skin and Marimonda will have your head on a pike."

"Then what do we do?" Theia asked as she took off her eyepatch and dried it. "We can't end up as fish food for this thing."

"I could shrink it and keep him incarcerated in this bottle," Olius said as he pulled out an empty alchemist bottle.

"Well, what's stopping you?" Hector asked as he surveyed the waters, keeping an eye out for the pink sea creature.

"Well, I have to concentrate on the spell for one thing; it takes a while to prepare it. Another problem is that this spell requires a good visual on the target to work and I don't see it anywhere," Olius responded as he pulled out his book and flipped through the pages.

"Then I guess we have to get him out of the water?" Regibus said. "Darvell, you want to go fishing?"

"Now is not the time for fishing Regibus. We have to take care of…oh. I see now."

Olius looked up from his book with a worried look on his face.

"Where are you two going? We can't have anyone splitting up—"

Splash.

"—now. Does anyone ever listen anymore?"

"Don't worry Olius, I'm sure Darvell and Regibus can handle themselves," Jade said as she finished drying her hair. "They are the two strongest people in this group."

"What about me?" Hector boasted.

"What about you?" Jade asked.

"Nothing," Hector mumbled angrily. "I didn't say anything."

Regibus and Darvell dove down into the murky water, the bright glow of Olius's staff fading behind them. Regibus grabbed a couple of his dreads and stroked them, the strands glowing a mellow mix of sea green and deep blue. As they dove deeper, Regibus put his arm in front of Darvell. He pointed down to show that the pink sea creature was swimming below them, its tail slowly moving up and down. A series of quick clicks and screeches filled their ears as it traveled through the water.

Darvell grinned and was going to reach for his greatsword until Regibus smacked his hand away from the hilt. He pointed upwards and reminded Darvell what Aurelina had said before. Darvell rolled his eyes and lowered his hand. Regibus cracked his knuckles and pulled his hand back. He punched through the water and a burst of condensed water fired out of his knuckles towards the beast. The burst of water dispersed across the creature and failed to have grabbed its attention. Regibus furrowed his brows and tried it again but with a much more violent thrust. The result was almost instantaneous as the beast was thrown down to the sea floor, hitting itself against some jagged rocks. The monster looked upward and growled, a quick burst of clicks and screeches escaping its thin snout.

Regibus went to look at Darvell, only to find him already swimming upwards. Regibus looked back down to see the monster swimming up at him with its mouth all the way open. Regibus's eyes opened wide as he started to make his way up. Darvell and Regibus emerged from the water and swam towards the nearest platform. They threw themselves on it as Darvell gasped for air while Regibus was scrambling to get back on.

"Did you find it?" Hector asked.

Before any of them could say anything, a thunderous screech erupted from the water. The pink monster rose out of the water and opened the hole of its head, another ear-shattering scream echoing through the cave. However, unlike the other screams, this one rattled and caused all of their bones to ache. Hector suffered the most pain because the suit he was wearing violently banged against his body from the vibrations in his armor. Everyone tried to shake off the piercing scream but it appeared to echo through the rest of the cavern, getting stronger the longer it persisted. The creature began to swim towards everyone as they were still suffering the effects of the screech.

Darvell looked up from the pain and saw that the beast was charging towards Jade. Her eyes were closed due to the pain as she clutched her ears. Darvell gritted his teeth as he uncovered his ears and dashed towards Jade. The beast opened its jaws as it reached Jade only to take a heavy bite on the stone as Darvell grabbed her and rolled her to safety. The stone shattered, forming cracks across the platform.

Olius pried his eyes open and saw the creature slinking back into the water. Olius took out his book and flipped through the pages, stopping on one section and throwing the book on the floor. Crackling blue energy escaped his mouth, small symbols forming within the air as he spoke.

"Exsurdo!"

The deafening screech suddenly ceased as everyone slowly uncovered their ears. The vibrations in all of their bodies began to hurt less. Hector opened his mouth to speak but nothing came out. He began to freak out and started to scream silently. Olius slapped him across the face and gestured his hands to tell him to calm down. Suddenly, the ground shattered once more as the pink beast crashed through the center of the platform. Everyone fell on their backs as they scurried away from the shattering cracks.

Theia narrowed her eyes and got up from the ground, pulling out an arrow from her quiver. The arrow was black and smoky, devoid of any other color. The shaft was ghostly and translucent, turning white as Theia touched it. The light around the arrow seemed to grow dim and hazy as she pulled back on the bowstring. She waited for the creature to show itself, waiting patiently with her arrow at the ready. Once the creature rose from the water, she let go of the arrow. It flew through the air towards the creature, exploding into a plume of black mist upon impact.

Theia's vision grew dark until the only thing she could see was pitch black darkness. She looked around for a bit and started to see white echoes of everyone, including the beast that was swimming underneath them. Theia pulled out a couple of exploding arrows and began to fire them towards the position of the beast. The others could only see Theia shoot at the ground, causing more cracks to form on the platform. Olius pulled out his staff and mouthed the magic spell again to reinforce the stone.

Chantal ran up to Theia and signaled her to stop destroying the only thing keeping them from sinking. Theia signaled to the ground, the beast was down below. Chantal moved her hands to say she didn't see anything. Theia smacked her head and gave a long kiss on Chantal's lips. Chantal blushed as her eyes turned black, the ghostly echoes forming around her. She looked around and could now see what Theia was seeing. Theia pointed down towards the ghostly image of the swimming beast as it made its way back up. Chantal cracked her knuckles, pulled her fist back, and began to punch the stone platform. Olius felt the vibrations under his feet and turned around to see Chantal punching the floor.

Chantal's last punch successfully broke off a piece of the stone platform. As the beast began to swim upwards, the piece floated down and smacked it in the snout. The beast let out a gurgle of bubbles as it sank to the bottom of the underwater lake. The pain in everyone's bones faded away as Olius snapped his fingers and everyone could hear the quiet sloshing of the waves.

"What happened to not hurting the goddamn fish?!" Aurelina yelled.

"I thought the piercing scream went away," Theia mumbled under her breath.

Chantal snickered as Darvell held back his chuckle. Hector frowned as Auerlina groaned angrily. She walked over to the hole and looked down at it. She could see the pink of the sea creature's skin fade away into the deeper parts of the water.

"At least it's immobile now. I can just heal any of its wounds when we capture it," Aurelina said as she got up.

"Then we can try an alternative to capturing it. Regibus, take this bottle and open it with the spout facing the monster. The bottle will suck it up and we can have Aurelina heal it when we reach the surface," Olius ordered.

Olius handed Regibus the clear bottle. The neck of the bottle had a blue ribbon wrapped around it with what appeared to be Olius's name written on it.

"Olius, why does this bottle have your name on it?" Regibus asked as he grabbed it.

"I used to sell magic bottles on the black market for money. I needed some form of income and selling magic stuff was the most practical."

"Can't you just make gold?" Darvell asked.

"Darvell, that would destroy the value of gold and flood the market, which would then cause a price boom in the price of materials," Olius explained.

"What?"

"Just go get the stupid fish so we can leave." Olius groaned as he turned back to Regibus.

Regibus shrugged his shoulders and dove down to get the pink sea monster. As he swam to the bottom of the lake, he could see the stone rubble piled on top of the creature. Regibus gently landed on his feet and slowly walked towards the creature. He examined it as its eye bled out from the center due to a small stone that pierced through its cornea. Along its skin were deep cuts and wounds which made the once pink skin seem a lot more red. The snout was bent downwards with a few rows of teeth missing from the lower and upper jaws. Regibus rubbed his chin and shrugged.

I'm sure it's fine. Olius and Aurelina can fix it anyway.

Regibus grabbed the bottle and pointed the opening towards the fish. He pulled off the cork with a quick yank and almost immediately, a spiral of water enveloped itself around the fish and rocks as they were shrunk and moved into the base of the bottle. The bottle stopped its sucking and Regibus jammed the cork back into the opening. He put the bottle in front of his face and could see the fish lying on a bed of rocks that got sucked up as well. Regibus put the bottle in his pocket and made his way back to the surface. As he reached the top, he plopped himself on the ridge of the remaining platform and handed Olius the bottle. Olius and Aurelina examined the fish and they both made a face.

"It's practically dead! What the hell you guys?" Olius complained.

"I asked you guys to make sure it didn't get hurt! Theia and Chantal, what were you two thinking?" Aurelina angrily said as she walked up to them.

"Hey! We got the fish and you two can just fix him right up," Theia scoffed.

"Don't give me that! If the damages were minimal we could have cleaned it up with ease. These kinds of wounds take years to heal, even with magic. That's time we don't have!"

Chantal stepped in front of Aurelina and pushed her back. Chantal cracked her fingers and gave her a menacing glare. Aurelina looked at her with an expression of awe and anger.

"I don't need your sass either, Chantal; this is just as much your fault as hers."

As the three continued to bicker, Darvell walked up to Hector.

"Don't you think you should help her?"

"I wish I could. But between Chantal and her, I'm sure I'd get my ass handed to me if I got either one angry at me."

"Fair enough."

Regibus moved forward and interjected before the fight got any more serious.

"I don't want to bother anyone but I think it's time we start heading out."

Aurelina huffed and made her way towards the cavern's watery exit. Theia and Chantal also made their way out as they angrily conversed. Regibus sighed as Jade walked up to him and awkwardly patted him on the back.

"At least you got them to stop, good job," Jade complimented.

Jade made her way to the exit leaving Regibus reassured. She dove back into the water as Olius made his way in.

"This group isn't going to last," Olius grumbled.

"Don't say that, we've all fought before," Hector said as he patted Olius on the shoulder.

"Yeah, but this is different. This journey is either going to bring us together or have us at each other's throats," Olius argued as he stored his book away.

"With that mentality it's going to happen," Darvell scoffed. "We'll all be fine once we've properly kicked ass."

"Darvell, you can't solve group issues with fighting. We are literally trying to prevent any more fighting amongst us," Olius interjected.

"Olius, a good group has got to have some variation," Regibus stated. "Without it, we'd be bored all the time."

"Are you willing to sacrifice group security for fun?" Olius asked, his question on the border of sounding like rude sarcasm.

"I would," Hector butted in.

Olius turned around and gave him an angry glare. Hector gulped and reached slowly for his shield. Olius groaned and made his way back to the exit.

"Let's just get going. We need to leave this jungle now."

CHAPTER 12

Darvell was the last one to rise out of the water. He could see Aurelina storming into the wagon as Theia and Chantal were talking by a tree. Theia was trying to calm Chantal who was punching a rather large hole into the tree. Olius was pacing back and forth nervously as he held the battered and broken fish in the bottle. Hector and Regibus seemed to be the only people who weren't consumed by the heavy atmosphere of stress. But they looked worried that the group would disband after coming so far. Jade was nowhere to be seen, probably surveying the area. Darvell frowned, walked towards Olius, and snatched the fish. He put the bottle over his hand and lit his hand on fire. Olius screamed in fear and tried to grab the bottle back but Darvell held him at bay with his tail.

"What the hell are you doing Darvell?!" Olius screamed. "Are you trying to get us killed?"

"Maybe I am! I'd rather have some godly being tear us limb from limb than tearing ourselves apart," Darvell barked back as he kept Olius away from the bottle. "Why the hell are we getting all worked up about some stupid fish?"

"Some people don't know how to not fuck up a simple task!" Aurelina yelled from inside the wagon.

Chantal stopped punching the tree and began to walk towards the wagon. Theia grabbed her and tried to restrain her.

"Look at us!" Darvell pointed out. "We've broken down only twice and we're not even halfway into this place! We're much more than a group you guys, we are a family."

"Okay sure, we're a family. Can you please give me the only thing that's keeping us alive now?" Olius pleaded as he tried to grab the bottle.

Darvell narrowed his eyes and closed his fist. Olius's face beamed with relief as he reached for the bottle. Darvell opened his fist again and a roaring flame spewed forth from his palm. The little fish boiled alive as Olius's face went from relief to ice cold fear. Aurelina poked her head out to see what was going on, her jaw dropping as she laid eyes on the fire boiling the fish. Darvell stopped boiling the fish and threw the bottle as far as he could into the underbrush.

"Did he just..." Hector whispered to Regibus.

"I think he just did," Regibus replied. "I think he also knows what's coming next."

"Darvell. Do you know what you just did?" Aurelina quietly growled as she came out of the wagon.

"Yes," Darvell said triumphantly. "I got rid of the problem."

"No, you didn't. You made our problem even worse than it is right now! Marimonda is probably on her way to kill you all right now!"

Everyone looked around listening for the violent stomping of a god despite not knowing what it would sound like. However, none of them heard the sound of stomping or even the angry shriek of a furious deity. Aurelina looked around with a puzzled frown.

"She should be here right now," Aurelina said as she looked around.

"Well, I guess she didn't love that fish as much as you thought," Darvell said smugly.

"No, something is wrong. She would have felt that fish die miles away. Something has happened to her."

"I can confirm that idea," Jade yelled as she came from down the path.

"What do you mean?" Regibus asked.

"While I scouted ahead, I saw that I didn't return here so I decided to make my way back to the wagon. As I made my way back, I heard a vicious growl out in the distance and a surge of divine magic coursed through the jungle. It couldn't have been you Aurelina, and my best guess would be it came from Marimonda," Jade explained as she reached the group.

"This is great news! We can leave now and not have to deal with Marimonda," Olius rejoiced as he made his way to the wagon.

"We can't just leave," Aurelina argued. "Doesn't it bother you guys that she's dealing with something that's taking up all her attention to the point she forgot about us?"

"Even more of a reason to leave Aurelina," Hector replied. "If a goddess is having trouble dealing with it then what chance do we stand?"

"I don't know about you guys but I'm willing to fight this thing." Darvell grinned as he cracked his knuckles. "It also wouldn't be a good idea to let that thing roam and catch us by surprise later on."

"We can't just blindly go into this fight Darvell," Olius insisted. "It would be—hey hey! Don't just go charging off!"

Darvell was in mid-run as he turned his head and smiled. Olius groaned and rubbed his temples. He looked back at the others and pulled out his book.

"We all know Darvell's ready to fight," Olius stated. "What about the rest of you?"

"I think Cutthroat can fight. If he isn't, you know you have me," Regibus assured.

"I'll do my part," Hector said as he raised his spear. "I also have Nugget to help me."

"Chantal needs to blow off some steam. I think this is the best way," Theia said as she pulled out her bow. "As for me, I'm ready as well."

"My mother would get worried if something happened to her. I'm sort of obligated to help in a way," Aurelina reluctantly agreed.

"So, what do you say, Olius?" Darvell asked as he gripped his greatsword. "Are you going to fight?"

"Let's go kick some ass then," Olius groaned as he readied his book.

"Then get on the coach and lead the way! Everyone else, prepare yourselves," Darvell cheered as everyone made their way into the wagon.

Out of anyone in the damn world to be the chosen one, it had to be Darvell, Olius thought to himself as he got on the coach seat.

As Darvell dragged the cart through the jungle, dashing around corners and over rocks, Olius held tightly to the coach seat, holding the compass in front of him to measure the strength of the magic in the area. The compass spun violently towards the right.

"Turn right!" Olius yelled.

Darvell steered the cart to the right and the compass readjusted itself to pointing straight ahead.

"Marimonda is dead ahead!"

"Ha! Brace for impact!" Darvell cheered.

"Wait! No no no no!"

Darvell stopped in his tracks and bent his knees to jump into the air, taking the cart with him. As the cart flew through the air, Olius screamed while Darvell laughed maniacally with joy. Darvell and the cart landed and skidded across the dirt ground, coming to a halt as he and Olius took a sudden look around. There were no sounds of birds or small critters scurrying about, only the unending visage of a battle that had taken place.

As Darvell unhitched himself from the cart, he slowly approached the battlefield, putting his hands on his revolvers as he continued to take it all in. The bodies were hanging from vines by the throat, gently rocking back and forth, or impaled by wooden spikes jutting out of the ground. Some of the bodies seemed to belong to Zlo's army, although the blood on their armor made it difficult to distinguish the lion crest that made them identifiable. Those that didn't die at the hands of the plant life seemed to have been torn asunder by some of the crocodilian beasts native to the jungle. However, as Olius hopped down to inspect with Darvell, they both could see that something had ripped open their thick, green hides and split open the soft underbellies. Thrown across the ground were the wooden shards of shields that the crocodilians probably used to defend themselves. Many of the shattered weapons that could be seen looked like they belonged to both Zlo's soldiers and the crocodilians. Olius bent over to get a better look at the ground, having seen a large human footprint left amongst the wake of the dead.

"This might explain why those guardians were scouting the jungle. They weren't just looking for us, they were looking for the actual intruders," Olius said as he rubbed his chin. "Then this might also explain why Marimonda hasn't ripped us apart yet."

"Olius, what the hell are we dealing with?" Darvell asked.

"Something that can cause so much destruction that it caught the attention of a goddess," Olius concluded, a shiver escaping with his explanation.

As Chantal got out of the wagon, she felt a surge of pain

through her head and she fell onto the floor. Theia jumped from the wagon and helped her up.

"What happened Chantal?" Theia asked as she lifted Chantal from the floor.

She shook her head and moved her hands to explain, another jolt of pain surging through her.

"Chantal says that the magic here is strange, almost painful to be around. I feel a little pain in my eye but it's nothing to write home about," Theia said as she rubbed her eyes.

"My body is kind of tense but I'm feeling fine," Jade replied. "Something or someone around here is the cause of this."

"Well we're not going to find them here, nothing but corpses," Hector nervously said as he got down from the wagon.

"But the compass led us here for some reason," Olius worried as he looked at it again.

Olius narrowed his eyes towards the compass and could see that the arrow was bending and splitting apart. Olius yelped and threw the compass away. They all watched it explode.

"The magic here is fluctuating horribly. The compass couldn't handle the pressure," Olius said as he looked back at the others.

"Great, now we're lost and have no idea where the source of the magic is coming from," Aurelina grumpily said.

"Then we should just look the old fashioned way," Darvell proudly stated.

"You don't mean it do you?" Olius whined.

"Exactly that, we'll use our eyes," Darvell said with a smile as he started to look around.

"That'll take forever! We don't have that kind of time," Theia said as she gestured to the jungle around them. "This place is huge!"

"With that attitude it will take forever," Darvell countered as he walked away from the group. "Quit your whining and let's go!"

Darvell made his way into the underbrush and disappeared

within the jungle. Regibus walked over to Olius and tapped him on the shoulder.

"Can't you make another compass? One that can handle some magical overload."

"Oh, I forgot I could do that." Olius chuckled as he scratched the back of his head. "I keep forgetting I'm a wizard sometimes. I'll start working on the new compass, the rest of you make sure Darvell doesn't wander off too far."

As the others left to look for Darvell, Olius hopped into the wagon and headed to his workshop to work on the new compass.

"Darvell! Where are you?" Hector yelled out into the jungle air.

"Do you really think it's a good idea to yell out loud when there's something in these monster infested jungles ready to kill us?" Theia questioned.

"I'm sure it'll be fine. We've taken on all sorts of monsters during our time here, we can handle a few more," Hector beamed confidently.

"You say that Hector," Jade said as she led the group through the jungle. "But keep in mind that there's a strong possibility that something in this jungle might not even be from here if Marimonda is having trouble with it."

Hector gulped and gripped his shotgun as he looked down at the ground. As they continued to walk through the jungle, they came across a large set of ruins scattered across the floor. A large, grey ziggurat stood amongst a clearing in the trees. It reached just above the treetops of the jungle, four ramps of weathered and vine eaten steps leading to a yellow, stained marble altar. Atop the larger blocks that made up the ziggurat, vines and moss made their home on the broken stone monuments of Marimonda. Some of the statues were missing their heads or arms; others were completely in half or covered in a vicious net of vines. The bright blue sky could be seen above as a few wisps of white clouds floated by. The trees around the ziggurat were thicker and far darker in color. They seemed to choke and narrow the paths around the jungle. Their branches extended farther outward, almost wrapping around other branches near them as heavy green vines dropped downwards to the ground.

As they walked around, Chantal felt her knees weaken until she couldn't walk anymore. She sat down near a stone pedestal while the others looked around.

"Hey Aurelina, what is this place?" Hector asked.

"Well, a few hundred years ago, people used to come here and worship the gods who didn't like to walk amongst them. They felt it would be better to set up towns and centers dedicated to their idols on their holy ground. It was going well until settlers were popping up way too fast and taking up all the space around here. So the gods declared this place and the others deeper in the Garden of the Gods forbidden from people. Those who were real fanatics were probably killed by monsters or something; I wasn't here when it happened."

"So they just sent monsters to kill them?" Jade asked.

"Oh heavens no, the monsters are free to do their bidding. Their homes are here as well and people intruding would cause them to kill."

"I'm sort of relieved that the gods won't send monsters to kill us, but at the same time worried because the monsters don't have anything holding them back," Hector stated.

"It'll be fine. Nothing my strong and handsome knight can't handle," Aurelina said as she gave Hector a kiss on the lips.

"Ha ha, of course," Hector blabbered.

"Can you guys focus? We're trying to find out what's causing all of this," Jade said.

"I'm sorry Darvell isn't here but that doesn't mean you can rain on our parade," Aurelina scoffed.

Jade rolled her eyes and walked off towards one of the temples. Regibus frowned and started to walk with her. As soon as he reached her, she began to walk a little bit faster. Regibus groaned and caught up with her again.

"What do you want?" Jade asked, crossing her arms.

"Can't a big brother hang out with his favorite little sister?" Regibus said, putting his hands out as if he were suggesting a hug.

"Of course he can…" Jade slowly said.

Regibus's eyes widened as he let out a smile.

"If he were a good brother in the first place," Jade quickly countered.

Regibus's smile faded as he slumped over. Jade scoffed and started to walk away. Regibus tightened his fist and ran up next to her.

"What's wrong with you?! I'm trying to make up for lost time and you're shunning me for trying! What do I have to do to make it up to you?"

"You already know," Jade recalled as she inspected the temple ruins.

"I'm not telling you, it's for the best Jade," Regibus argued, his voice suddenly stern.

"Then you still suck," Jade said as she turned around and glared at him.

Regibus shook his head and left Jade alone. Theia walked over to Chantal and examined her. She was starting to pant and blush as she limply moved her hand towards Theia's.

"Something's not right here. Is anyone else's bandanna wearing off?" Theia asked, her voice becoming more concerned.

"No, I'm fine," Regibus said as he came back to the center of the field of ruins.

"I'm okay as well," Hector responded.

"Then Chantal's feeling the force of the magic. I'm having second thoughts about finding Marimonda."

"I'm with Theia. I'm not fond of my aunt anyway. Even if Chantal is kind of rude, it pains me to see something happen to her," Aurelina said as she flew to the top of one of the pillars.

Chantal looked up and weakly moved her hands.

"Gee, thanks," Theia translated.

Suddenly, there was an explosion on the other side of the field. Everyone but Theia and Chantal ran over to the site of the explosion to see Jade flying through the air and landing right in front of them. They looked forward and saw One walking towards them, a thick chain wrapped around his hand. Following him was a squad of fifty imperial soldiers marching at his left and right. He looked at the group and laughed as he yanked the chain forward. The chain extended through the crowd of soldiers towards the back.

"I was tasked by Zlo to find all of you and kill you by any means necessary. However, you idiots have done me a favor and came right to me. All that's left is the fun part of seeing you all die."

"Yeah right, we'll show you who's an idiot!" Hector said as he raised his spear.

"Ah yes, the powerless one is going to show me," One mocked.

Hector lowered his spear a bit and quivered.

"Give it up One! All of you are nothing but a bug in the eyes of the gods!" Aurelina retaliated.

"That was in the past my dear angel. Dark magic courses through our veins and although we cannot surpass the gods yet, we can surely go toe-to-toe with them!" One bellowed as he pulled his sword and slammed it on the ground with a violent thud.

"Well Darvell kicked your sorry ass once," Jade weakly yelled as she slowly rose from the ground. "That means he can do it again!"

"Is that so?" One asked, his voice beginning to erupt with laughter. "Where is the pathetic fool any—"

One was then shot in the face, leaving a golf ball-sized hole right in the middle of his forehead. Everyone turned around to see Darvell aiming his revolver at One. Darvell frowned and walked towards the others as he unsheathed his greatsword. One, still conscious, laughed maniacally as his body began to reform, strands of dark, ethereal string filling the wound in his head. Darvell gripped the hilt of his greatsword, holding back his rage until the moment was right.

"It seems that it was a good idea to bring some assistance with me," One said, slowly jostling the chain he had in his hand.

"Thank you, sir."

"I wasn't talking about you; most of you are going to die anyway!" One exclaimed without looking at them.

The soldier was going to retaliate but the other soldier next to him grabbed his shoulder and shook his head.

"Anyway, it would be a shame not to let the monk see what I have to kill all of you," One continued to say to the group.

"What do you want with Chantal?" Theia retaliated as she and Chantal ran to the group.

"Not me, archer. Someone else wants the pleasure of taking her down."

One pulled on the chain and a low growl could be heard from behind the wall of soldiers. They parted to the left and right to reveal a hidden figure, its body hulking forward. It was covered in deep scars, poorly hidden by a tattered black cloth. The cloth had a hood attached to it that covered most of the head. Along his wrists were thick iron bands held together by a chain connected to the chain One was holding. He wore no shoes while his brown baggy pants were covered in fresh bloodstains. He stopped before One and stood up straight, revealing a little bit of his neck. A large cauterized and stitched wound could be seen from the front. Theia's and Darvell's bodies began to tense as soon as they realized who was under the hood. Chantal looked up at the ominous figure in fear, her voice freezing up if she had one.

One laughed as he dropped the chain, causing the man to rip off his shackles and remove his hood. On his face was a large hand-shaped scorch mark. His eyes were white as quartz while his teeth looked like thick yellow fishhooks. His physique was more muscular as thick black veins pulsed slowly, almost to the point of not moving, across his grey body.

"I would like all of you to meet the new and improved Nezer!" One shouted at the others, his arms thrown forward.

CHAPTER 13

Everyone stood in fear as they saw Nezer stand by One, his veins pulsing across his wounded body. Chantal's eyes widened as tears flowed down her cheeks, seeing her brother turned into an undead monster. She felt her legs fill with the desire to flee but, paralyzed by fear and despair, was unable to move at all. Nezer stood hunched over, silently staring off into space as the others prepared themselves. As One watched intently for their reactions, he could see the despair in Chantal's soul and laughed. Theia clenched her teeth as she took a step in front of Chantal.

"We had to sneak back into the village to get his body and head. We couldn't lose such a valuable asset, right Nezer?" One asked mockingly.

Nezer stood there quietly with a stoic face. One rolled his eyes and continued to taunt the group.

"At least he doesn't talk back. So tell me Darvell, are you ready for a rematch?"

"I don't know. Two on one doesn't seem so fair to me. Although, I'd still kick both of your asses," Darvell taunted back as he admired his greatsword.

"Oh no, I can't stay. I have too much work to prepare for

your demise. I want it to be special. Nezer on the other hand would love to do it for me."

One raised his hand and the familiar purple haze enveloped him. As it faded, he was gone and Nezer was left standing in front of the wall of soldiers. They looked at each other and at Nezer, who quietly stood there.

"Is he going to do anything?" whispered one of the soldiers.

Nezer suddenly tensed up and a black energy formed around his hands. The black light reconstructed itself into two large axes. The handles were made of black Damascus iron with iron bear heads on the butt of the axe heads. The axes were connected to the iron shackles on Nezer's wrists as thin ghostly chains jingled with his stiff movements. Nezer's teeth began to thicken as heavy drool poured out of his mouth. His quartz white eyes began to crack as lines of dark red danced across like lightning. He broke into a sprint, his heavy foot leaving a print in the soft earth, and charged towards the group.

"I guess that's the signal."

The soldiers charged, their spears pointed forward, as Darvell and the others pulled out their weapons. Darvell took flight, his heavy wings stirring up dust as he rose, as Aurelina followed suit. Darvell breathed in and let out a blast of fire from his mouth, scorching the ground below as soldiers dove out of the way. Aurelina took her knives and imbued them with divine magic. She dove down closer to the soldiers and threw three of them. The knives exploded as bright light blinded the soldiers that were too close to the blast radius.

As the soldiers fell, Nezer charged through the fire and light, unfazed by either, and charged towards Chantal. Olius, who was firing bolts of blue arcane energy, saw where Nezer was heading.

"Theia!" Olius yelled, "he's after Chantal!"

Theia, who was in the back firing arrows, narrowed her eyes and shifted her gaze towards Nezer. She pulled back on the bowstring and sent an arrow flying towards him. As the arrow hit him, Theia saw that the arrow didn't faze him as he maintained his charge. Suddenly a black aura formed around the arrow and caused the wood and iron to decay. Nezer continued his charge towards Chantal and raised both of his axes in the air. Chantal rolled out of the way as Nezer swung them downwards. Olius and Regibus ran over to Chantal to help stop Nezer's onslaught. Olius extended his staff and shot a ray of frost while Regibus extended his arm forward as a flash of green raced across it. The humid air around him became cold as water formed across his body. As the water enveloped itself around him, the ray of frost froze the water and encased him in a thick block of ice. Suddenly, the ice began to crack as Nezer broke through it and rushed towards Chantal once more.

"Damn it!" Regibus growled. "It didn't even slow him down!"

"It seems that they have done something to his physical state. If he were brought back to life normally, ice that thick would have stopped him," Olius responded as he looked through his spell book. "You guys keep him controlled while I figure out what happened to him."

Regibus nodded and ran towards Nezer, forming a cutlass from the water in the air. Meanwhile, Darvell descended from the sky and pulled out his greatsword. He began to swing left and right, his blade slicing through soldiers as streams of blood flew through the air. Aurelina fired a beam of light at the soldiers and saw that Hector was being attacked. She flew to him as Darvell looked up and smiled. The soldiers felt uneasy as they saw him unfurl his wings and stand up.

"I have all of you to myself." Darvell laughed, smoke pouring out of his mouth.

Darvell raised his greatsword and slammed it into the closest soldier. He breathed out a short burst of fire and scorched the soldiers around him. He swished his tail, knocking some of them back. As Darvell finished killing the soldiers, he breathed heavily as he looked at the bodies.

"I guess that's that," Darvell panted, sweat forming on his hands. "Time to go fight Nezer."

Before he could go and help the others, he saw the corpses of the soldiers rise from the ground. Their once human faces were replaced with ghastly black eyes and white skin. They raised their spears in an eerie unison and extended them forward towards Darvell.

"Well shit."

Darvell quickly reached for his revolvers and fired a couple of shots towards the soldiers. Unfazed, they continued to shuffle towards Darvell. He took a step back and started to run towards the others. The soldiers charged towards him as hellish growls escaped their mouths, like a symphony of hornets buzzing through the air.

Aurelina dove down to Hector, but not before seeing the soldiers come back to life. She gasped and flew faster to Hector, who had finished killing the soldiers around him. She plucked a couple of feathers and quickly jammed them into the eyes of the soldiers. The soldiers screamed, light pouring out of their eyes and mouths, before crumbling away into dust.

"That bastard must have cursed these soldiers to turn undead once they died. Do you mind telling me who the hell this guy is?" Aurelina yelled.

"That guy over there is Chantal's brother. Darvell killed him after we all learned he was a traitor to Chantal's village. I guess they brought him back to life. He was a lot more talkative back then," Hector said, still in slight shock at seeing a human turn into dust.

Nezer growled and continued to swing at Chantal with his axes. His eyes never looked at Chantal directly, and his swings didn't look precise. It was like looking at an invisible puppeteer maneuvering their marionette. However, despite the lackluster coordination, Nezer managed to create small cuts on Chantal's body as she sluggishly tried to keep up with Nezer's violent attacks. Her orange aura began to slowly fade away as her stance began to suffer.

"Leave her alone!" Theia yelled as she nocked an arrow on her bowstring and aimed.

The arrow's head was made out of white iron with two long fins protruding backwards. The shaft was made entirely out of a slick black material, almost like rubber. Theia let go of the arrow, watching it fly into the lower half of Nezer. He grunted as he looked down at the arrow. The shaft began to loosen as strands began to extend outward, wrapping themselves around Nezer's entire body. He tried to rip the strands apart only to have them wrap around tighter, crushing his body and bones. Nezer began to lose his balance and fell to the ground with a thud, twitching wildly to release himself from his binds.

As Chantal sighed with relief, she and Theia could see Darvell punch and slash at the zombified soldiers trying to overwhelm him. He was violently yelling with every swing, bursts of fire and smoke pouring out of his mouth as he tried to keep them at bay. They began piling on top of him and biting into his body. He tried to burn them off but their unrelenting desire to eat him did nothing to deter them.

"Somebody help Darvell!" Theia yelled as she fired a couple of arrows into the mob.

"Hold on!" Hector yelled as he reached for his shotgun and shield.

Hector ran towards the swirling mass of zombies, smacking the ones on his left with his shield and firing his shotgun in front of him. Some of the zombified soldiers turned their attention to Hector and they began to move towards him. They extended their hands towards Hector and grabbed him by the arms and the legs.

"Get off me!" Hector yelled as he tried to stab and slash with his spear.

Aurelina's ears twitched as she heard Hector scream, quickly turning her attention towards him. She immediately raised her hands as her eyes began to glow. She spoke, her voice echoing louder as a horrible buzzing of wings filled the air. A large swarm of locusts began to fly through the air as it dove down and filled the area. As the swarm descended, they started to gnaw at the zombies, reducing them only to bones.

"What are you doing Aurelina?!" Olius yelled as he backed away from the swarming storm of locusts.

"I'm saving Hector, what does it look like I'm doing?" Aurelina responded, her voice booming in Olius's ears as she stared at him with heavenly white eyes.

"Hector and Darvell are still in there!" Olius yelled. "They'll get eaten alive as well!"

Aurelina's white stare broke as she opened her eyes in worry. The locusts' buzzing grew louder as the swarm dispersed all over the rocky field. Everyone shielded their eyes as the locusts violently flew around, smacking into everyone.

"I'm sorry! I panicked and I—" Aurelina worried as she swatted at the locusts.

"Just call them off!" Olius loudly said, trying to get his voice to overpower the sound of the swarm around him.

"I can't, I lost my concentration on them. I'll have to take some time to regain control." Aurelina rapidly looked around. "Just give me a few minutes. You and the others take care of the undead soldiers and Nezer. You'll need to finish them off completely with light, okay?"

Olius nodded in confirmation as he ran to regroup with anyone in the swarm. Aurelina flew out of the swarm and put out her hands, chanting the spell again to regain control. Meanwhile, Chantal looked back and saw that Nezer's wrappings were being ripped by the biting and gnawing of the locusts. Nezer then ripped apart his confines and let out a deep, bear-like growl. Chantal grabbed Theia's attention and pointed to Nezer, who was turning around to face them. The locusts, despite being a bothersome menace, hardly made Nezer flinch. As he stared at them, one of the locusts crawled onto his eye and stood on top of it.

"I guess he really is undead," Theia coldly stated. "Are you sure you are up for this?"

Chantal weakly nodded and put up her fists as Theia pulled out another arrow. Nezer growled quietly as a violent purple glow emerged around him. Chantal could feel her body weaken as she stared at Nezer's glowing body. She then collapsed as Nezer's eyes met hers.

"Chantal!" Theia screamed as she caught her in her arms.

Nezer walked up to them as the storm of locusts flew around and buzzed violently in the air. Theia looked up to see the dark silhouette of Nezer standing above them. His body was obscured by the locusts swarming around them. All that Theia could see was his silhouette and the menacing, purple glow of his two eyes.

"Forgive...me," Nezer growled through his teeth.

Nezer raised one axe in the air, swinging it down towards Theia. She closed her eyes and waited for her death. She held on tightly to Chantal's body, a tear escaping her closed eyes.

Bang.

Theia felt the spatter of ice cold blood hit her face as she opened her eyes. She looked up to see that Nezer's hand had been blown off of his wrist. Theia looked back to see Jade aiming her rifle. On her face was a translucent mask made out of emerald green light with an opaque black visor where her eyes would be. The entire mask made Jade's face look featureless, adding to her stoicism as she put another bullet into her rifle. She reloaded the rifle and aimed at Nezer's head. Angrily, Nezer ran towards Jade and raised his other axe in the air. As Nezer reached her, she put out a thumbs-up. Nezer slowed his charge, confused, before he felt Darvell tackle him in the side of his stomach.

Nezer got up from the ground and looked up at Darvell, who was bleeding heavily from wounds across his body, a thin trail of blood dripping down the sides of his mouth. Yet, there was a confident smile as he held his greatsword, letting the tip of the blade hit the ground. Nezer scowled as he gripped his axe and bared his teeth. Nezer and Darvell rushed towards each other, roaring loudly as the clash of steel resounded through the swarm of locusts.

Jade dashed over to Theia and Chantal. She could see Theia sobbing as she caressed the still body of Chantal. Jade took off her mask and began to inspect Chantal.

"She's dead, Jade!" Theia bawled as tears rolled down her face. "It's my fault; I wasn't able to protect her."

"She isn't dead, Theia," Jade comforted as she touched the side of Chantal's neck. "She's just unconscious. Give her this and hopefully she'll wake up soon."

Jade handed Theia a rather miniscule vial with a clear liquid swirling inside. Jade stood back up and disappeared back into the locust storm. Theia uncorked the vial and began to pour the liquid into Chantal's mouth.

"Please be okay Chantal," Theia pleaded through her stuttering.

Chantal slowly opened her eyes to find herself in a familiar room. She looked around and could see that it was her home back at the Neveralpa Mountains. She felt the warm roar of the fire in the fireplace as she stood up. The room was filled with hanging wind chimes and scented candles emitting a nostalgic smell of pine and oranges. For some odd reason, the overall feel of the room was smaller than what Chantal remembered. As she walked around the creaky wooden floor, the room began to shift slowly to center on a cradle being rocked by a man. Chantal walked towards the cradle and saw that it was her father. He turned around and smiled, getting up to hug Chantal. She jumped into his arms, knocking him a bit back as a quick chuckle escaped his mouth.

"Chantal, it's so good to see you again. Before you say anything, I'd like to congratulate you for freeing the kingdoms," Amos said, his voice warming Chantal's heart.

Chantal blushed and moved her hands asking where she was.

"Well my dear, you are in what some call the space between the mortal realm and the spirit realm. I felt your spirit quaver so I brought you here to let it rest. "

Chantal moved her hands slowly, asking if she was strong enough to continue going forward.

"It's okay my sweet child. You've made it this far and I know you can keep going. If not for yourself, do it for the ones you love," Amos said as he stepped back and winked.

Chantal smiled and moved her hands for one final question.

"You would like to know what happened to your brother? He simply has lost his way like I once did. You can make him whole again, Chantal."

Chantal angrily moved her hands, declaring that Nezer was too strong to fight.

"Too strong? From what I remember, you always won when you two were roughhousing," Amos laughed as he slapped his knee. "But it would seem that dire situations require solutions. Stare into the fire over there."

Chantal looked over to the fireplace and could see the fire flicker in and out and turn blue. Chantal walked over by the fire and stared intently into it, feeling her skin get colder instead of hotter. She felt that cold breeze nestle through her body, bringing back a flood of memories. She then slowly turned into ash that flew into the cold blue fire. Amos returned to rocking the cradle as he watched over the two children inside. One child was holding a stuffed brown bear while the other held a small green snake with orange bird wings protruding from its spine.

Chantal opened her eyes as she abruptly got up and looked around. The swarm of locusts was still active as she saw a glimpse of Darvell and Nezer's fight. Nezer had Darvell by the throat, chucking him forward with a heavy grunt upon releasing him. Darvell impacted the ground and slid through the dirt, coughing blood as he lay on his back, unable to get back up. Nezer shuffled over to his blown-off hand and grabbed it. He put it back into his bleeding wrist as purple strands of flesh enveloped itself around the wound, stitching the two pieces together. Nezer flexed his fingers and summoned both of his axes.

"Chantal! You're okay!" Theia exclaimed as she embraced her.

Chantal took Theia by cheeks and kissed her before she got up and cracked her knuckles. As she walked away, leaving Theia dumbfounded, Nezer turned his attention to Chantal and bared his teeth. Dark purple smoke began to cascade off Nezer, enveloping him tightly as it took shape. The smoke took the form of a tattered black leather cloak with a bear skull hood, pearly white teeth pressed against Nezer's head. The purplish smoke then wrapped around his hands into leather gloves in the shape of bear claws. Both of Nezer's axes scraped against the ground as he shuffled towards Chantal.

As the others finished off the undead soldiers, Aurelina was able to finish reciting her spell to dispel the locusts. As they flew away, everyone could see that in the middle of it all were Nezer and Chantal, circling around each other. Jade ran towards Darvell and looked over his wounds.

"You need to stop being so headstrong," Jade scolded.

"But...it's my specialty," Darvell joked, coughing as he slowly got up.

As Jade helped Darvell back to safety, the others watched Nezer and Chantal stare each other down. Chantal had regained her strength, her bright orange aura glowing stronger and brighter. She breathed in slowly and held the air before just as slowly letting it out. Nezer snarled as spittle flew out of his mouth, layered hellish growling gurgling out of his mouth.

"We have to help her," urged Theia, making her way to the group.

"None of us are strong enough to go toe-to-toe with Nezer and Darvell is too weak right now to help her," Jade explained as she pulled out some bandages.

"We would only distract her anyway," Olius stated as he stared at Chantal. "I can feel a surge of magic coming from her, something that will be able to defeat Nezer."

Chantal closed her eyes and took another deep breath in. She began to search deep in her head for all the times she had spent with her brother out amongst the piles of snow, the stories he had sat down to tell her so she could fall asleep and the times he had saved her from the other kids around the village. She focused on his face, full of color and life. She opened her eyes and looked at what stood in front of her. All she saw was grey and death, a pale imitation of what her brother was. Chantal focused her thoughts and separated the two from each other, splitting apart the memory of her brother from the vile darkness she could see. Now all that lay in front of her was evil, one that she felt needed to be vanquished.

She put her arms up, fingers pointed forward as she gently moved her legs apart and bent downwards slightly. The orange glow around her began to morph into green and then blue, alternating between those three colors. Then Chantal took her right foot and stepped back as she placed her left foot forward. She put her right arm by her side, closing her fist as she put her left hand in front of her, her palm facing outward. She stopped glowing, the aura disappearing altogether. Chantal opened her eyes and let out her breath as she looked towards Nezer. She narrowed her brows and put out her other hand, bending her fingers towards her to commence the fight.

Nezer shuffled forward as Chantal mirrored his footsteps before the two of them began to run at each other. Nezer lunged forward, waving his axes wildly with as much force as he could use. Chantal slithered between each strike, ducking and leaping over them as she studied her brother's movements. Once she felt the ground beneath her feet again, she ducked between his legs and grabbed his ankles. She gripped them tight as she pulled them with her as she rose from the ground. Nezer quickly fell forward, putting his hands out to stop his fall. As he did, Chantal grabbed him by the end of his cloak and abruptly pulled him back up. She took her free hand and punched the lower half of his back, sending a surge of pain into his spine.

Nezer growled fiercely, regaining his balance, as he turned to face her. With a faster flurry of swings, he cut through the air as he tried to hack her into pieces. Chantal, forced to stay close fearing that a misstep could end her, used her fingers and quickly guided the axes away from her. She began to study the slashes and ducked underneath the last one, grabbing the axe by the shaft to propel herself away from him.

Nezer saw Chantal suddenly leave his sight and looked around for her, turning around and receiving a roundhouse kick to the face. Nezer, dazed by the impact, watched through his blurry vision as she was about to deliver another kick. He put out his hand and grabbed her by the ankle before flinging her behind him. Chantal tumbled through the air as she hit the ground with a brief thud.

"I can't watch this. I need to help her!" Theia cried as she pulled out her bow.

"Don't Theia," Olius warned as he put his hand in front of

her. "This is just like the time she fought her father. She's grown a lot along this journey so trust her, she can do this."

Theia looked back at the duel, almost causing her lip to bleed from biting it. She pushed Olius's hand away and pulled out an arrow. Streaks of white light cascaded off the arrow as it flew towards Nezer's head. To Theia's disappointment, the arrow found no purchase as it exploded with one look from Nezer's piercing purple eyes. Theia was caught in his demonic gaze, stricken with fear as her body lifelessly collapsed.

Chantal caught a glimpse of Theia's collapse as it caused her body to tense. She rose from the ground and ran towards Nezer, leaping into the air as she struck the bridge of his nose with an open palm. Dazed again, Chantal concentrated her strength into her foot to strike at his head once more. Nezer, expecting another kick, grabbed her foot before it could reach his head. However, Chantal propelled herself up with her other foot and kicked him with that one instead. The force of the strike forced Nezer to let go, stumbling backward and growling with rage. As she landed, Nezer threw a blind punch in hopes of striking her. Chantal dashed out of the way and got back on her feet only to see Nezer going for another punch. She put up her hands and redirected the punches away from her as she slithered between his strikes.

As Nezer threw out one last punch, Chantal grabbed it and breathed in quickly before throwing Nezer above her and into the ground. As she backed away, Nezer slowly got up and cracked his shoulders. Chantal breathed in heavily, feeling her lungs hurt as she cracked her fingers. Nezer ran towards her as she stood still, putting her closed fists beside her. Once Nezer reached her, he threw his punch, landing it across Chantal's face. However, as he did, Chantal grabbed Nezer's arm and pulled him in closer. Her fist, barely an inch from his chest, touched him as a ripple raced across his body. As Chantal let go, she watched Nezer's body fly backward into a boulder, cracking in half as he impacted it. His head split apart as the scar around his neck burst open, a stream of blood pouring out.

Chantal wobbled slightly before she spat out some blood, collapsing from exhaustion. She stared at Nezer, his lifeless body leaning against the rock. Her eyes began to water as she slowly got up and crawled towards Nezer. Tears began slowly gliding down from her eyes as she buried her face into her hands. She tried to hold back the image of her brother but the sight of his corpse broke her in the final moments of her concentration.

Olius stared at Chantal before he reached for his book, stopping at a page of reanimation. He read through the pages and suddenly began to smile. He rushed over to Aurelina, who had just finished healing Darvell.

"I think I found something," Olius said as he approached Aurelina. "I think there might be a chance that we can bring back Nezer."

"What?" Aurelina said, surprised at the notion. "Undead don't have souls that can be brought back, how does Nezer still have his?"

"He had far more autonomy than the other undead," Olius explained, quickly showing the pages of his book to Aurelina. "It must be because they wanted to preserve some aspect of his intellect. I'd argue they transformed him into a lesser lich."

"If what you're saying turns out to be true, I think we could revive him," Aurelina suggested. "But what about the mind control problem?"

"I can look into it and see if anything is still there," Olius confirmed as he looked back, seeing Chantal slowly laying herself across the ground as she went to sleep.

"Then it's settled. Darvell, get up," Aurelina ordered. "We need you to go get the wagon."

"Ugh...my bones hurt," Darvell groaned. "A few more minutes."

"Come on, get up," Aurelina groaned as she summoned her halo, gently waving it over Darvell's body.

Darvell rose from the ground as he felt his strength slowly come back to him. He sighed and trudged towards the direction of the wagon. Olius walked over to Theia, who was watching Chantal from a distance, biting her lip.

"You aren't going to go over there?" Olius asked. "She could really use you right now."

"What would I say to her, Olius? We just killed her brother again and I overheard that you and Aurelina want to revive him? What for, to kill him again?"

"Well in hindsight he can't die anymore...But that's beside the point. We've come a long way and I've never seen Chantal break like this. I'll leave it to you but if it were me, I would already be with her."

Olius walked away, leaving Theia staring at Chantal from a distance. She sighed and walked over to Chantal as she sat down to kneel beside her. Chantal weakly opened her crying eyes and looked up to see Theia. She smiled and lifted her head to put it on Theia's legs. As Chantal slept on Theia, she looked up and saw the once bright sky turning into dusk.

The still night hung above the shimmering green jungle. The quiet song of the local birds filled the sky as the stars sparkled above, giving off a bright and radiant shine to the group below. A few hours earlier, Darvell brought the wagon to the field, and everyone began to prepare themselves for the night. Everyone except Theia and Chantal, still by Nezer, still outside. Chantal had been asleep for a while and the longing for sleep was starting to overpower Theia. Before she could fall asleep, Darvell walked by and dropped a bunch of rocks in front of her, startling her as she quickly opened her eyes.

"What the fuck Darvell?" Theia angrily yawned.

"What? I'm making a fire for you. Aurelina says it gets cold during the night around here," Darvell said as he arranged the rocks into a poorly made circle. "Damn it, how do you make a circle?"

"You don't have to do this, you know. I'm sure it won't get that cold."

"Aurelina said so and it's the least I should do for you three."

"Three?"

"Yeah, Nezer over here was mind controlled from the start. I guess when he first met either One, Zlo, or any of those assholes they overpowered him and rearranged his mind."

"So he wasn't always like this?" Theia asked.

"No, Olius used some weird magic to contact Jaihind back in the Northern Kingdom and asked what Nezer was like. He explained it was for a resurrection spell and apparently he is an 'honor and strength are what matters' kind of person," Darvell explained as he grabbed a log of wood and lit it on fire. "So he is sort of a stick in the mud, but he isn't evil by nature."

Theia looked down at Chantal and played with her hair. The crackle of fire filled the cold air as Darvell lit his cigar. He took a deep puff and looked at a sulking Theia. He moved his cigar closer to Theia.

"Want to try some?" Darvell offered. "I promise it isn't bad. It has a good strong flavor."

"I really don't smoke; it isn't good for the lungs."

"Don't be such a wuss. One puff won't do you any real harm."

Theia furrowed her brows towards Darvell as she reached over for the cigar. She moved it towards her mouth and the cigar emitted a noxious dark smell of either burning coal or melting iron. Almost gagging at the smell, Theia put one end in her mouth and took a short puff. The taste of the smoke was just as bad as the smell, leaving a small scorching sensation in her throat. The smoke left her mouth in a small cloud as she pounded her chest, coughing.

"What is in this thing?" Theia complained, her voice raspy with the lingering smoke.

"Just some tobacco sprinkled with other stuff," Darvell said before he took a long drag.

"Like what? I swear if it's something that'll kill me—"

"No, of course nothing deadly," Darvell interjected, the smoke flying out of his mouth. "Just some spicy herbs to add flavor."

"This isn't flavor, Darvell," Theia argued. "This is like eating red hot ingots."

"I guess they aren't for everyone, pass it back then."

"Tell me something Darvell, what are you going to do after we finish this?" Theia asked as she handed the cigar back.

"I feel like we always have these talks. Why are you so interested?" Darvell joked before taking a puff from his cigar.

"Because, I find it hard to know what to do after we save the world. Our names will be known, we'll be regarded as heroes all over. I have no idea how to cope with all that fame. I'm sure it would go to your head."

"Maybe, but I'm doing this as a job with a little revenge on the side. For me, there are no heroics involved."

"So what are you going to do? Slink away and just leave society after saving it?"

"Of course not, I'll still be doing mercenary jobs after this," Darvell explained. "Planning for the future was never one of my strong suits."

"Neither is planning at all," Theia remarked jokingly.

"Ha ha, very funny. But I'm serious, we've all heard kid stories of people going and saving the day. But they never tell us what happens after that, we just assume they're living the good life. Now that we've been given the chance, who says more adventure is in store for us? I'm sure you and Chantal will continue to flirt and date, Aurelina and Hector will get hitched, Regibus will go back to being the vessel for Cutthroat's treasure exploits while Jade tries to find a loophole and Olius will probably go back to his castle and establish a 'democracy' so he can stay away from kingship and keep reading about magic."

"A what?"

"A 'democracy.' I have no idea what that is, he keeps using too many big words. He says it's something that lets people vote for a leader every couple of years. It's really complicated stuff that I have no intention of paying attention to."

"Well that's Olius for you. It's getting late; I guess we should get some rest now."

"You're right. I'll come back with some pillows for you guys."

Darvell got up from the ground and headed back towards the wagon. Theia looked around and picked up Chantal to lay her across her body. She gave her a kiss and they both leaned against the rock where Nezer was, leaving the crackling of the fire the only sound emanating in the night.

CHAPTER 14

As the crack of dawn broke through the skyline, the burning embers of the late night fire flickered away as Theia and Chantal quietly snored while the others slowly woke up from their beds. Olius was the first to walk out, carrying a cup of tea in one hand and swirling a yellow vial in the other. He breathed in the air and furrowed his brows at the slightly colder air. He shrugged it off and walked towards Nezer, sipping his tea. Olius looked at the slumped over corpse of the vicious killer, peaceful and at rest despite the bloodstains on his grey body. Olius finished the tea and poured the yellow liquid into the crack of the skull. The yellow water mixed with the pool of black sludge and started to close the gash, magically glueing together from the concoction of the viscous black and yellow liquids. Once the entire crack was closed off, the grey body of Nezer changed from its dead, grey color to a similar hue to Chantal's skin.

"Looks like the potion worked," Aurelina whispered as she walked up to Olius.

"I guess so. It's sort of a good thing Darvell got possessed at the beach; this second look into this possessive magic is very interesting. How long until he wakes up?" Olius responded quietly, gesturing to move away from the slumbering group.

"It won't take long. They didn't have to break out any strong magic to possess him since he was mind controlled for so long. Is it me, or did this place get colder?"

"Strange isn't it? I thought that the jungle was permanently hot, it appears I was wrong," Olius said, looking up at the sky. "Do you think Nezer's presence somehow changed the climate around the jungle?"

"It's a possibility, divine and undead magic are very powerful things and using both could have some adverse effects on more than just climate. I'm just glad Nezer here didn't have access to any stronger magic or this place wouldn't have lasted long," Aurelina said, scratching the back of her head.

"Let's hope we don't have to run into this too often. It's bad enough we have to deal with the environment killing us, we could have all sorts of people on our ass who could be working for Zlo."

"It would be a pain to deal with that problem."

"Indeed. I guess we should start leaving soon then? Don't want to waste any more time hanging about."

"Okay, but you have to wake Darvell up. He gets cranky and I'm not running that risk,"Aurelina said.

"I thought it was Hector's turn this time. I don't want to get pelted with his fiery morning breath after the entire bottle of whiskey he drank last night."

"I'll go wake up Hector then."

As Aurelina rushed to get Hector, Chantal sat down by Nezer to wait for him to wake up. Theia accompanied her as the others finished fixing themselves for the rest of the journey. Hector walked out of the wagon with black soot on his face and a few singed hairs as Darvell followed suit, shouting apologies.

"I'm sorry!" Darvell yelled. "I don't know why the hell I have morning breath this bad."

"Well learn to control it! Sooner or later, none of us are going to have hair on our heads," Hector yelled, wiping some of the soot from his eyes.

"Well, wear your armor next time."

Hector rolled his eyes and headed towards a nearby lake to wash off the soot. Darvell looked around and saw Theia and Chantal sitting by Nezer. He sighed and walked over with his hands in his pockets, whistling quietly as he stood over them. Chantal moved her hands and Theia sighed.

"What did she say?" Darvell asked.

"She asked if you were just going to stand there," Theia said. "She's having a moment, Darvell."

"Well I don't think this moment is going anywhere. Chantal, if you want I can bury him properly. I don't think Olius and Aurelina's magic juice worked properly."

"That won't be...necessary."

The three quickly turned towards Nezer as his eyes stared blankly back at them. Although his body was back to normal, his eyes had become glazed over with a dim white light, his pupils nowhere to be seen. He slowly got up, stumbling around once he was on his two feet. Chantal began to cry as Nezer put his cold, clammy hands on her face.

"No need to cry, sister. I'm just glad you didn't give up on me. I'm grateful that all of you didn't give up on me. Well, almost all of you," Nezer said as he stared off into the distance, Darvell walking out of his gaze.

"Can you see anything?" Theia asked as she helped Chantal off the floor.

"No and yes. I can't see how I used to before this magic was introduced into my body. But I have a new pair of eyes that lets me see you all as bright, colored lights."

"Sounds trippy," Darvell said with a hint of interest.

"Where are the two who helped me come back to life? I would like to thank them personally," Nezer said, slowly moving his head around.

"Would you like me to get them? They shouldn't be too far..." Theia said.

"That won't be necessary, Theia," Olius said as he walked over with Aurelina. "It seems that Nezer is finally awake, how do you feel? I need to make sure that there aren't any side effects lingering inside you."

"I feel nothing but rejuvenated. As if this body isn't my own."

"Well you should expect to feel that way for some time," Aurelina repiled. "Olius and I had to use a basic resurrection spell with some added ingredients to purify your body and soul to remove any control Zlo had over you."

"How come I can't see normally? All I can see are lights."

"Well, this is divine magic. What you see is how I perceive all of you, it's just I can see your souls and bodies since I'm a full-blooded divine being," Aurelina explained.

"This brings some comfort I suppose. The real problem I have, is where do I go now?"

Chantal perked her head up and signed what could be seen as a question. Nezer sighed and put his hand on Chantal's shoulder.

"I can't go back to the village, Chantal. I have done too much damage back home and I am ashamed to show my face to our father," Nezer said, his voice a bit distant.

"You could always come with us," Theia reassured. "There's plenty of room in the wagon."

"I am truly grateful for your offer, but I have done the same if not more damage to your group as well." Nezer thanked her with a smile that suddenly turned sour. "Also Darvell's soul morphed into a color that gives me the impression of...disapproval."

"I didn't say anything," Darvell responded as he put up his hands defensively.

Chantal raised her hand to slap Darvell, but Nezer stopped her before she could go into full swing.

"He's right Chantal. I would be uncomfortable as well if I were to join the group anyway."

At this moment in time, Regibus and Jade walked up quietly arguing before they reached the rest of the group. Nezer's face furrowed and turned to Aurelina, blindly staring at her.

"Would it be possible to stay here? I feel natural here and I don't think I'd like to go back to the cold of the mountains."

"Here?" Aurelina asked. "I don't know, I would have to talk to Marimonda and I don't know if she'd be—"

"Overjoyed to have a new addition to the jungle!" Marimonda declared.

Suddenly, everyone but Nezer drew their attention behind Aurelina as Marimonda appeared. They all took out their weapons and pointed them at her. She sighed and put her hands up in the air.

"I come peacefully. I came by to thank all of you for getting rid of those soldiers. It seems that they were focused on weakening me by destroying some of my beautiful jungle and subduing me. If it hadn't been for your timely arrival they might have succeeded."

"Cut to the chase, why do you want Nezer?" Theia asserted as she pulled back harder on the bowstring.

"Since you killed my guardians, I need a new one in the meantime. I would be glad to accept this one as I work on better guardians."

"I mean, not to be disrespectful, but I believe I have no more magic in me," Nezer said as he patted his body.

"Not true," Olius interjected. "In fact, I believe in a few days you'll feel like yourself again."

"Then it's settled! Nezer, you can stay here," Marimonda said as she walked over to Nezer.

"Nezer, are you sure you want to stay?" Aurelina asked.

"It's my best option right now. I feel better here anyway," Nezer responded with a smile.

Chantal walked up to him and stared with teary eyes. Nezer didn't stare down at her and instead stretched his arms out to embrace her. Chantal slowly hugged him as Nezer let out a single white tear. He bent down and whispered into her ear.

"I'm proud of you Chantal. Surely you can make the world better with these."

Chantal suddenly felt a strange feeling in her hands as Nezer grasped them tightly. A muted white glow cascaded off his hands and wrapped around her hands before he let go. She backed away and saw brown, fingerless gloves on her hands. Located on each knuckle was an iron stud that glistened underneath the sun. She looked back at Nezer and gave him a smile as he did the same.

"We best be off then," Regibus said as he adjusted his belt. "There is still much to cross before we reach Zlo."

"The rest of you may finish getting ready. I would like to talk to you, pirate," Nezer said as he put his hand on Regibus's shoulder.

"What do you need him for?" Jade questioned.

"This does not concern you right now. Maybe in the future he will heed my words when conversing with you," Nezer replied stoically without looking at her.

Jade gasped and was going to retaliate until Darvell put his hand on her shoulder. He gestured to move along towards the wagon. Grumpily, Jade swung her rifle on her back and made her way over. Nezer directly looked into Regibus's eyes, something he had not done with anyone else. He lowered his eyes and Regibus became nervous.

"What can I help with?" Regibus stuttered.

"Not me pirate, you. I see two souls within you, something very unnatural even without this sight."

"Oh that? That's my great grandfather, Cutthroat Alexander. Is that all you were worried about?"

"No pirate; let me finish. Where you have surplus in souls, the other you were talking to has none."

Regibus narrowed his gaze and breathed heavily. He pushed Nezer's hand off his shoulder and pushed him away.

"Listen pal, I may have not met you until yesterday but you have no business saying that. Your vision must be fucked up or something," Regibus barked.

"I have no idea how to fix this; nor I know how it works. But what I'm saying is true. Is she your sister, pirate?"

"How would you know?"

"The way siblings argue varies, but there is a common interest of safety for each other in every discussion. I may not know the cause for your discourse with your sister but know that whatever it is, it's in your best interest. I have nothing more to say."

Nezer then walked away into the jungle, disappearing almost immediately from Regibus's sight. He stood there, contemplating what Nezer had said. Cutthroat then appeared on Regibus's shoulder and looked towards the ground.

"I've known some gods in my life Regibus and when they're serious, they mean it. Even if Nezer is only one-fourth god or something, he was telling the truth."

"How long have you known?" Regibus said quietly, trying not to get himself any angrier.

"I just learned today Regibus; I'm a ghost, not a god. You can't ask her about this."

"Why not?" Regibus responded crudely as he made his way to the wagon.

"Because she's going to use it against us. The typical 'I can't do it but you can?' It will look bad on us in front of everyone," Cutthroat explained.

Regibus stopped in his tracks and tightened his hand into a fist. He felt torn between his secret, finding out what was wrong with Jade, and trying to protect her. He sighed and resumed walking.

"I guess you're right. We'll keep it to ourselves but just so you know, you're becoming more trouble than I expected," Regibus declared, his voice harsh.

"I'm glad you're seeing that it is. Are you going to kill the deal then?"

"No, not yet," Regibus reluctantly countered. "Without you I have no magic and I still need you to take care of Jade."

Cutthroat growled and disappeared in a wisp of smoke. Regibus hopped into the wagon and was met with Aurelina waiting by the door. She looked pensive as she looked out the wagon arch.

"What did Nezer need you for?"

"Nothing, the simple things about family I guess. His intuition is pretty good, he figured out Jade and I were siblings."

"Okay then. Have you seen Hector? I looked all over the place for him but he's nowhere in the wagon."

"I think he went to the water to take a quick dip. I'm going to go find Olius; I have some things to ask him."

"Well, have fun then."

"Actually, before I do, can I ask you something?"

"Depends on what it is."

"You said you had the same vision as Nezer but only better. What's my sister's soul like?"

"It's a muted emerald color. It's mostly still since she's a collected person but it gets brighter when she's more emotive."

Regibus gave her a stern look, furrowing his brows as he looked away. Aurelina stood up straight and watched Regibus leave without a word. She turned back to the jungle and continued to wait for Hector.

CHAPTER 15

As Hector finally made it to the wagon, looking more refreshed and less covered in smoke, he sat down at the common area of the wagon in front of the fire. He felt drowsy and mesmerized by the dance of each flame swaying back and forth, accompanied by the crackling of the wood, gently closing his eyes. As he went to sleep, he could feel his body get heavier.

Hector opened his eyes, looked around, and saw that the room was normal. However, there was something odd about the atmosphere, as if he was being watched. He looked up to see a giant eye staring down at him. He watched its unblinking presence stare at him, gripping at his soul right through his own eyes. The weight became unbearable as the pupil of the eye began to grow, a thin spectral hand slowly descending towards his face. With every ounce of his body, Hector jumped out from his seat and pulled out his shotgun. It felt weird in his hands, as if it wasn't his gun. Hector looked down and saw a large, black snake hissing back at him. He dropped the snake and fell to the floor.

Upon impact, the scenery violently changed, giving Hector painful vertigo. He looked around and saw he was back at *Woodhurst,* sitting in front of the pub. It was burning a lot more than he remembered as he watched the fire consume his home again. He could hear the screams of the cannibals inside, burning and melting due to the heat. However, he didn't see Darvell lighting the fire. He saw himself with a blazing torch and a wicked smile on his face. The imposter turned around to look at Hector. His eyes were devoid of any color, only a black that reflected the burning fire that he had created.

Hec...tor. Come...to...me.

Hector tried to move, but his body didn't even budge. The imposter dropped the torch and reached for the spear on his back. It wasn't like his spear; it was black and covered in barbs. As the imposter exited the building, Hector could feel his presence make him nauseous. A black haze surrounded the imposter as it reached Hector. It raised the spear in the air and began to laugh, gnashing its sharp teeth as it hollered. It thrust the spear towards Hector's face at full power. He winced, only to reopen his eyes in a different area unfamiliar to him.

The room was enormous and spacious. Its walls were lined with black stone, pockmarked with holes in the shape of eyes. Red drapes hung from the top of the walls as a matching rug lay across the floor. Built into the walls were stained glass windows, depicting scenes of war and devastation. Hector looked closer and could see that the scenery in the stained glass moved as it depicted the nightmarish images. In front of Hector was a throne made of pure obsidian with two braziers of solid iron burning ferociously. Draped on top of the throne was a huge skeleton of a bat, its eye sockets letting out two plumes of black smoke. There, Hector saw someone sitting and staring at him as it sat on the throne.

Its appearance was obscured by an onyx cloak. However, two large crimson horns protruded outwards, jutting out like disfigured rhino horns. Their tips were plated in gold as they glistened in the surrounding fire. Resting on the armrests of the throne were the hands of the figure. Thick, red fingers slowly tapped against the obsidian throne. Hector tried to move away, but his body moved forward instead. The figure smiled, its white teeth contrasting against the pitch black shroud.

Hector stopped moving as soon as he was only a few feet in front of the devilish silhouette. The figure towered over Hector, unmoving like a statue until it raised its hand. A solitary finger extended forward and pointed at him. Hector felt his body crush against itself, as if a heavy weight were being added to his shoulders. His blood began to boil as his bones suddenly became cold.

"I'll see you soon, Hector Montagine," the devil growled in a foreboding voice.

It raised its crimson hand and snapped its fingers. Hector felt his body lunge backward as he was pulled away from the figure, eventually finding himself falling into darkness. The force of the fall began to pull on him harder, almost ripping him limb from limb. Suddenly, the pull stopped as Hector was abruptly impaled in the chest. He looked down and saw his spear protruding out with blood gushing all over his jacket. Hector could feel his body grow weaker as he tried to scream for help. Nothing came out; nothing but silence as Hector slowly died on his spear.

Hector rolled and mumbled on the sofa, muttering to himself. He violently moved to the left and right until he woke up in a cold sweat. Hector reached over to touch his face and felt small crystals all around. He turned to his left and saw Olius taking down notes in his spell book.

"What the fuck are you doing?"

"I'm taking notes on dream magic. It's been very interesting ever since Darvell had his and this book doesn't have a lot of notes on oneiromancy. I saw you sleeping so I decided to use it as an opportunity."

"Well, can you stop? I don't like having my mind being prodded with magic."

"You might change your tone if I tell you that you could get magic powers from it."

"Really!"

"No, I'm joking. Oneiromancy magic is nearly impossible to manage even for people who were born with magic in them. You'd have the same chance of developing magic from this as Darvell being able to come up with a functioning plan."

Hector gave Olius an angry glare. He got up from the couch and began to take off the crystals.

"Oh come on, that was a joke!" Olius yelled. "That was funny."

"I'm going to sleep again. I don't want to wake up with anything else on my face."

Hector left the room as Olius rolled his eyes and picked up the crystals.

The night stars glistened as the once dense jungle lightened up, the flora becoming more relaxed and open. Darvell continued to drag the wagon until he reached a clear end to the jungle. He looked around and breathed in the cool air as he took off the reins and stretched his arms.

"I think I can get Attila out now."

"Way ahead of you," Jade said.

Darvell turned around and saw Jade holding the Attila statue in her hand.

"Hey! Be careful with that, you're holding my horse right there."

"I'm careful, don't worry. I came out here to talk to you about some stuff," Jade said as she put Attila down.

Upon backing away, the statue began to crack and glow. With a quick blast of light, Attila appeared, neighing with excitement.

"It's nice to see you, girl. Sorry you had to stay like that for awhile; I didn't want you getting sick or anything."

Attila neighed and placed her head on Darvell's shoulder.

"I love you too. So, Jade, what did you want to talk about?" Darvell asked as he placed the reins on Attila.

"I want to know if you have an actual plan, Darvell. I don't think anyone is going to want to charge in blindly."

"I haven't heard any opposition," Darvell suggested as he jumped onto the coach.

He turned to Jade and was met with a disapproving look. Darvell slowly turned away and started to drive the wagon.

"You need a plan Darvell; no one is going to charge right in with you."

"You say that but quite a few people have. I just give off that feeling of confidence," Darvell said with a cocky smirk.

"Well that's going to change; I'm going to have to teach you how to plan for the worst."

Darvell groaned loudly, scaring the nearby birds in the area.

"Learn! You're already teaching me how to read. What else are you going to do, teach me how to eat with manners?"

"You have been a little sloppy," Jade said quietly.

"No, no, no! I'll look past learning how to read and I'll give a passing glance to planning. But I will eat like a madman if I want to," Darvell argued.

"If you say so. Speaking of which, we still have to practice writing your name."

"Ugh! Fine, take the reins."

Darvell shoved the reins towards Jade and crossed his hands.

"Good, now take out a paper and some charcoal and let me see how much you know right now," Jade asked.

Darvell pulled out a piece of paper from his pocket and a piece of wood.

"Darvell, I said a piece of charcoal," Jade angrily ordered.

"Hold your horses, I know what charcoal is."

He took a deep breath and breathed onto the tip of wood, eventually making a charcoal tip.

"What am I writing again?"

"Your name. It doesn't have to be neat or anything, just write your name."

Darvell moved away from Jade and hunched over his writing process. He scribbled violently on the paper. Jade tried to look over and see what he was doing but Darvell put his wing between them. A few hours passed and Darvell was still writing on the paper. He was starting to emit smoke out of frustration and Jade accidentally inhaled some. She coughed and rubbed her burning eyes.

"Darvell, it doesn't take someone this long to write their fucking name."

"No wait! Hold on, I'm almost done. Give me like...a few more minutes and I'll be done."

"In a few minutes I'll have two black lungs!" Jade yelled. "Just show me the paper."

"No!" Darvell whined.

"Give me the paper Darvell!"

They began to fight as each one of them pulled on one end of the paper. Darvell tried to blind her with a quick flash of light from his wings, but Jade put up her hand and reflected the light back with an iron hand. Darvell covered his eyes, letting go of the paper. Jade looked at the paper and sighed. It was nothing more than a bunch of drawings of everyone in the group. However, upon closer inspection, the drawings somehow spelled out Darvell's name. The drawings themselves were also very good despite their childish designs.

"Darvell, this is pretty good. How did you come up with this?"

"Well, I was drawing the D and then it came to me. It looked a lot like Theia's bow so I drew around the D. The two L's in my name looked like Hector's spear or my revolvers. As for the A, it's supposed to look like you are leaning against your rifle. I think the R is a pirate hook since Regibus is a pirate."

"What about the V and the E?"

"Oh, the V is Olius's little soul patch and the E is a snail."

"A snail?" Jade asked, confused with the choice.

"It was hard coming up with ideas, okay? I was trying to write my name as well."

"Well at least you wrote your name. I'm proud of you."

"Thanks I guess. I just don't know when this is going to come in handy."

Jade thought about that question for a while and started to blush at coming up with no answer.

"You have nothing do you?" Darvell said sarcastically.

"Of course I do. Names are very powerful in the world of magic, Darvell. We all have a true name that is unknown to us. Sometimes, people will learn a devil's or a demon's true name to have power over them. So you want to be careful with your name Darvell, it can be their greatest weapon."

"I don't know. A big enough sword and two guns seem good enough for me," Darvell replied as he received the reins from Jade.

Jade rolled her eyes as she moved closer to Darvell slightly, continuing to drive under the night sky.

As Olius picked up the crystals, Regibus watched him from afar. He had a pensive look on his face as he watched him pick up the magic rocks.

"If you're going to watch me, the least you could do is help me," Olius said without looking up.

"How'd you know I was standing here?" Regibus questioned.

"When I was traveling around in my nomadic years, I put a spell on me to help detect magic. I can feel everyone's magic as if it were pins and needles on my skin. Well, everyone except Hector."

"Shut up!" Hector yelled from somewhere in the wagon.

"Doesn't that hurt?" Regibus said as he picked up the gems.

"Not really, it used to but now I've grown accustomed to it," Olius said as he finished picking up the crystals. "Mind if I ask what you came looking for?"

"Since you know a lot about magic, I'd like to learn more about it," Regibus explained as he took a seat. "I want to be a better team member."

"Of course, I could teach you about—"

"Jade. How did she get her powers?" Regibus sternly demanded.

Olius gave off a disappointed expression and sighed. He leaned against a nearby wall and flicked his finger in the air, causing a nearby chalice to float towards him as wine from the barrel floated into the chalice.

"You want to know about her?" Olius pointed out as he gestured the chalice at Regibus.

"Yes. I need to know since she already knows how I got mine. I want to make sure she didn't do anything stupid getting them."

"Like you?" Olius said snarkily.

"Leave my decisions out of this," Regibus rebuked. "Tell me what she has and how she got it."

Olius sighed as he pulled out his book and flipped through the pages. He stopped and quickly read through the paragraphs of messy calligraphy and symbols haphazardly scattered across the musty tan pages. He closed the book and snapped his fingers, a small burst of light appearing above his hand. A circle within a square within a circle appeared as Olius began to talk.

"She has learned a modified transmutation magic. She can take her entire body or parts of it and morph them into different materials. She seems to be fond of morphing into iron or gems but she isn't limited to just those materials. I'm not sure if she can do liquids and gases but solid morphing I'm very sure of."

"How did she get them?"

"Transmutation is easy stuff, Regibus; even I can do it. I don't because it's not my style. I'm just surprised she can pull off such high level skills like pulling out bullets from her hands. Most people can only alter themselves, but creating objects out of your body is next level."

"Does that require more training?"

"To be honest with you, she shouldn't be able to pull that off. She doesn't seem like an innate magic user according to you two not having any magic as kids. It's off-putting."

"What can you make of it then? Is there anything you can do to get power like that?"

"This feels like an interrogation," Olius acknowledged. "To my knowledge, some people can teach this skill or they just consume something. Nothing life-threatening at all can occur from her type of magic."

"Nothing? So it's just regular acquired magic?" Regibus asked.

"No, there isn't anything you can use against her," Olius sassed.

"You'd think. Have you ever heard of selling your soul?" Regibus said. "What about that?"

"Oh please, no one is that stupid to sell their soul for magic. It's everywhere!"

Regibus furrowed his eyes and drank the rest of the wine. He left the room and Olius fuming.

"You're welcome!" Olius yelled. "Ungrateful."

CHAPTER 16

The wagon continued to drive until it stopped at a large gorge. Darvell and Jade hopped off and examined the gorge, in awe at its immense size. The two ends were miles apart as the farther one looked down the gorge, the darker it became, until there was nothing but black.

"I guess we made it. This place is pretty intimidating," Darvell said as he rubbed his chin.

"Didn't Olius say that there was a bridge somewhere?" Jade asked as she looked for one.

"I did say there was a bridge. In fact, we are in the right place," Olius said as he walked towards them.

"Where is it though? All I see is a large gorge and a few miles of oblivion down below," Darvell said.

"You both fail to see the magic of this place, the bridge is right here."

Olius began to walk to the edge, Darvell and Jade biting their lips in fear.

"Hold on! How sure are you?" Jade questioned.

"I have the utmost confi—"

Olius was cut short as he began to plummet. Darvell and Jade ran to the edge to see Olius hanging on to his staff, having wedged it between some rocks. He looked up and nervously smiled.

"Okay, so I was wrong. Please help me up," Olius pleaded.

Olius finished dusting himself and looked around. He took out his book and flipped through the pages. Darvell looked at it and tried to make out some of the words, unable to glean any important information from it as the letters and symbols melted into each other.

"That book can't solve everything we come across." Darvell scoffed as he looked away from the book. "I've never had to read about fighting people. I just did it!"

"Never underestimate the power of a book, Darvell," Olius replied as he slowly walked towards the edge, checking for the bridge with his staff. Suddenly, Olius's staff hit something solid as he passed it over the gorge. He flipped the pages of his book and began to speak, his voice slightly echoing as he spoke.

"Revelare!"

The air near the gorge began to sparkle as a stone bridge revealed itself. The three of them could see that the bridge's path was made from large stone tablets, each one expertly carved to resemble the face of a dragon. At the beginning of the bridge were two dragon statues, covered in vines and grime. Although they were faded and old, they emitted a dignified aura as they raised their front claws in the air. Their wings curved backwards as they stood on their hind legs like rampant lions. Darvell walked up to one of the statues and gazed into its stone eyes. He felt his head hurt as the eyes of the statue looked into him, unblinking and burdensome.

"Darvell, are you okay?" Jade asked as she tugged his hand. "You look confused."

"I'm…I'm fine, I think. Olius, what is at the bottom of this gorge?" Darvell questioned without parting his gaze from the statue.

"The book doesn't say. I guess the writer never ventured down below. Why do you ask?"

"Something...something is calling to me," Darvell whispered as he turned his gaze to the gorge.

Darvell walked towards the end of the gorge and looked down. He could see only a dark pit the farther he looked. Yet, he could feel something was down there. Darvell took a step forward, his heart pounding loudly as his wings twitched violently. The fire from his wings alerted Jade and Olius, who were busy analyzing the bridge.

"What are you doing Darvell?!" Olius yelled as he ran up to him.

"I'm going to see what's down there."

With that, Darvell leaped from the edge and plummeted downwards into oblivion. Olius and Jade looked over the gorge to see the bright fire that Darvell emitted, watching it shrink as he fell further into the black abyss.

"We have to get the others. Get the wagon ready, we're going down there," Jade commanded.

"Understood, I'll get the wagon flying and—"

"No, you already did that once with the ship. I know the wagon is smaller but we can't have you expending all your magic all the time. I have a better idea that can get us down there."

Darvell plummeted deeper into the gorge, never looking back up. The fire from his wings lit his way as he observed the dark void around him. There was nothing but shadow surrounding him. However, he could feel something in his wings and tail that made them twitch. He dove down further, his fire shining brighter as he went down. Suddenly, Darvell could see something in the distance that reflected his fire. He focused his attention on it and saw that it was an opening, almost dragon-like in design.

"Holy shit! There is a bottom!"

"What do you mean there's a bottom?" Olius yelled.

Darvell turned around and looked back to see Olius and Hector on the wagon, plummeting a few feet behind him. The wheels were replaced with large blue crystals that gave off a vibrant hum. The wagon hovered downward quickly as it trailed behind Darvell. Hector was sitting in the coach seat, struggling to guide the wagon as it descended down the cavern.

"You guys don't see it?" Darvell yelled.

"It's hard to see anything with the darkness of this gorge," Hector loudly stated.

"It's down here guys! Just look down and you can—what the hell!"

Suddenly, the stone mouth of the dragon opened up. Darvell opened his wings to slow his descent, forgetting that the wagon was behind him. He crashed into the coach seat and found himself sitting next to Hector. As they flew into the dragon's mouth, Hector gripped the reins and pulled up to slow them down.

"Hold on!" Hector yelled as he guided the wagon towards the light.

As the wagon flew downwards, the light began to shine brighter. The glow gradually became too bright, forcing Hector and Olius to cover their eyes. Darvell, on the other hand, grabbed the reins from Hector and continued to drive the wagon towards the light. He stared towards it, seeing figures move through it. As he reached the light, he could see a glass barrier in front of him. He took his revolvers and fired two shots into it, laughing hysterically as Hector and Olius screamed in fear from not knowing what was happening. The glass barrier shattered as the wagon passed through, grabbing the attention of everyone down below.

Darvell opened his eyes slowly, looking around to see where he was. He could feel a painful sensation all over his body as he moved his head. He could see iron bars to his left while the walls that encased him looked like obsidian. However, the rocks looked smooth, layered upon each other like bricks. The pain in his body began to subside as he slowly woke up. Darvell tried to sit up but upon doing so, he heard the familiar jangle of thick heavy chains wrapped around his wrists and legs.

It's always chains, isn't it?

Darvell looked forward and could see an empty cell in front of him. However, its size was immense, almost the same size of a whale. Observing even more, Darvell's cell was the same size as the one in front of him. Darvell walked towards the bars of the cell and looked around. There he saw what appeared to be a giant black dragon standing guard. His wings were filled with holes and a green mist emitted from his mouth. Darvell scurried back, his chains clattering and clanking along the way. He brushed up against the wall, breathing heavily as he heard the steps grow louder as they approached his cell. He tried looking for a place to hide but his cell was empty. Darvell crouched as much as he could and covered himself with his wings.The dragon peered past the wall and examined the cell. He didn't see Darvell anywhere and began to panic frantically.

"Oh no! He's escaped!" the black dragon bellowed.

He rushed away from the cell as Darvell peered from behind his wings. Once he stood up, he looked at his chains and smiled. As Darvell began to melt the chains, he could hear the stomping of dragon feet from the other end of the hallway. He clenched his teeth and growled.

I'm going to have to yank these chains, no time to melt them.

Darvell grabbed both chains and pulled on them. The pain in his body surged through him as he not only pulled off the chains, but the wall they were attached to. As the wall crumbled away, Darvell stood in awe that turned into fear as he saw an entire kingdom's worth of dragons flying and walking around. He felt miniscule amongst them all as the sound of thunderous flapping wings filled his ears. He could see bright orange lines marked into the walls that illuminated the large cavern city. Suddenly, Darvell could hear screams coming from one group of dragons that was walking by.

"He broke through the cell! Get the guards!"

Darvell nervously looked around as more dragons turned their attention towards him. He could see dragons flying down from up above with black armor adorning them. He turned and ran back into his cell, trying to flee the scene. As he walked back in, the black dragon that was guarding him was in the cell.

"The abomination is loose! Capture him!"

"That's awfully rude," Darvell responded.

The black dragon took a deep breath in and breathed out a stream of steaming black liquid. Darvell dodged it and watched the splash burn through the stone floor, leaving a gaping hole. Darvell looked up at the dragon and narrowed his eyes. He put out his hands and lit them on fire. The black dragon raised its claw and tried to crush him, missing him as Darvell rolled away. He jumped and slashed at the dragon's leg. As the talons harmed the dragon, it reared up in pain, knocking the iron cell door open.

Darvell ran out the door and through the various hallways until he found a room with a chest and stacked weapons. He ran over to it and punched a hole through it. The chest wall shattered and what lay inside were dragon-sized weapons, varying from swords to shields. At the bottom of everything were Darvell's sword and guns, which looked puny in comparison to everything else. Darvell crawled inside and grabbed his weapons, sighing in relief that they weren't destroyed. Crawling out of the chest, Darvell stood up and dusted himself.

"Okay, it's time to find the others and get the hell out of here."

As he exited the room, he looked around and saw a large door that looked like it led outside. He ran towards the door and gripped his sword. He stepped back and took a large arcing swing in front of him, shattering the lower half of the door. As the cloud of destruction passed, Darvell could see dragon guards waiting for him with crossbow bolts aimed at him in all directions. The crossbow bolts were the size of tree trunks while the arrowheads were made of the same black rock Darvell saw in his cell.

"We have you surrounded, do not resist or we will shoot," one of the dragons said from the impenetrable wall.

Darvell looked around and weighed his options. An idea popped into his head as he leaned against his sword and tried to feign confidence.

"How about we stop fighting, I'm a dragon just like you guys."

"You are not a dragon! You are an abomination to our draconic blood!"

Darvell furrowed his eyes at the response, his posture stiffening as he grabbed the handle of his greatsword.

"I don't like being called an abomination," Darvell growled.

"What are you going to do about it?" the dragon said as he laughed afterwards. "Look at you!"

An unsettling movement could be felt in the wall. The other dragons moved slightly away from him as he laughed. Darvell smiled and cracked his fingers.

"Any of you who don't want to be burned, move away."

Almost immediately, the dragons backed away from the laughing guard. His laugh began to dwindle as he looked to see his compatriots backing away even farther. He looked down at Darvell and saw him extend his brass wings. Unlike the other times, they glimmered brighter than usual as the fire blazed off them. Before Darvell could breathe out a torrent of flame, a booming and violent voice sounded out.

"Halt!"

Everyone looked up to see a brass dragon, larger than any other dragon Darvell had come across. He landed in front of

Darvell, his wings extending outward, and a thick tail thumping the ground. The earth he stood on shook as Darvell almost lost his balance. He could see the dragon's face, aged with wisdom and tense with wrath.

"Who are you?" Darvell questioned meekly as he held his greatsword.

The giant brass dragon adjusted itself, puffing up to look bigger. Darvell could see that the white hairs dangling from its snout were lit at the ends, emitting a black smoke but never actually burning the hairs. He could see in his eyes an ever-changing fire against a coal black iris. There were no whites in his eyes, only fire and darkness. The dragon's teeth were pasty and white, ending in pointed tips that haphazardly interlocked with each other. A closer look could show that, despite visible old age, the dragon's entire body pulsed. His scales fluttered, opening and closing with every twitch. Almost like a sea of brass, its waves of scales rippling across the surface. Although his wings weren't on fire like Darvell's, they emitted an unbearable heat towards the other dragons, causing them to rear back to not get burned. The dragon bent its head down to Darvell and spoke, almost breaking his eardrums in the process.

"I am the almighty dragon of brass! I am Ignis, the Scorcher of Injustice! Who might you be; abomination of our blood?"

"I'm Darvell Letholdus, the Brass Half-Dragon! Mercenary for hire and son of Marius Letholdus!" Darvell roared, not nearly matching the ferocity the other dragon had.

The other dragons murmured and whispered amongst each other. The old dragon reared back up and examined Darvell's wings. He looked closely, seeing that his wings were the same shade of brass he had. Flicking his forked tongue outwards he quickly grabbed Darvell. He began to crush him, Darvell pushing back as much as he could. Ignis then took flight and left the scene, leaving the other dragon officials to calm down the area.

CHAPTER 17

As Ignis held Darvell in his grasp, he could see that he was taking him to a large swirling stalactite. The stalactite was immense, extending from the top of the cavern and reaching all the way to the floor. Various dragons could be seen coming in and out of the stalactite as they flew through the air. At the very top was a polished white area with statues of dragons decorating the entrance. Ignis flew upwards and landed at the top, forcefully throwing Darvell onto the floor. He landed on the ground and passed Darvell, prone on the ground. As he got up, he could see that the area here was only for decoration, treasure laid haphazardly across the marble floor as four enormous pillars held the entire stalactite in the air. Their smooth black texture had familiar markings, almost decipherable by Darvell.

"You claim to be the son Marius. Is this correct?" Ignis questioned, his aggressive tone riding his tongue.

"Yeah, is that hard to believe?" Darvell groaned as he dusted himself off.

"It is. I have not seen my son in quite some time. I find it... surprising that he would have a son. I would have thought the outside world would have killed him first."

"Well you would be surprised," Darvell murmured under his breath.

"I am still uncertain that you are my blood."

"How can I prove it then?" Darvell asked, puffing up his body.

"Simple," Ignis said, his brass scales shifting in hue as he lowered his head closer to Darvell. "Let me hear your roar."

"What?"

"All dragons have a roar, child. Each one is unique to each family and they are passed down through bloodlines. Our bloodline has the strongest roar in history, ferocious yet respectable. So, show me if you are really family."

Darvell gulped as he looked up at Ignis, his judgmental eyes piercing him. Darvell took a step back, breathed in deeply and slowly let it out. He had no idea what a dragon roar sounded like, especially one that was supposedly unique to his family.

You'll be fine. Just yell and I'll help you.

Darvell darted his eyes around the area for the source of the disembodied voice. Darvell shrugged and took in a deep breath once again. His throat began to heat up as he let out a violent and ear-numbing roar. He had created something he had never heard before, yet it felt like what he was doing was right. The roar disturbed the bats hanging from the cavern roof as he finished. Darvell panted heavily as he looked up at Ignis looking down at him. He could see that his stoic expression had not changed, except for a little tear of fire rolling down his snout. He began to chuckle to himself and began to laugh, almost roaring in delight. Darvell nervously laughed as Ignis was then engulfed in flames.

"Oh shit!"

As the flames dispersed, Darvell could see a tall old man in Ignis's place. His robe was long and flowing, covered in foreign runes and designs. His brass scales had turned into brass-colored skin with visibly more patches of scales on them. His eyes remained the same color but they had a more welcoming gaze. Underneath the robe was a white set of linen clothing emblazoned with a design of two upright dragons on the front. The white hairs he had on his head and on his beard were plentiful and still lit at their ends. Ignis walked towards Darvell and hugged him.

"It is wonderful to see you grandchild! It's been decades since I've seen someone of my flesh and blood."

"Decades?" Darvell asked quizzically.

"Yes, decades, our brass kin are rare in existence although not outright gone. There are others who have brass but our family's blood was much more sought after."

"I see. By the way, where are you keeping my friends?"

"Your friends are in the common area for the leaders of the Citadel," Ignis explained.

"What!"

Darvell stormed through the halls, charging past dragons that quickly moved out of the way. Ignis quickly apologized to the others as he caught up with Darvell.

"I know you are furious but the Citadel is huge, don't you need me to guide you to them?"

"No need, I can smell them from here," Darvell growled.

They both turned a corner and walked down a hallway that led up to a doorway. It was guarded by two silver dragons who both held large spears as they stood side by side. They looked down and frowned as they pointed their spears at him. Ignis walked in front of Darvell and towered over the two silver dragons. They looked up and saw his stoic face, quivering a bit as they lowered their heads.

"Is the little one with you, my lord?" one of the silver dragons managed to ask.

"The little one is my grandson. You best pay respect towards him."

They both looked down and saw a little Darvell walking past them, banging on the doors.

"Of course my lord," the two dragons said as they pushed back on the doors, letting them enter.

Darvell entered the room, fuming mad as smoke billowed from his tail. He looked around the red carpeted floors and white walls to see piles upon piles of gold and treasure. The walls had paintings of Ignis and other dragons on them. The ceiling above them had three hanging chandeliers. Suddenly, Darvell turned his attention to the far off corner of the room. He could see a small section of high-end chairs surrounded by a high class round table. There, he saw everyone eating heartily and merrily. Hector turned around and almost choked on his food as he saw Darvell standing by the door, wings flaming and outstretched.

"Um guys, Darvell is back."

Olius stood up abruptly, bumping into the table and walked towards Darvell slowly.

"It's so good to see you Darvell—"

"Shut your face!" Darvell roared. "You guys just left me in prison?"

"We made a better impression on them than you did Darvell," Olius explained. "Ignis here was kind enough to bring us here while you recovered from your wounds and calmed down."

"What happened?" Darvell asked.

"I can answer that!" Regibus yelled. "Once we hit the floor—Olius thankfully stopped us before we crashed and destroyed the wagon—guards began to come from all corners of the area and you decided to fight them. You would have won if it weren't for someone knocking you out cold with a tail whack right into the head," Regibus explained as he made the motion of a slap.

"Not just any guards, they were the best of the best. The Enforcers are considered by many to be the best trained dragon squadron since the formation of the Agon-Dray Averncay. When I heard someone singlehandedly took down four guards I thought it was an exaggeration. Now that I know it was my grandson, however, I'm sure he could have taken down more if he were given the chance," Ignis bursted out as he laughed away and pounded the gold in his pile.

"Grandson?" Theia asked. "Darvell is actually related to you? I thought you just had the same last name."

"Our name is revered and not to be taken lightly, no matter if Darvell is not a full dragon," Ignis said as he picked up a pile of gold. "We dragons tend to look down disdainfully at other creatures."

"What if he had divine blood in him?" Jade questioned. "Do dragons at least respect that?"

"Well, a good part of the Citadel is very devoted to the Old Flame. I'm sure if he did they would be able to overlook his human side," Ignis explained. "Why do you ask?"

"It just so happens that Darvell is also the son of an angel," Aurelina said as she reached for a glass of wine. "More specifically a Valkyrie."

"Really?" Ignis beamed as he raised his head in joy. "This is great news! The Council will be overjoyed to hear this."

"Who?" Olius asked.

"Oh it is not important right now. You can all continue eating. I have to go and discuss things with some other dragons."

Ignis left the room in a hurry, leaving the others to enjoy their meal.

"I wonder where they got this chicken," Darvell mused as he took a seat next to Jade.

"Aren't you still angry?" Hector asked.

"I still am. You guys left me to rot in a prison cell!" Darvell barked as he began to fill his plate.

"Not all of us," Regibus said as he reached over for some hot bread. "Jade here kept saying that we should have done something. Actually, she hasn't eaten or said anything since you were knocked out."

Darvell looked over to see that everyone else's plates were full except Jade's. Her plate was clean and still shone under the bright light of the room.

"Well at least someone cares about me," Darvell promptly said.

"I just wasn't hungry, that's all," Jade trilled nervously.

As they all sat around and ate, Darvell couldn't help but look around the room. He noticed that everything was bigger, sized to match the dragons' needs.

"Olius, is there any other reason why dragons don't like mixed blood?"

"Well, dragons are a proud race from what I've read about. Throughout time, they have been symbols of power and absolute reign; some old nations were governed by dragons. Man, to them, are nothing more than lesser beings. When we were able to match and sometimes surpass their power, they grew bitter for quite a while. This was the Dawn of Flame, a time where dragonkind and humankind fought viciously. However, during this time of fire and iron, some dragons and humans began to sympathize with each other. Some humans spent their entire lives protecting dragons that had saved them. Some grew bonds stronger than any shackles a master blacksmith could make. The dragons of old despised this; they outcast dragons that began to familiarize themselves with humans. Once they had left, the norm had been set that humans were lesser beings in spirit, but as rivals, they were second to none."

"What caused the war to end, Olius?" Theia asked as she wiped her mouth.

"Well, both sides agreed that the war should end. Kings and dragon lords made peace with each other, stopping the killing of any more offspring if no more villages or kingdoms were burned to the ground. The rest is history as they say."

"So, does our presence offend anyone? Are we spitting in their eyes so to speak," Hector worriedly asked.

"In a small way, yes. Aurelina and soon to be Darvell are okay since they are both angelic in blood and Darvell is also dragonkin. As for the rest of us, let's try to not anger anyone," Olius explained.

"No worries guys, if they try to pull anything funny I'll make sure to knock 'em all out again!" Darvell cheered as he took a swig from a mug.

"I hope it doesn't come to it, I don't want the guards to be humiliated again," Ignis said as he entered the room. "I would like all of you to accompany me to the Council Room. My associates and I would like to see you all together; we must speak with you about a few things."

"The Council wants to see us?" Hector nervously asked.

"Yes, they are intrigued about your arrival," Ignis explained as he pointed to Darvell. "Especially about you, grandson."

"Well let's get going then," Darvell said as he wiped his mouth and got up from the table. "I want to meet these other dragons."

Darvell walked towards the door and tried to push it open, not realizing that the door needed to be pulled. A sudden feeling of dread overcame the group as they watched Darvell bang his head on the door.

"I feel you should let us do the talking," Theia admitted as she pulled the door open.

CHAPTER 18

The group walked down the hallways, surveying the scattered loot and gold along the walls, as they made their way to the Council Room. Compared to everyone else, they all looked like ants to the sight of the dragons flying around or walking the halls. Jade walked up to Regibus and tugged on his shirt.

"How are you holding up?" Jade asked.

"What do you mean?" Regibus responded, happy that he didn't have to start the conversation this time.

"All this gold lying around," Jade pointed out. "Isn't it enticing Cutthroat?"

"No, I've made sure to 'turn him off' so to speak," Regibus said as he looked around.

"Well that's good to hear."

"Mind if I ask you something Jade?" Regibus asked, his voice getting lower.

"What is it?"

"Do you feel intimidated by any of this? We've both heard stories of dragons going extinct when Zlo took over. But here we are, amidst so many."

"I don't feel all that intimidated," Jade responded. "Dragons are just as equally vain as they are intelligent; they can be very predictable if you know which one you are dealing with."

"What about Darvell? We both know he is far from intelligent," Regibus chuckled.

"True, but he's more human than dragon," Jade corrected.

Their conversation was cut short as they turned a corner, walking towards a gilded door made of solid iron. On the door were ten dragons, all of different designs, posing around a circle. The emblem on the door was a dragon's claw gripping a rolled up scroll. As the doors opened, the group was led inside by Ignis to a low lit room. Candles floated through the air, dimly lighting the room. There was a large table made of smooth black rock, sprinkled with shimmering pieces of metal embedded inside. Behind the table were nine gargantuan dragons, quietly murmuring to each other.

As the doors closed, Ignis took flight and sat between the red and gold dragons as he addressed them both in a rough tongue that no one could understand. The murmuring ceased as the dragons shifted their attention to the group, who were so miniscule that the dragons had to lean forward to see them. Hector began to quiver, causing his armored jacket to rattle as Olius gulped in fear.

"What do you call yourselves?" the black dragon slurred, his voice hissing as he spoke.

"We...we...we are uh, we are the...," Olius stammered, trying to avoid breaking down.

"We are some kick ass people and I'm one of you guys!" Darvell gleefully cheered, pushing himself to the front with a boisterous smile.

Hector vomited as Aurelina went over to heal his sickness. Jade frantically reached for her gun while Chantal stood in front of Theia, her fists up in the air. Regibus only stood there pale as a skeleton while Olius walked over to Darvell and angrily whispered at him.

"Darvell, these are ancient dragons!" Olius quietly yelled. "Show some more respect!"

"No worries Olius, these guys are technically family!" Darvell consoled as he gestured to all of them.

"I assure you that the only family you have in this court is Ignis here," the white dragon corrected in a harsh and cold tone, his glacier blue eyes narrowing judgingly.

"Frio, that's no way to talk to him," the green dragon argued with a honeyed tone in her voice. "He is family, at least by race. As for you Zuur, try to be a lot less intimidating. You've scared the one in the armor half to death."

"But he is more than just family, he is an heir to the Council seat for Ignis," the silver dragon quietly acknowledged. As she spoke, little snowflakes could be seen forming around every breath she took. "We have dozens of heirs but Darrous here is Ignis's only heir. Does it matter if he's full blood or not?"

"Ugh, it's Darvell—"

"Mind your tongue boy, we are debating," the gold dragon sneered. He puffed out a short burst of fire as he turned to the silver dragon. "All I'm saying, Argenti, is how can we really tell he is of angelic descent as well?"

"Some simple magic will work," the blue dragon interjected. Her wings let off small sparks of blue lightning with every movement of her body. "But I don't see why we should let him in because of it; he still isn't a full dragon."

"Times have changed Aurum; angelic descent is not as rare as it used to be," the copper dragon spoke, her silvery voice escaping her heavily scarred mouth. "As for you Inpulsa, don't be so rude. We have all shared our disapproval for each other's heirs but we must give this one a chance, for Ignis's sake."

"Aeris is right. But might I propose something?" the bronze dragon said as he gestured towards Darvell. "How about we have Darrous here decide for himself? What do you think, Rubrum?"

"A marvelous idea, Aes. Darrous, do you wish to be the heir to Ignis's throne?" The red dragon snarled as he moved his gaze towards Darvell.

All the dragons began to look towards Darvell, who was playing with the barrel of his gun while they were talking. Darvell looked up and nervously smiled.

"Sorry, I wasn't paying attention. What was the question?"

The entire Council groaned as they slumped over and growled in exasperation.

"I already don't like him," Frio said as he looked towards Ignis.

"Fair enough, it was a long shot anyway," Ignis said as he reached over for a large chalice.

"I'm sorry to interrupt everything, but as you can see Darvell is not the most competent," Theia apologized as she took a step forward.

"Hey!" Darvell roared.

"Would you mind telling us what is going on?"

"Well since you are the first out of all of you to actually take initiative," Aurum responded, his golden scales shifting in the candlelight, "dragons live long but we are not immortal. We need heirs to take our place after we die. As of right now, we all have about one hundred different heirs. Ignis here only has... him." Aurum snarled as he pointed to Darvell.

"Honestly, I feel hurt right now," Darvell said, taking out a cigar.

"Smoking isn't allowed in the Council Room, Darrous," Aeris angrily scolded.

"How come? At least three of you look like you breathe fire so I don't see the problem," Darvell pointed out.

"Darvell, for once just listen to someone," Jade said as she reached over for the cigar.

"It's out of courtesy, Darvell. Frio and Argenti here have

weak lungs when it comes to heavy smoke. That's why they must sit far from Aurum, Rubrum and I," Ignis explained.

"Enough of this!" Frio roared as he slammed his claw on the table. "We must decide if Darrous is good enough to be heir."

"Actually I don't want to be an heir," Darvell announced. "I don't think I can."

Everyone turned towards him, mixed emotions across everyone's faces. Olius walked forward and decided to explain.

"You see Council, Darvell has been given a godsent mission to kill Zlo so being—"

"Zlo! You, by the Oracle, were sent to kill that spawn of evil and chaos?" Argenti stammered rapidly, her hyperventilating creating larger snowflakes around her mouth.

"Boy, you do know that you will surely die," Zuur said, his tongue flicking from his mouth.

"Not so, he was told by the Oracle herself that he can kill Zlo," Aurelina mentioned.

"How can you prove this?" Inpulsa snarled.

Aurelina rolled her eyes and extended her feathery grey wings. Her bright yellow halo formed above her head as the dragons stood in awe.

"A daughter of the Oracle! Ignis you lucky bastard, your grandson is the chosen one!" Aes congratulated.

"You guys already knew?" Darvell questioned.

"I had a vision come to me during one of my prayers," Aurum explained. "The Oracle spoke to me and told me that an heir of the Council would be the heir to fell Zlo. She didn't tell us specifically whose heir it would be. We argued and argued on who it would be but we would never suspect it would be Ignis's."

"If Darrous must go on this adventure then he cannot be heir by default. Council members cannot have been in contact with any divine missions. Makes it hard to deal with political obligations," Frio said with a hint of satisfaction in his voice.

"Then I am to be without an heir?" Ignis stoically stated.

"Isn't there a loophole of some sort?" Regibus asked. "I mean, no offense Darvell, but you're not the best with high stakes politics."

"It's fine. Everyone's been saying shit about me lately." Darvell sighed with a shrug.

"The human may be on to something," Rubrum said, scratching his chin at the idea. "We would have to check the archives. This meeting has ended; we will continue this discussion again tomorrow. May I speak to you all after they leave?"

"Us? What do you want with us?" Theia said nervously.

"I would like to speak with all of you," Rubrum said, his eyes flaring with fire.

As the other dragons left the room, the group was left in the gaze of Rubrum. He looked down at all of them and examined them. He smiled and moved closer to them as he went past the table. His size was bigger than the others, Ignis barely matching his stature. Hector felt as if he was going to throw up again, Aurelina rubbing his tummy to ease the pain. As Rubrum stood in front of them, his size began to shrink in a bright eruption of fire. As everyone shielded their eyes, Darvell stared down the light, smiling as he did it.

"It may be too intimidating to talk to all of you in my true form," Rubrum explained as everyone uncovered their eyes.

They could see that he wore a scale covered robe that matched his tone of dark red. His black hair was like coal while his fluorescent white teeth shone with his smile. The trim of his robes had rubies and sapphires sewn in while the back of the robe had hanging crimson tassels. His brown tanned skin showed hardly any scales, as if he were just a regular human being. He would have been able to pull it off if it weren't for the cinder-colored eyes that looked at everyone with an eager stare.

"I would like to apologize for our bickering and arguing earlier, the tendencies of us dragons seem to never go away. I would also like to welcome you to Drakon. This place has been a sanctuary for all dragons alike. As some of you may know, Zlo has ridden the world of Darrous—"

"Darvell. It's Darvell," Darvell interjected.

"Darvell's kind were almost eradicated from the face of the earth. They have begun to rise again, but Ignis is the only one to survive of the Letholdus reign," Ruburm said with a quiet tone, his hands clasping together. "Or so we thought until you came along. Even if you were not bound by the strings of fate we understand if you do not want to be here. The fate of ancient dragons like ourselves is very dull and dreary. However, I have pored through the archives looking for a loophole in the laws we had created."

"You are a democratic system?" Olius asked, intrigued by the idea.

"Not entirely. When our kin of brass were on the verge of disappearance, we decided to band together and hide ourselves so it would not happen to anyone else. After much toiling and discussion, we agreed that those who showed remarkable leadership and knowledge that could help the Council would be allowed to serve in it. Ignis would be able to lead the little remaining brass dragons that lived and the rest of us could lead our kin, making sure we could prosper through these dark times," Rubrum explained, snapping his fingers as smoke flew around them and formed chairs to sit on.

"What does this have to do with me?" Darvell asked, growing restless from all of the talking.

"You see Darvell, dragons don't live forever as it has been stated. Even though we are all ancient dragons, Ignis is...ancient. He will not live very long and an heir must be procured. If we were to allow the public to vote in another brass kin, desires would erupt and our way of government would surely collapse in the long run. If humans applied what we have they may have a chance but dragons come from a different creed of life. Then, I remembered that all of our heirs are also our kin. No matter what age or generation they are from, if they have our blood then they can be chosen."

Everyone, except Darvell, furrowed their brows. Rubrum chuckled a little and sighed.

"It seems that most of you understand where I'm going with this. I can assure you I can't find another way."

"What are we talking about?" Darvell asked absentmindedly.

"So Darvell only has to…ugh…find someone and make an heir?" Aurelina uncomfortably asked.

"Not just anyone right?" Jade quickly asked.

"Why do you care?" Regibus questioned smugly.

"No, she is right," Rubrum interrupted. "It would ruin the reputation of the Letholdus family name. For your grandfather's sake Darvell, please don't go out and do it with a common wench."

They have that in a dragon society? Darvell thought to himself, keeping his thoughts hidden from the group. "Of course I won't," Darvell confidently replied.

"There is one more thing. The bearing of children is frowned upon here if there is no pact between the father and mother."

"Like a blood oath?" Darvell asked with concern in his voice. "I'm willing to do that but nothing more."

"No, it's—" Rubrum began to explain.

"Oh he has to sign a contract of some sort," Hector jested.

"It's not that either. Let me finish—"

"Is it like alimony?" Regibus asked.

"No that would come after, if it ever comes to it," Rubrum laughed.

"Wait!" Olius yelled. "Darvell has to marry someone?"

Darvell's eyes widened as he looked to Rubrum, hoping it wasn't what Olius said.

"Exactly." Rubrum smiled as he leaned in his chair.

"Hell no! I'm not marrying anyone!" Darvell roared. "I'm

too young to be held down! I don't care if Ignis and I share blood."

"Darvell, be reasonable!" Rubrum pleaded.

"Nope, I'm walking out of here and that's final. I'll fight my way out of here if I have to! None of you can make me get married!"

Darvell felt something hit him in the back of the head, causing his vision to go black. He fell to the floor with a thud as everyone saw Jade standing behind him, the stock of her rifle in the air.

CHAPTER 19

Darvell slowly opened his eyes, looking around the decorated room. On the walls were trinkets and musty books stacked on shelves. Their spines were gilded with faded golden titles that Darvell could barely make out. Regaining more of his senses, he could feel his body was lying across a fur bed. He tried to get up but his body ached as he tried to move.

I really have to stop getting knocked out.

Lying back in the fur bed, Darvell looked above and could see various torches hanging along the walls. At the other side of the room was a door cracked open silently. Sizzling meat could also be smelled once Darvell regained his sense of smell. The pain in his body began to ease as the feeling in the rest of his body came back. Darvell got off the bed, wobbling for a few seconds before stabilizing himself. He shuffled towards the door and passed through it.

He found himself in a kitchen with a figure standing by a stone stove. She turned around to reveal herself as Jade. Darvell mouthed some words but nothing came out. Suddenly he looked down and saw a small child tug at his shirt. The little girl had long curling black hair and a white dress on. She had a familiar fiery glow in her eyes that made Darvell feel as if he were staring into a mirror. The girl smiled and spoke, causing a ringing pain in Darvell's head.

"Wake up Darvell."

Darvell woke up in a cold sweat on the Council Room floor. He could hear faint and muffled talking behind him. As he got up, the deafness in his ear began to fade.

"What the hell were you thinking?!" Hector shouted.

"All right, I overreacted," Jade admitted angrily. "But Darvell was probably going to get himself in trouble so immobilizing him would help."

"But you knocked him out cold!" Theia retorted as she pointed to Darvell. "He hasn't moved for an hour."

Darvell rubbed the back of his head as he felt a large sore. The pounding in his skull began to subside. Regibus turned around and helped Darvell get up.

"Glad to see you back up." Regibus smiled as he extended a hand outward. "I was starting to think Jade might have knocked you out for good."

Darvell tried to say something but as he spoke he could only mumble and drool. Regibus narrowed his stare as Darvell got up, wobbling and trying to keep his balance.

"Oh no," Regibus realized, his eyes widening. "We have a problem here people."

"What is it, Regibus?" Aurelina asked, walking over towards Darvell.

"Jade might have hit him too hard in the head."

Darvell made some angry mumbling noises as spittle ran down the sides of his mouth. Aurelina sucked her teeth as Regibus rubbed his chin nervously.

"Damn, she really did mess him up," Aurelina said as she

grabbed Darvell's head and examined it. "I might be able to fix him if I can find the right spell."

"Can't you do it just now?" Regibus asked. "Doesn't healing magic just heal?"

"There are certain levels of healing," Aurelina informed, pointing to some random parts of Darvell's head. "There is regular 'I'm bleeding and I need to be healed' healing and 'One of my organs is internally bleeding and I don't know which one' healing."

"So Darvell is the latter?" Regibus asked.

"Yes. I know his brain is damaged but I'm not sure where. If I just blast him with healing magic in the wrong spot, something could go wrong," Aurelina confirmed as she let go of Darvell's face, wiping the spittle from her hand. "Best case, nothing happens. Worst case is that the damage becomes permanent."

"What's going on over there?" Rubrum asked as he walked over. "What's wrong with Darvell?"

"Jade might have knocked him too hard," Regibus responded. "He just lost the ability to speak."

Rubrum's eyes widened, he ran up to Darvell and grabbed his face. He looked directly into his eyes and could see the blank stare in Darvell's eyes. Rubrum let go of his face and began to pace the room, biting his black nails, muttering to himself.

"Ignis is going to kill me!" Rubrum yelled. "I need all of you to take him to Aeris. Once there, she can help fix this hopefully. After that the rest of you are free to explore the Citadel. Let's keep it between us and say that Darvell...hit his head on something."

"You would be surprised how accurate that is," Theia laughed.

Jade went to help get Darvell but Chantal stepped in front of her. She shook her head at her and Jade backed off. As Chantal and Hector guided Darvell through the halls, Jade lagged behind with her head hanging. They reached the middlemost part of the Citadel and made their way to the medical wing where Aeris worked. They walked through the halls, walking past all sorts of dragons. They looked up nervously at them, seeing every single one of them tower over the group.

A few minutes of traversing the halls, and they reached an open pair of iron doors that led into a huge room that stretched out for what seemed like miles. There were rooms upon rooms full of injured dragons. They were covered in bandages and splints all over. Some had deep bite wounds marked around their bodies, bleeding profusely as they stained the bandages.

"I wonder what happened to all of them," Hector wondered.

"We've been having some complications in the mines," Aeris mentioned as she walked in front of them. Floating beside her was a scroll and a rather large feather, dripping ink onto the scroll below it.

Everyone looked up and could see Aeris, the copper dragon from the Council, stand in front of them. Her scales were a pale shade of copper that shifted under the torchlight. Her body was slender with her wings folded by her sides. The horns on her head were thin and curved back along her head. Near her face, scars could be seen on her bottom jaw that looked deeper as she got closer. There were puncture wounds and scrapes that were sewn together, creating awkward overlapping sections.

"So tell me," Aeris said as the scroll and feather disappeared from her side as she looked down at the group. "What seems to be the problem?"

"As you can see, Darvell had an accident. He hit himself super hard and ended up dumber than he was before," Olius explained.

Darvell angrily dribbled and groaned as he shifted over to Olius, almost falling as he took a step forward.

"Well just enough where he still understands when he's being insulted," Olius remarked.

"Rubrum told us that we should leave him here to get better,"

Aurelina mentioned. "If you want, I could stay here as well and help you with everyone here."

"I would be in your debt. The medical staff I have with me have been working day and night trying to keep up with the injured," Aeris thanked, her toothy smile unsettling some of the group. "Down the hall is my second in command, Asclepius. He can show you what everyone needs help on."

Aurelina nodded and walked down the hall. Aeris lowered her head and looked at the others.

"As for the rest of you, I'm not sure if any of you have the proper medical knowledge to help. You can all leave and enjoy yourselves around the Citadel. Darvell will be better in no time at all," Aeris assured.

As everyone thanked her and got themselves ready to leave, Jade felt something tap her on the shoulder. She turned around and saw Aeris behind her, towering over her.

"I would like to speak to you privately, help me bring Darvell to my office. Most of the other rooms are too big for him so I might need to apply a more personal touch."

"Are you sure?" Jade asked.

"Of course, I'm sure the others will be too busy for you to apologize to them," Aeris stated, a quiet chuckle escaping with her words.

"What are you talking about?"

"Just bring Darvell into the room. I'll explain everything in due time."

Jade narrowed her gaze and guided Darvell to the room. As she guided him through the halls, she could see him dribble as he tried to speak. He tried to formulate words, occasionally biting his tongue as he moved it around. Jade winced as he bit his tongue too hard, letting out a pained groan. She stopped walking and turned around to face him. All she could see was the blank stare against his face. She let out a tear and stared towards the ground. She then felt a hand touch her shoulder, which made her look up to see that it was Darvell trying to say something. He groaned and moaned, squinting his eyes in pain, trying to formulate some sort of response.

"What is it Darvell?" Jade begged.

"Ugh! Ugh! Argh!" Darvell groaned angrily.

Jade's hopeful face began to quietly sob. As she began to cry, Darvell approached her and embraced her. He clutched her closely and tried to sing a song using his mumbles. His song, although inconsistent and rough on the ears, made Jade feel calm. Suddenly, a cough came from behind her.

"You know, it's not healthy to fall in love with patients," Aeris acknowledged, her voice sounding a lot closer.

Jade rubbed her eyes and turned to face Aeris. She could see that Aeris had turned into a beautiful young woman dressed in an elegant nurse outfit. The gown was a deep copper rose color, with puffy sleeves and a frilly bottom. The half apron she wore was a deep black with two copper buttons outlining the pocket she had in front. The entire gown reached the bottom of her ankles, revealing her bare copper scaled feet. Her hair was wrapped up in a messy bun held together by two copper rods engraved with flowers. Her eyes looked like melting copper that refused to be cooled. Her sweet smile would have been more endearing if it weren't for the numerous scars, now more apparent against her tan skin.

"I don't often show this form. Many of my people find it to be undignified for my position in office. However, in my earlier years, I found that this form would help more of the humans I worked with."

"You worked to heal people?" Jade asked, wiping a tear from her eye.

"When I was younger, I lived by the coast and loved to talk with the sailors and villagers. I remember a time when a great sickness overcame them. I had seen the sickness before so I decided to take this form and cure them. They used to call me 'the All-Healing Mistress by the Sea.' It was a long title but I loved it, so I decided to practice medicine. So please, come inside and we'll talk about the situation."

Aeris motioned her hand to a door that formed to her left. They walked through it and Jade and Darvell found themselves in a small office, poorly lit by a single black candle that surprisingly didn't melt with the white fire roaring on its wick. The walls were decorated with artworks portraying landscapes, mostly seashores and beaches. On the oak desk in front of them were a couple of wooden statues of dragons gingerly placed next to a trinket that continuously smacked some orbs back and forth.

"You can lay him here, child. I'll get the medicine to ease his pain," Aeris said as she pointed to a nearby bed before continuing to rummage through a chest.

Jade guided Darvell to the bed and laid him across it. Darvell yawned and closed his eyes as Jade took a seat on a wicker chair. Aeris pulled out a couple of jars and put their contents into a boiling pot.

"I haven't caught your name yet," Aeris said as she pulled out two china cups.

"My name is Jade."

"Well Jade, it'll be easier to help Darvell if you told me where you hit him."

"I didn't hit him," Jade countered.

"Trust me Jade, I wasn't born a century ago. You were the farthest from the group and you stuck by his side. You even shed tears for him when you felt that he wanted to say something but couldn't. Either you love him a lot to see him go through this or you did the deed. Right now, I'm thinking it's a little bit of both."

Jade bit her lip as Aeris poured the steaming liquid into the china cups. She smiled and took a seat across from Jade.

"It seems that I'm right. Listen, there is no shame in owning up to one's mistakes. So tell me, where did you hit him?"

"I hit him in the back of his head. I thought it would just halt him for a bit but I didn't know it was going to do this to him."

"The anatomy of a dragon is very complicated, both in our original and transformed appearances. After all my years tending wounds, I've found out that we all share a similar weak point when we are in human form."

"The back of the head?" Jade questioned.

"It's one of the many reasons we prefer not to morph. Luckily for our patient, some simple medicine and your angelic friend's abilities will make him feel better," Aeris explained as she took a sip. "I might have to talk with her once she finishes helping Asclepius."

Jade sighed in relief. She took a long sip from the teacup and could feel the taste of a strong yet sweet flavor course through her mouth. Jade couldn't help but look at the scars Aeris had on her face. Aeris put down her cup and looked towards Darvell.

"I got the scars from Zuur."

"Hmm?"

"You are a very perceptive Jade, but so am I." Aeris laughed as she looked at Jade. "I could see you wondering."

"I was...but I didn't want to seem rude after all this hospitality," Jade apologized as she lowered her cup.

"Don't fret, child. I don't really get to talk to anyone now, so much work down here. Would you mind if I told you what happened?" Aeris suggested.

"I would be honored to listen."

"You see, it all happened before the Council was ever formed. It was even before the Citadel or Zlo's attacks were ever a thought in our heads. This was when dragons ruled the world, some with an iron claw while others preferred to live nomadic lifestyles. When I was younger and lived in my village by the Varuna Sea I came across Zuur one day, flying low near the ocean for some fish. He was enchanting and knowledgeable; he knew how to talk his way into my heart. Believe it or not, I managed to do the same with him. But our scales were different, I with my copper and he with his black. To intermingle with the other dragons was frowned upon by each and every type. But we didn't care; we loved each other too much to settle for an eternity without each other."

"What did you do?" Jade asked, her eyes sparkling as she stared intently.

"We did what anyone madly in love would do: we left what we had and we settled for somewhere across the mountain ranges. I found people to help over there and it would have been wonderful if it weren't for the eradication that plagued our brass-scaled siblings. Every dragon flocked here to protect themselves from the onslaught. We each tried to find the people in our village but they had been lost to the murder spree Zlo had led across the world," Aeris recounted, her voice growing more distant as she remembered those darker times.

"I thought only brass dragons were hunted?"

"My sweet child, do you think Zlo would only limit himself to brass dragons? He had to keep his power somehow," Aeris weakly joked. "It was an immense show of might to kill so many of us."

"I guess so," Jade admitted, shuddering at the realization.

"We had lost everything but each other. That was until we met the rest of the Council. We had all lost something dear to our hearts and we decided together that we would start anew in leading our people, thus the Council was formed."

"You really made a life for yourself."

"Alas, some beliefs never die. The people still resented the mixture of race, and the love Zuur and I had for each other was only known by the Council. We did our best to hide it; it's been easy so far. Our love could never fully blossom into what we wanted. Especially the way he is now."

"What happened to him?" Jade said, putting her cup down.

"It happened one fateful day when Zuur came back from the

mines. He was designated to lord over the mines and all of its workers. His group was attacked by an unknown assailant and he returned, permanently damaged in the head. Some soldiers went back into the mine and captured it. When he came to me to be healed, I couldn't find out what happened to him. I had to learn and learn what was wrong with him."

"What did he find in the caves?"

"It was a horrible monster that lurks in caves and eats whatever flesh walks in front of it. Nimh, thanks to her knowledge of nature, told me that the eyes of this beast had scarred Zuur, shattering his mind. I wasn't able to cure him, only soothe his pain," Aeris said, her choking voice trying not to collapse.

"Is that why you know so much about this?"

"Yes it is. However, my sadness stems from the fact that I cannot cure him. I went to embrace him one day and...he lashed out in fear. He bit me where the scars are and sprayed acid, the very thing that we both exhaled. I reared back in pain and I saw him stare at his mistake. Driven by shame and horror of what he had become, he became reclusive and introverted."

"Is he still like this?"

"By the mercy of the Old Flame, I was able to convince him that I forgave him after ten grueling centuries of me pleading to him that I still loved him. Now, he only confides in me as I help him keep calm when the debates in the Council begin to rile him up. Sometimes, however, I think he still feels horrified at what he did."

"Is the slurring part of the damage?"

"Yes, he used to speak fluently but he now tries to keep his ideas short and blunt."

"I'm sorry that all of this has happened."

"You have nothing to feel sorry about Jade. I still have Zuur and wonderful friends that I can call my own. I'm just glad you wanted to listen to an old dragon's tale."

"It was beautiful." Jade smiled as she finished her tea. "I just can't help but feel that you are telling me something."

"What would that be?" Aeris said, her smile returning.

"That you know the group doesn't like me being around and yet Darvell insists that I stay with them. Even after losing his speech, he still finds it in himself to comfort me."

"You're correct child. I may not know the extent to your exclusion but I know what it feels like to be cast off by others. Just know that even if the world judges you, the love from just one person will ease the pain. I believe I should get going; I don't want to leave your friend Aurelina doing all the medical work. Darvell's condition is simply a hard blow to the skull, perhaps in the temporal region. Your angelic friend may have an infinite pool of healing but I know where to apply it. I have some medicine and magic that can cure him. Feel free to stay here and keep Darvell company."

"Thank you, Aeris."

"My pleasure," Aeris said with a slight curtsey.

Aeris got up and left the room, leaving Jade alone with Darvell. She continued to drink the tea, looking at Darvell as he peacefully slept. She put down the cup and walked over to him. She took a seat on the bed and played with his hair as she watched him snore quietly. Jade slowly laid herself across the bed with Darvell. She closed her eyes and felt Darvell lay his hand across her.

I love you Darvell.

CHAPTER 20

Olius walked around the Citadel, admiring the artwork and designs on the walls. He happened to come across another large stone door. Inscribed on the doors were runes unfamiliar to Olius. He pulled out his book and flipped through the pages until he came across a list of alphabet translations. He took out a feather and began to inscribe the symbols onto the page. They disappeared and new words appeared on the page.

"Knowledge is power?"

The space between the doors started to glow with a bright blue light. The doors opened inwards to the room on the other side and revealed countless bookshelves packed to the brim with books and scrolls. Dragons of every color and size flew around the room, taking books with them and perching themselves on various hanging poles to review the books. Olius beamed with excitement at all the possible things he could learn from the dusty pages and tomes that surrounded him. As he walked into the room, the doors shut behind him. He saw that all the bookshelves were in the air, emitting a sparkling shine at the bottom.

"Autem."

Olius began to fly upwards as he felt light as a feather. He stopped at the first bookshelf he came upon and read through the titles. Olius furrowed his brow at the sight of the titles of the books, all foreign in script.

"I can't read any of this. I'd get tired halfway through just translating every page."

Olius put the book back and looked for any section with titles that he could read. He turned to his left and came face-to-face with a large and menacing blue dragon staring right down the middle.

"Oh—"

"What are you doing here, child?" The blue dragon snarled, her face moving in closer to Olius's. "How did you get in?"

Olius could feel every beat of her bright blue wings, the wind pushing against him. Her snout was large and wide with rows of yellow, sharp teeth. Her shoulders were broad with two rows of frills traveling all across the body. There were occasional streaks of fluorescent blue lighting dancing across her wings. Her horns were thick and curved upwards along her head until they went back down, ending at a point behind her head. She stared at Olius, her annoyed pure white eyes staring him down.

"You must be Inpulsa," Olius squeaked. "I got in by saying the password."

"That is written in our tongue and I know the half dragon is too stupid to read, let alone teach you our tongue." Inpulsa snarled, hiding her laugh behind her harsh words.

"Well, I am a gifted mage. Reading and translating foreign languages is child's play," Olius responded, trying to sound confident.

"I see..." Inpulsa responded sarcastically. "Well, I'm sure a superior mind like yours can help me with something."

"Oh, of course."

Inpulsa grabbed Olius and she flew upwards towards an opening in the roof of the room. She passed through the hole and they both entered a large room with scrolls and books haphazardly placed around it. Floating candles lit up the room as

Inpulsa set him down on the floor. Olius dusted himself off and watched as a burst of blue lightning engulfed Inpulsa. As Olius recovered from the flash, he could see that she had morphed into a tanned woman wearing a white silk shirt partially tucked into her black pants. She had blue framed glasses on her face that expanded her pure white eyes which crackled with dim flashes of light. She had short black hair with blue tinted braids going across her head. She walked past Olius and pulled out a small box and handed it to him.

"Take a look at this box and tell me what you think it is," Inpulsa ordered, crossing her arms as she judged his movements.

Olius took the box and analyzed it, quickly and swiftly inspecting all of its sides. There were runes on all six sides of the cube, their shapes extremely foreign to Olius.

"This seems to be a box with a foreign language on it."

"Yes I know that, I wouldn't have asked you if that was my question," Inpulsa snarled. "Do you know what box it is?"

"No! Don't tell me! Is this the Box of Babel?"

"I see you are well informed. Yes this is the Box of Babel. The owner, Mirmi of Solmon, was an avid puzzle maker with a vast understanding of riddles. This box was a riddle of language and I have been struggling for centuries trying to figure out its runes."

"That explains the mess," Olius joked as he looked around.

"I'm not usually this disorganized; I've just been so frustrated with this confounded box!" Inpulsa growled as she pointed at the box.

"Well what have you tried so far?"

"I've looked through countless books, dead languages and active ones, trying to see what it is. I used to venture outside to find the area Mirmi lived to see if any lost villages provided him with an unknown language. Alas, I haven't found a single one."

"Did anything come with the box, any inscriptions explaining how to solve it?"

"There was but the inscription is so broad. I remember that

it went like this: 'The mute has no need for speech. They convey everything without saying a thing.' I think it was some bastard's graffiti," Inpulsa explained.

Olius scratched his chin as he moved the box around his hand. He focused on one rune and tried to start there. Inpulsa saw the concentration on his face and slithered over to him to see what had caught his attention. Olius took his finger and ran it across the rune, feeling the space inside the etchings. He closed his eyes and felt that the rune was the beginning for the letter "T." Then it changed into a different design, possibly from another language, yet it still meant "T." Olius kept going until he went through a bunch of different languages until he finished tracing.

"Well? What is it?" Inpulsa excitedly asked.

"I have no idea how you didn't think of this sooner! The designs are foreign to you and I because they aren't symbols at all!"

"They aren't symbols? How does that make…It makes perfect sense! Of course Mirmi wouldn't write it in a language that one race would know by heart. He would want to write this in something no one would understand and what better way to do that than writing the runes in every language possible?"

"How come you couldn't figure it out?"

"Dragons are a proud race, child. The mixing of other languages with mine disgusts me. I guess it took a race open to anything to solve this puzzle," Inpulsa said, holding her nose up high.

"That's awfully nice of you to say."

"Don't let it go to your head; we still have a lot more experience under our belt than you."

"Fair enough, let's finish this puzzle then. I want to know what's in the box."

As they continued working on the box, Olius read out loud

the letters the languages made and Inpulsa wrote them down. They looked at the word the box created.

"Theson," they both said in unison.

They stared at the paper for a few more minutes.

"I have no idea what this means," Inpulsa said, defeated.

"Neither do I," Olius said, looking through his book.

"What's that for?" Inpulsa said, her stern voice shifting into curiosity as her white eyes observed the book.

"It's my magic book. I have had it ever since I was a baby."

"Can I have it?" Inpulsa bluntly asked.

"No," Olius rudely declined.

"I see."

They continued to stare at the word, the flickering of the candles making up for the lack of conversation. Inpulsa looked at Olius and Olius looked back at her, concern in his stare.

Hector walked around the Citadel looking for a place to get something to eat. His stomach rumbled loudly as he tried to read the signs that hung above the doors around the halls.

"I can't read any of this. I'm too starving to think about anything right now."

Hector walked towards the end of the hall, his stomach rumbling louder, until his nose caught the tantalizing smell of cooked meat. He walked towards the smell and into a large room filled with weapons and armor. He walked around some more, trying to find the source of the smell. The armor around the walls was huge and elegantly designed, as if they were statues rather than armor stands. The smell began to get stronger as Hector turned a corner and came across two large dragons sitting at a table.

On the right was a large white dragon, muscular with two thick horns on each side of its head. The horns on the right had a couple of chips in them while the ones on the left were shiny and pristine. The snout of the white dragon was thick and outlined with a frill that danced along the lips. His eyes were fierce, a thick sloped forehead above them. His tucked wings looked wide and were riddled with holes. The dragon on the right had fair, silver scales and was far thinner than the white dragon. Her horns were tame and miniscule, barely arching around her head. Her wings, also tucked in, had a white shine to them. Between them was a table full of food, steaming and elegantly prepared. On the table was a plate with a lake-sized bowl of steaming soup, and a field-sized plate of what appeared to be a whale, roasted and garnished with gigantic vegetables.

"Argenti, this is the best meal I have had in a while. I find it hard to believe that you had time to make this with your nose stuck in those books." Frio laughed as he ripped a piece of whale off and ate it.

"Thank you Frio. I found a wonderful cookbook in the library this morning. What we are eating here is a couple native dishes from the frost giants up north from here. I found these dishes quite interesting because they each have a unique history to them," Argenti said, her bright smile showing itself at the compliment.

"Frost giants you say? I remember killing a few of them when I was commander during the Coldthorn War. They did not stand a chance against us with their ice spears," Frio cheered in a raucous and boisterous voice.

"Interesting," Argenti said, her smile fading a bit. "I guess..."

Frio and Argenti looked at each other awkwardly and continued to eat. Hector shook his head at the two and started to look at the food again. Frio groaned and looked towards the direction where Hector was hiding.

"We can give you some food if you're that hungry," Frio growled through his scowling mouth.

"I promise he won't hurt you," Argenti consoled.

Hector walked out and sheepishly headed towards the giant

table. Frio reached over and picked him up, Hector hoping his white claws wouldn't pierce through his armor. Frio gently placed him on the table, between him and Argenti. Hector reached over for a piece of the whale and began to eat it. Although most of it was fat, the texture was chewy and it felt like eating meat.

"So what's your name little guy?" Argenti asked sweetly.

"Oh don't talk to him like that; can't you see he's a soldier?" Frio retorted.

"But look at him! He's so cute and adorable. I don't believe he's hurt a soul in his life."

"I know a thing or two about killers Argenti, this kid has the look of a killer." Frio laughed, his coarse and hearty voice echoing through the room. "Am I right?!"

Hector looked blankly into space, remembering the time he was forced to eat his only childhood friend. He nervously laughed as he took a bite of the whale chunk he had in his hand.

"No, no. I haven't killed anyone at all," Hector denied poorly.

Frio smiled as Argenti raised her eyebrows in surprise. They continued to eat, the silence quite discomforting to everyone in the room, until Hector broke it.

"Are you guys like…dating?"

Frio choked on his drink while Argenti coughed uncomfortably as she looked away. Hector gulped, thinking he had hit a bad nerve in the two.

"Boy, you shouldn't throw around things like that! Such allegations, right Argenti?"

"Oh yeah, of course. That would be silly!" Argenti stammered.

Frio looked at her and his cheeks turned slightly blue. He reached over for his drink and nervously drank it. Argenti started to blush as well and got up from the table, almost knocking everything over.

"Ugh, I have to go. I think I left some of the books unorganized. I'll talk to you later. Goodbye, Hector."

Argenti shuffled out of the room, leaving Frio and Hector

by themselves. The table had been cleared of the delicious food, leaving only scraps and dirty dishes. Frio sighed as he finished off his wine, looking ahead of him where Argenti sat.

"I feel bad now," Hector glumly stated.

"Don't feel bad kid, I don't even think it would work if we were given the chance. She and I are too different. I was a warlord and she is a historian. I guess my presence gives her a bad taste in her mouth since I'm a constant reminder of my race's destructive nature."

"You were a warlord?"

"Yes, my dear boy. I was a proud 'Prince of War' among my people. The white dragons are by far the most ferocious killers since we came from an environment so scarce in materials."

"So you are good at fighting?"

"I consider myself the best of my race," Frio bragged, his teeth glaring with his smile. "Sometimes the best out of everyone."

"Could you teach me how to fight?!" Hector asked as he jumped up.

"Teach you to fight? Dear boy, how have you managed to get this far then?"

"Well I've pulled my weight most of the time, but I feel that I'm not the most useful sometimes. Out of everyone in the group, I don't have a single magic power."

"That is mighty impressive, even for me. These lands are filled with all manner of beasts that could kill any human without a second thought. You just being here is a sign of either skill or dumb luck."

"Even so, I want to be better," Hector insisted. "I want to make sure my friends can rely on me like I can rely on them."

Frio slowly nodded in confirmation. He scratched his chin and got up from the table. He walked around, looking at his collection of armor. He turned to Hector and frowned.

"You don't have the heart of a warrior, Hector. You are too kind to be one."

Hector looked distraught. He began to get up slowly, grabbing his things.

"However, you have the heart of a knight. You possess the determination to strive forward although all odds are against you. You walk amongst gods as if you were with them, yet you don't boast. You know you are mortal, as we all are, and I am proud of that. So you must not fight with ferocity like your dragon friend or like anyone else. You must fight like you are defending justice. I can sense it in you that you want ills to be corrected and wrongdoings to never be enacted. So I will teach you how to fight with dignity, finding every opening possible to win. You must promise me something in return."

"What is it?"

"Do not rely on my teaching for everything you come across. If it seems it will come in handy then so be it. Yet, the adaptability of a fighter is what makes them a deadly foe. You must remain open to every opportunity and with your best judgment, do what you think will create the best outcome. Do you understand?"

Hector beamed with excitement as he jumped from the table, not realizing that the height was too high for him. He fell a good few feet, Frio looking at Hector suddenly sprawled out on the floor. Slowly but surely, Hector got up with a smile on his face.

"I'm okay! I'll be back as soon as possible." Hector winced as he finished getting up.

"I'd stop by the medical bay before you come and train," Frio suggested. "Just to make sure you didn't break anything."

"Will do!"

Hector quickly left the room, his armor clanking loudly through the halls. Frio sighed and shook his head. A little smile curled on his face as he started to pick up the dishes.

CHAPTER 21

Regibus could feel his head pounding, as if a hammer was jamming nails into his brain and ripping them out. His vision was blurry with the occasional black spot forming. There wasn't anywhere in the Citadel worth visiting due to the pain, except going back to Aeris to get some medicine. Regibus stopped and looked around and turned a corner to recuperate. Suddenly, the pain began to feel like a voice trying to speak.

"Cutthroat I swear, if you have something to do with this..." Regibus grunted as he rubbed his eyes.

"Listen Regibus, there are piles upon piles of gold around here!" Cutthroat angrily growled, his voice poking through Regibus's head. "Let's just grab some!"

"No, we are not doing that. This is their stuff and we are not taking it."

Upon saying that, Regibus felt his legs stop moving. He fell to the floor and face-planted onto the carpet. Regibus tried to get back up but his arms went stiff as well.

"Listen, I didn't come back from the afterlife just to help my grandkids. I came here because you promised me some riches," Cutthroat said, his voice coming out of Regibus's mouth. "If I can't have the ones I lost I might as well get some new stuff. So let's get going!"

Regibus felt his body move upward sporadically as he took an awkward step forward. He felt his vision grow worse as he continued to walk. Once his vision was completely gone, he could no longer control his movements. Blind to the world around him, Regibus began to panic.

He's encroaching too much in my head. I have to find a way—

You aren't doing anything until I get my gold!

What!

We share a body Regibus; therefore, we share a mind.

Regibus struggled, trying to regain control of his body again. The smell of metals filled his nose, alerting him that Cutthroat had managed to find something. He forced in another sniff and suddenly knew what Cutthroat found.

Gold.

That's right! We'll just take a couple and be on our way. They won't miss anything at all. There is so much here!

Don't you dare touch anything!

Who are you to tell me what to—

Regibus's vision came back instantly as he felt his body come back under his control. The return however was unpleasant and painful, like was knocked against a stone wall. He found himself in a pile of gold coins piled up to an enormous scale. He looked around and saw that the room he was in held not only gold, but all sorts of treasure. Mountains upon mountains of emeralds, rubies, sapphires, silver coins, bronze coins, platinum coins and various diamonds were piled on shelves, pots, boxes, with some scattered everywhere on the floor. Regibus got up and walked around in utter awe at the amounts of treasure in this room.

"This place is crazy. I bet you could buy a kingdom with it."

"To be realistic, you could buy all four if you know how to bargain," a voice echoed from around a corner.

Regibus stopped in his tracks as he saw the bronze dragon

walking towards him, holding a couple of papers in his talons. He looked over at Regibus and examined him. He got up into his face, Regibus staring him right down the center of it. His metallic white eyes pierced right through him. The dragon snorted and backed off, returning to his accounting. Regibus stood there in shock as the thudding of the dragon shook him out of it.

"I see that the wretched ghost has finally left. He was getting on my nerves; I thought he would never leave."

"What…What ghost?"

"Don't play dumb with me pirate, your seafaring stench couldn't mask the magic emanating off you. I'm pretty sure Zuur could even tell. I'm just glad he got what was coming to him."

"Do you know what happened to him?"

"Not sure. Inpulsa would know since she dabbles in the stuff. I do remember something about a curse? I wasn't paying attention, the treasure logs are way too backed up to be listening to the magical world."

"Curse?"

"Yes, yes, curses and whatnot. Do you mind leaving? I have some busy stuff to take care of."

"Oh...of course."

Regibus walked out of the room, the doors closing behind him with a loud thud. Regibus looked at his hands. He tried to summon Cutthroat, flicking his hands then clenching his fists. No matter how hard he tried, he couldn't feel his presence.

"Oh shit."

"There sure are a lot of injureds coming in," Aurelina said as she inspected the wounds of a red dragon.

"What's more surprising is that they all have the same injuries," Asclepius stated, lifting the wing of a black dragon. "Bite wounds, deep cuts, and for some reason extreme bludgeoning on the legs and arms. I've never seen these types of injuries on such a large scale."

"It's also strange that most of these dragons come from the mines. It's as if there is something in the caves that's fighting back." Aurelina yawned, looking over the medical papers.

"You've been working for quite some time. I'm sure even gods need to sleep once in awhile."

"No...no, I'm fine," Aurelina yawned. "I just need some coffee."

"As Aeris's right-hand man, I suggest you take a break. The rest of us can take it from here."

"I guess you're right. I'll be back in an hour then."

Aurelina left the medical bay and decided to walk around the Citadel. The hallways she walked led her into a large stone balcony that overlooked most of the buildings below. Aurelina could see multiple lights gingerly floating through the cavern acting as miniature suns for the dragons. Up on the balcony were multiple pillars holding up the floor. They were gilded with gems in intricate patterns, depicting scenes of dragons flying through the air or swimming through water. Suddenly, Aurelina heard heavy footsteps behind her and the sound of a faint conversation. Aurelina moved behind one of the pillars. She could see Ignis in his dragon form talking with another brass-colored dragon.

"As you know, you are my most trusted advisor. So it would only seem fitting to have you marry my grandson to keep the lineage going," Ignis said.

So this must be the girl. I thought Rubrum was the only one who was coming up with this plan.

"I am humbled by your choice, Ignis. I'll be sure to provide a good offspring for the Council," the dragon declared, her voice striking a familiar nerve in Aurelina's brain.

The two dragons continued down the hallway as their conversation continued. Aurelina walked from her hiding spot and widened her eyes. A gleam of white light raced across her eyes as her vision changed. She could see everything in a blurry glow except for a bright flame flickering back and forth that took over Ignis's body. However, Aurelina gasped as she laid her eyes on the glowing mass of dark purple energy pulsating like a dying heart. Aurelina then felt her body fly backwards as something wrapped around her.

Aurelina woke up once more and found herself in a dark room lit by a couple of hanging candles. The thing that had grabbed her unraveled and slithered into a corner. The room was covered in leaking pores with a bubbling, green liquid slowly dripping from clean cut holes. Some of the holes were stuffed with jewels and diamonds but not in any order, as if they were flung around crazily. There were small pools of acid on the floor, not digging into the ground but just sitting there. Aurelina looked towards the dark corner of the room, looking to see if anyone was there.

"Hello? I know someone is in that corner, I can see you," Aurelina threatened.

"You can't see me; I'm silently sneaking so you can't see me," the voice slurred with an audible lisp.

"I was kidding but now that I know you are in that corner, tell me why you dragged me here?"

The voice cursed in the same harsh tongue as a pair of shale white eyes slowly opened. The eyes blinked, momentarily covered with a thin green film, as they continued to stare at Aurelina.

"I still haven't gotten your name. But from looking at where we are and how you talk, I guess you must be Zuur."

"Yes, how did you know?" Zuur asked, his snout poking through the shade.

"You have a very distinct...voice."

"I know I have a lisp, I've been cursed with it ever since...it doesn't matter. I must ask you two things. I suggest you don't let the others know of your findings."

"How come?"

"I do not yet have proof to question Ignis's advisor. She suddenly rose through the ranks, too quickly if you ask me. I've been tailing her and have learned she has no immediate family members around Drakon. The others have not paid too much attention but I have, I do it in his best interest."

"Seems like it's stalking," Aurelina accused.

"I owe him my life after he saved me. Also, you're in no place to judge. I can sense from you that you agree with my notion."

"Well you're right about that," Aurelina admitted. "What was the second thing?"

"I heard you can heal those who are injured?" Zuur asked as his head poked through the shadows. "Is this true?"

"Yes, why do you ask?"

"My condition was not always like this. I ventured into the caves one fateful day and was met with an ambush. I was beaten into an almost catatonic state and I returned a different dragon. I want you to cure me," Zuur begged as Aurelina felt his body shift.

"I've heard about your condition already. I believe Darvell is going through the same thing. However, if I couldn't heal him, what makes you think I can heal—"

Zuur slid a book towards Aurelina. The book was leather bound and huge. However, as soon as Aurelina went to grab it, it shrunk to a much more human-sized book.

"You stole this didn't you?" Aurelina gasped.

"It was not my best moment but I want to be at my best for her again," Zuur sheepishly stated, his voice whistling through most of his words. "She was far too busy helping others so I thought I could take this into my own hands."

"I find it romantic," Aurelina beamed as she flipped through the book. "I'll help you, but you have to help me make sure that brass dragon doesn't pull anything, okay?"

"You have my word," Zuur said as he revealed himself.

Aurelina watched as Zuur lumbered out of the shadows to reveal himself, his hulking figure crunching the gems beneath his feet. His snout was pockmarked with holes dripping green acid as misshapen teeth of different sizes and shapes somehow interlocked with each other. His tucked in wings looked like thick leather, ripped in some parts and stitched with what looked like numerous spools of string. Zuur's posture was hunched and snake-like as he looked at Aurelina. He blinked again and smiled.

"Now keep yours."

Darvell tossed and turned on the medical bed, his body heating up inside. He could feel his blood boil as he clenched his hands, impaling his claws into his palms. His vision fluctuated from vibrant colors to static lines of grey and white. With each passing vision, his headache worsened even more until he opened his eyes. He looked up to see a sky of grey. He lifted himself up and looked around. This was the same place that he had met his father, an infinite field of low flying smoke and grey coloring.

"Hello! Anyone out here?" Darvell yelled as he began to look around for signs of life.

"You don't have to yell," Scales said as he instantly appeared behind Darvell.

"Holy shit! Don't do that!" Darvell shrieked as he jumped.

"My bad. Listen Darvell, we have some problems. You see—"

"I thought you were too busy helping with the other gods?"

"We are in recess right now but that's beside the point," Scales explained. "It seems that your stumbling with the other dragons is preventing the journey from moving forward. Yanusu suddenly started bickering with himself and that's how we found out."

"Who's Yanusu?" Darvell asked. "What do you mean he started bickering with himself?"

"Yanusu is a god that helps keep track of the beginning and end of adventures," Scales said. "We put yours on top priority and suddenly his left began to mutter while his right told him to be quiet."

"Two heads? That sounds cool!" Darvell beamed.

"It kind of—wait! We need to stay on track!"

"Yeah, you said my adventure has stopped. How the hell is that possible?"

"That's partly my fault. I came down to the first dragons and explained to them that the binding laws of marriage must come first, before anything. So your quest is literally on halt since we have a divine law prohibiting your divine mission from proceeding."

"Isn't the Oracle the most powerful god?" Darvell pointed out. "How come your word is higher than hers?"

"That's also her fault. She agreed with me and that law has since stopped many adventurers from many races."

"Can't you just get rid of it? You are gods after all."

"You know how many people stopped their adventures for marriage? They'd be fuming if we just got rid of it!" Scales yelled as he threw his hands in the air.

"Then what are we going to do?" Darvell asked, beginning to quaver.

"I don't know! What's even more worrying is that we can't figure out who you are marrying because we can't pinpoint her soul. We have no way of influencing this at all."

"Can't you go down there and talk to them, get them to give this up and find a new way?"

"After all that happened to the brass dragons? I don't

think they want to even speak my name at all." Scales laughed nervously.

"Forgive my intrusion but I believe I have a say in this," a voice said from behind them.

Darvell and Scales looked back and saw Marius walking over to them. His brows were furrowed while his stride was quick and furious.

"Darvell cannot marry this woman. His Semi-Divine nature violates the laws put into place before you decreed that marriages are binding. The marriage goes against the will of the gods and a divine mission. He cannot get married!"

"You're right!" Scales cheered. "The new question is how we can tell the Council about this."

"That is the question indeed," Marius concurred.

"Are you sure you won't make an appearance?" Darvell asked. "It would take a lot of pressure off us."

Scales scratched the back of his head and sighed.

"You're probably right. I just don't know how they'll react. If they don't hate me then I might be able to tell them that the wedding can't happen."

"It sounds like a plan, just not an entirely good one," Marius stated. "But it's better than nothing."

"What should I do then?" Darvell asked.

"You just try to keep yourself out of trouble. You're in no shape to do any fighting or talking," Scales ordered.

"Why can't I fight? I feel fine for fighting."

"You are in a very serious position Darvell," Marius explained. "Your mind is in a very fragile state right now; any unnecessary stress could erase you and replace you with a true dragon's mind."

"Aren't dragons smart, why would something like that be bad?"

"A true dragon is like a primal form," Scales explained. "You will know nothing but killing and simply be an animal."

"Oh, that would make the journey difficult to manage."

"I believe it is time we must part ways, son. I'll help Scales prepare for his arrival, try to stay out of trouble?" Marius asked.

"Wait!"

Darvell opened his eyes and looked around. He growled quietly, sat up, and touched his forehead. He no longer felt the painful heat that he'd had, in fact he felt rather cold. He looked down to see Jade sleeping beside him. He smiled and got up from the bed and looked around the room. He headed towards the door and walked out into the hallway. As he walked a few feet away from the door, he stopped in his tracks. He didn't know if he should leave the room. His stomach rumbled and he looked to see if Aurelina was still around. Seeing that she wasn't, he smiled and made his way to the closest kitchen possible. As he made his way down the hall, a figure peered from behind the corner on the opposite end. Her silhouette glowed in the dim light, a white devilish smile peering out of the shadows.

"Such a nice place you have here Nimh, it's quite lovely," Theia said as she reached over for her cup of tea.

"It is quite nice isn't it? I would like to thank you two for accepting my invitation," Nimh thanked, her quiet voice hanging delicately in the air.

They drank tea in the open air of the magically grown flora, sitting on a hanging platform suspended from a large jungle tree. The ambience around them would have convinced anyone they were in a jungle if it were not for the dull rock ceiling above them. Colorful flowers blossomed on the thick vines cascading from the trees as the dirt floor was littered with large grey stones covered in blankets of moss. The platform that hung from the large branch was like a birdcage dangling from a golden hook, gripping firmly to the dark brown branch. The singing, glowing light of multiple will-o-wisps flying about kept the jungle lit to its fullest.

Nimh's humanoid form was almost an extension of the very jungle she resided in. Her greenish brown skin was covered in swirling thin lines of green scales that sparkled under the faint lights. Her flowing cape resembled cascading leaves of all colors as a crown of flowers and thorns lay gently on her head. An earthen dress detailed with rising vines and flowers hugged her body, as if it were her very skin. Her pristine yellow eyes held within them pitch black irises.

"If you don't mind me asking Nimh, why invite us to tea? Olius swore that the dragons wouldn't really like our presence," Theia asked as she put the white china cup down.

"Well the young wizard is correct. The people here would shun you. That is why we want you to stay in the Citadel. The guards are under our control so they wouldn't dare say anything and it has been quite some time since we've seen humans. I'm especially fond of you two," Nimh smiled.

"Were you some mystical dragon in the jungle?"

"No dear, just a legend back in the day," Nimh quietly boasted. "'Nature's Messenger,' some would call me."

Chantal gestured her hands in a questioning manner.

"Chantal wants to know what you did to get the name."

"I would go around spreading nature to kingdoms I deemed too invasive on my land. Oh I had so much fun watching as my magic would spread through the streets; trees and flowers would spring to life with my mere presence."

"Did you kill a lot of people?"

"Only those who deserved it. You could not imagine the number of people coming into my home, killing the wildlife and burning down trees. They thought I had a treasure buried somewhere! Little did they know they were destroying it themselves."

"You don't have any treasure? Isn't that odd for a dragon?"

"It is, but the others hoard things that aren't normally

considered treasure. Frio hoards his large collection of historic memorabilia, there's Inpulsa with her scrolls and books, Zuur has exotic gems but he prefers to eat them, Aurum secretly hoards artworks, Aeris is too busy to have and maintain a hoard with her line of work, Argenti has this cute hobby of making ice sculptures, Rubrum used to collect letters from kings he was friends with until the war happened, and Aes, despite working with all the money in the kingdom, has a fondness for exotic clothing he likes to put on when he's in human form." Nimh chuckled, putting her hand on her lips.

Chantal tapped Theia's shoulder and asked another question.

"Chantal wants to know why you didn't say anything about Ignis."

Nimh bit her lip and swirled the tea in her teacup. Her yellow eyes darted away for a second as Chantal and Theia sucked their teeth, hoping they didn't ask something inappropriate.

"You don't have to answer if you don't want to," Theia said, retracting her question.

"No, no. You didn't hit a nerve or anything. It's just...out of all of us Ignis is the one who may have lost the most. Even before his bloodline and race were almost exterminated, he had to see his son leave."

"Do you know why?"

"He said it was a feud between them. The child no longer wanted to be like him. Instead he wanted to learn more about the world, maybe shed his skin for something more freeing. It did not sit well with him and he cast him out of the village."

"So it was remorse then?"

"No, even worse. Ignis thought his son knew it was only a temporary exile, to teach him some sort of lesson. Yet he never returned, and right then the killing of the brass dragons began. Ignis to this day blames himself since he believes he sent his son to be slaughtered."

"That's terrible."

"Indeed it is child; it goes to show you age is not proof of wisdom. Ignis is the oldest of all of us, by a few centuries, but he constantly mutters to himself about the mistakes he's made."

"I just want to know something, why can't Ignis find a new heir?" Theia asked as she poured some more tea.

"A human heir is very different from a dragon heir. Humans can procreate with anyone they wish and the child will be an heir," Nimh explained, swirling some honey into her tea. "No matter if the blood is royal or peasant; that child is an heir. A dragon heir, however, must have blood from the same dragon family and be raised in the same clan."

"I'm starting to understand," Theia said as she looked at Chantal, nodding in agreement.

"Indeed, Ignis has no clan anymore and Darvell is the only one left of his blood. Darvell's child, then, would be the only viable heir. Of course Ignis could have another child, but there's no one of his kind old enough who survived Zlo's onslaught."

"It scares me to know Darvell knows nothing about this."

Chantal drank her tea and nodded in confirmation.

"How so?" Nimh asked.

"Darvell isn't what one would call the brightest individual, certainly not the most well-mannered either. None of us have struck a nerve with any of you, and we are glad that we haven't, but Darvell soon might."

"You speak so rudely of someone who is destined to save us all, why is that?"

"I for one don't believe in entitlement, it's your actions that I first see," Theia explained, remembering her father as she sipped the tea. "I'm not sure about anyone else in the group," Theia added as she turned to Chantal.

Chantal shrugged, confirming she didn't believe in it either.

"Well it is good to see the lost child has made some good friends. I feel he won't be staying here so please take care of him.

If I know anything about bloodlines, they never seem to stop making the same mistakes."

"We'll do our best," Theia said with a smile.

Regibus walked towards the library door after a few hours of asking people where it was. He tried to open the door yet it was locked and too heavy to budge. He slumped onto the floor, breathing heavily from a lack of breath.

"I'm not going to get anywhere without Cutthroat helping me."

A few minutes passed and the thumping of feet could be heard down the hall. Regibus looked down the hall and saw a light blue dragon carrying a load of books and scrolls with him. His vision was weak yet it looked like he was heading toward the library. Regibus smiled and hid behind a corner, and waited for the dragon to open the door. He stopped by the door and began to speak in a harsh tongue. As the doors opened, Regibus snuck through the dragon's legs and found himself in a large library. He looked around for Inpulsa, seeing that she wasn't in the common area. He looked up to see a glass entrance to another room.

"She's probably up there. I wonder if I can get up there."

As Regibus stared at the entrance on the ceiling, Olius found himself summoning a shield to deflect blasts of lightning and magic from Inpulsa.

"Leave me alone!" Olius screamed from behind the shield.

"Give me the book! I want it for my collection!" Inpulsa hissed.

"I need it for my magic! Leave me alone!" Olius yelled. "Impetu!"

A spectral gust of blue light charged towards Inpulsa, forcing her backwards. Inpulsa, back in her dragon form, grasped her wrists and connected her arms together while she looked towards Olius.

"Ferro Saeva!"

As she pulled apart her arms, a long iron chain began to form. She gripped it and smashed the end onto Olius's shield, shattering it. As the magic barrier shattered, Olius cracked open the book and started to look for any useful spells. Inpulsa raised the chain again and brought it back down, knocking Olius to the side. As he slid across the floor, he looked downwards to see Regibus.

"Subcinctus!"

With a puff of blue smoke, Regibus appeared right next to Olius. He was still looking up until he realized he had changed positions. He looked down to see Olius slowly getting up, a trickle of blood running out of his mouth.

"What are you doing up here?" Regibus asked.

"I was helping Inpulsa with a riddle to get treasure. Now I'm fighting for dear life for this book," Olius responded, a bloody cough following afterward.

"Do not get distracted wizard!" Inpulsa roared as she flung the iron chain between the two.

Regibus and Olius barely jumped out of the way. Regibus landed on his feet while Olius landed on his ass again, a surge of pain rising up his back. Regibus pulled out his flintlock and looked at Inpulsa.

"Leave him alone!" Regibus threatened.

"Give me the book and we can forget about all of this," Inpulsa offered.

"What would the Council think about this?"

Inpulsa bit her lip and gave out a nervous laugh.

"The Council does not know my boredom! They all have their little pastimes but I have been cooped up under the earth for centuries reading the same books! I haven't seen a new piece of information in forever and that book holds spells that I may have not seen!"

"You...can't have...it...bitch," Olius weakly said.

Inpulsa growled and snapped the chain away into a puff of smoke.

"Listen here children, give me the book and I can give you a vast amount of treasure and knowledge. Just give me the book."

Regibus felt a sting in his arm. His eyes widened as a small smile appeared. Olius noticed the smile and was confused by it.

"What kind of treasure Inpulsa?" Regibus asked.

"All kinds of gold and jewels!" Inpulsa offered as she moved her claws around, small illusions taking form as she said them out loud. "Chalices made of pure silver that pour out the sweetest of wine, a silver gilded harp that plays by itself, robes worn by long dead kings made with the softest silk anyone can make. I can get you anything as long as you give me that book."

The sting in Regibus's arm began to hurt more as it traveled up his arm and into his body. Regibus did his best to hide the pain, smiling as he looked at Inpulsa. Olius scoffed as he gripped the book.

"We don't want your money you—"

"I want all of it!" Regibus yelled proudly, his voice echoing from out of nowhere.

Olius quickly jerked his head towards Regibus while Inpulsa smiled, her mouth curling towards the back of her head.

"Then give me the book, pirate." Inpulsa slithered, her eyes widening as she looked at the book. "Your treasure will be given to you."

Regibus walked over to Olius and stood over him. He reached for the book as Olius clutched it tighter.

"What are you doing?!" Olius whispered. "We can't give her the book."

"I'm tricking her," Regibus said. "Earlier Cutthroat was thrown out of my body but I can feel his powers coming back."

"How do I know I'm not talking to Cutthroat?" Olius questioned.

"Trust me," Regibus pleaded.

Olius bit down hard on his teeth, scowling at the idea of handing over the book. Regibus furrowed his brows and extended his arm forward again. Olius looked away and handed him the book slowly. Regibus grabbed it and walked towards Inpulsa. She smiled and reverted back to human form, eagerly extending her arms outward. Regibus stopped in front of her, still clutching the book.

"What's wrong? Why did you stop?!" Inpulsa snarled.

Regibus laughed quietly as the flesh from his face began to fall off. Inpulsa looked in disgusted horror as Cutthroat appeared in front of her. He threw the book back to Olius, pulled out two engraved flintlocks, and pointed them at Inpulsa.

"I'm back!"

Hector went back to Frio's abode and looked around to see where he was. Hector could see that the room had changed since the last time he was inside. In front of him was a large sand pit where a solitary man stood, inspecting the walls. The man was huge, maybe just as big as Darvell or Ignis. His skin was a pale white, much like the snow of the Northern Kingdoms he had seen before. The man had shaggy, frost white hair that turned into a long braid that travelled down his back. It had one large iron cap tying everything together at the end. The armor he wore Hector had ever seen. On his right shoulder was the top part of a wolf's skull, its two front fangs replaced with iron replicas. On the left was a shoulder pad that held up a faded white cape. On the cape was the symbol of a crouched dragon, holding a greatsword in its claws.

As the man turned around and grinned, Hector could see he

had a thick grey beard that covered more of his face than his own skin. He had a thick scar that slowly made its way down the bridge of his nose and buried itself within his greased mustache. His crystal white eyes, although pupilless, looked inviting and friendly. He wore dark brown studded leather on his chest and a checkered kilt of white squares with black stripes across the front of his chest and wrapped around his waist. His heavy leather boots hugged his legs as he walked towards Hector, waving his burly hand as stone stairs formed into the pit.

"Ah, Hector," Frio cheered. "It's nice to see that you actually came."

"I wouldn't miss this opportunity. I'm just wondering why you wanted to do it in human form. Doesn't it inconvenience you?"

"Although I am proud of my scales, I feel the need to give you the best training. So I opted for a more direct approach," Frio explained. "But enough of that, attack me!"

"What?"

"Take your spear and charge towards me."

Hector gripped his spear and gulped. He could feel that Frio was going to pull some trick on him. He put up his spear and charged towards Frio. As he reached him, he saw him open up his mouth and Hector instinctually moved out of the way. However, as he strayed away from him, he could see Frio kick some sand up into the air. As he shielded his eyes from the sand, he fell to the ground with a thud. He looked back up to see Frio extending his arm to help him up. Hector smiled and grabbed it, standing back up. Frio examined Hector's armor and let out a concerned sigh.

"What is it?"

"Your armor is quite heavy for you. What you have on is only good for foot soldiers," Frio pointed out as he looked at Hector. "You'll have to find a new set of armor to suit you. I have a couple other sets of armor somewhere around here, follow me."

As they walked out of the arena, it disappeared behind them at the snap of Frio's fingers. Hector felt as if the room had shrunk while he wasn't looking. Although the vertigo was slightly nauseating, it passed after a few seconds.

"It truly is amazing what magic is capable of, Hector," Frio said without looking back at him. "I was wary of it at first but I have Inpulsa to thank for showing me its endless possibilities. Here we are; some armor I have collected over the years."

Frio gestured to a large hall of armor stands, each one vastly different from the ones next to it. The hall seemed to go on forever, the torches on the walls disappearing as they reached the limit of Hector's vision. As Hector took off his armor, he was about to throw it into a nearby chest until Frio stopped him.

"Actually, I would like to keep this in a proper place. A memory of sorts."

"Really?"

"Of course Hector. I haven't been a teacher in a while and you have grown on me."

Hector smiled and handed him the handmade armor. He began to walk down the hall as Frio followed behind. Looking through the armor stands, one caught his eye. It had a dark breastplate with moveable shoulder pads. It shone in the torchlight, revealing the sculpted abs that the creator had bestowed on their creation. There was an elegant design in the center of the chestplate, a silver ingrained eight-pointed star within a circle. On each shoulder pad was an extended bird—possibly a dove—that pointed upwards. He put it on and somehow felt that this armor was built for him.

The suit of armor also had a pair of brown armored pants with the engraving of a horseshoe with a ribbon wrapped around the bottom of each pant leg. They were covered in the same dark armor that made up the breastplate. The armor plates on the knees were layered upon each other, bending as Hector moved them up in the air to get a better look at them. Putting them on, they hugged his legs, giving him a strange feeling of confidence. Lastly, he picked up a barbuta helmet with a silver cross on the faceguard. He turned the helmet around, admiring the craftsmanship of the silver studs lined across the bottom of it. He held it in his hand and put it aside for later. As he was about to finish picking out his new armaments, picking out some armor for his arms and hands of the same color to keep the color scheme going, Frio handed him a long silver shawl with two intertwined harps at the end and a pike shield engraved with an upright dragon holding two spears in its talons.

"I was given this scarf from an old spirit in the Vinson Mountains. I had given her some company during a horrible snowstorm and protected her from some of the local monsters. She promised that this scarf would protect me and all that I love. As for the shield, it belonged to a human companion I had once, a dear friend I consider my only equal," Frio confided, his voice letting off hints of melancholy.

"I'm really grateful for all of this," Hector said tearfully as he put the scarf on.

"Don't cry boy, it isn't really good for you," Frio said uncomfortably.

"Sorry...sorry about that," Hector said as he wiped his tears.

"Come! Don your new armor and let us duel. You have much to learn."

CHAPTER 22

Aurelina walked back to the med bay to return the book when she bumped into Aeris and Jade. She could see they had a look of distress on them, panting nervously as they stopped.

"Have you two been running all over the Citadel?" Aurelina joked.

"Yes! Darvell's gone!" Jade said as she caught her breath.

"He's missing?" Aurelina gasped, her feathers ruffling up uncomfortably.

"We have to find him," Aeris started. "His mental state can be prone to breaking more if he goes through any kind of unnecessary stress."

"The faster we find him, the quicker we can cure him," Aurelina said as she handed Aeris the leather bound book. "Zuur wants to speak with you after we find Darvell."

"Where did you—"

"We don't have time!" Jade urged. "We have to go find him!"

Darvell walked around the halls, looking around at the portraits of dragons hanging on the walls. Although his mind was in a feeble state, he remembered seeing these walls in his dreams. He sniffed at the air, trying to regain the trail of food he was tracking. As he walked, he could feel the air get colder as he went down one particular hallway. He lost interest in the food and followed the chilling air to a single small doorway covered in a thick sheet of frost.

Darvell looked at it with confusion and touched it. The immensity of the cold forced his hand back. He narrowed his eyes at the door and rubbed his chin, thinking of a plan to turn the cold doorknob. His eyes lit up with confidence as he bent down and breathed on it, letting out small bursts of fire. As he saw that the doorknob continued to remain cold, he angrily blew harder. As he did, he accidentally got too close and got his tongue stuck to the frozen metal. He chuckled as he tried to pull back, not being able to. Darvell let out a confused and angry grunt as he pulled harder, trying to free himself from his frozen conundrum.

"What are you doing?"

Darvell looked over to see a woman, slightly smaller than him, stand before him clutching a couple of books. She had snowy white eyes that glowed against her silverish skin. Her young features went well with the sun yellow hair that flowed down her head, the back being wrapped in braids that went across her head like cornrows. Her silver vest flowed down to her waist, stitched designs of snowflakes across the rim. The grey long sleeve shirt she had on was loose and wrinkled, ending with black cuffs.

"Are you okay?" the woman asked timidly.

Darvell nodded, pointing to his tongue stuck on the doorknob.

"I...I don't know what to do. Ignis never told us how to properly confront you, oh this is terrible," she stammered.

Darvell tried to calm her down. He took his hand and melted his way out by burning his tongue. He pulled back hard and fell to the floor, leaving a little bit of flesh on the handle. The lady looked at it and winced. Darvell got up and smiled, somehow not feeling the pain at the moment. The lady walked over to him and extended her arm for a handshake.

"I'm Argenti."

Darvell reached for the handshake and tried to speak, but nothing but mumbles came out.

"I guess you can't talk since you lost a bit of your tongue. Well I guess you don't need to introduce yourself since we all know who you are. You're Darvell, right?"

Darvell nodded happily as Argenti smiled. He noticed that every time she spoke a bit of frost came out, sometimes building up on her lips. He would have confused it for lipstick if he had not seen it before.

"Would you like to come in?"

Darvell shook his head yes as Argenti smiled and cautiously opened the door, trying to avoid the bit of flesh Darvell left on the doorknob. As they entered, Darvell was in awe; looking at the entire room was like looking into a painting of a wintery forest. There was a large knobby tree in the center of the room that had a small hammock hanging between two branches while icicles hung from various tree limbs. Although the room was covered in a thin layer of crunchy snow, there were flowers emerging from thick green bushes, all of them either white, silver, gold or a faint blue. Argenti walked to the tree and pulled down on a branch, watching it snap and regrowing back.

"Darn, I always forget which branch it is."

She pulled down another one and Darvell watched as a large compartment filled with books opened up. She neatly placed the books in her hand on the wooden shelves of the tree trunk. Darvell saw that the snow beneath his feet didn't melt away, as if it were in an untouchable state. Darvell began to think about the last time he had actually gotten to feel the touch of snow on his hands.

"I wish I could offer you something but all I have are books, and the Council said you can't smoke around me," Argenti sheepishly said as she turned to face Darvell.

Argenti looked at Darvell who was covering himself in snow as if he were at the beach. He looked up and smiled. Argenti laughed a little and took a seat on her hammock. She watched as Darvell continued to play in the snow, fascinated by it as if he had never seen it before.

He's nothing like Ignis, he's way too happy. It's actually a nice thing to see his stoic attitude doesn't run in the family.

"Hey Darvell, do you want to see something cool?" Argenti suggested.

Darvell stood up, some snow still covering his clothes. He looked excited and nodded his head. Argenti walked over to him and put out her hand in front of him. She blew into it, gently letting out a stream of cold frosty air as Darvell watched it condense from snow to ice. As she stopped the wind, she dusted off the excess snow and frost to reveal a little ice statue of Darvell holding his greatsword by the handle, the blade pointing downward. His wings were stretched outward while his tail was wrapped around the base of the statue. Darvell's face lit up as he admired the tiny ice sculpture, Argenti giggling at his childish smile.

"It's nice to see someone enjoying my ice sculptures. Maybe I can make some for you and your friends when this whole marriage ordeal is over with."

Darvell's face began to frown as soon as Argenti mentioned the marriage. Argenti saw his look of disappointment and sighed. She handed him the ice statue and patted his shoulder.

"Listen Darvell, I can see that you aren't up for something like that. I'll be honest with you, forcing you to marry someone you don't like or even know is beyond me," Argenti huffed. "I'd tell him, but I'm too scared."

Darvell looked at her and had a contemplative look on his

face. Argenti looked at him with a puzzled expression until she gasped at realizing his plan.

"You're going to tell him?" Argenti asked.

Darvell nodded confidently, handing the ice statue back to her. He was about to leave the room until Argenti stopped him, grabbing him by the shoulder.

"I'm...I'm...I'm coming with you. You just got here and he may not listen to you. I've stood by him for a long time and he might listen to me."

Darvell smiled, his pointed teeth slightly scaring Argenti.

"Don't do that! You look like a psychopath."

Darvell stopped smiling and chuckled.

Darvell and Argenti walked through the halls, heading back to the Council Room. As soon as they reached the door, Argenti grabbed Darvell by the shoulder and stopped him

"Wait, you can't speak. How are you even going to confront him?" Argenti asked. "We should have thought of that before walking all this way."

Darvell shrugged and pointed to his head.

"You'll think of something? I hope you know what you're doing, just know I'm with you."

Darvell smiled and gave her a hug, leaving Argenti dumbfounded but happy. They turned the corner to see the Council doors open to Aurum, Ignis, Rubrum, and a rather large figure standing amongst them. The dragons Darvell had seen so far stood taller than him by a couple of feet but this dragon was taller than all of them. The scales on the dragon glistened brightly, almost divinely, under the chandelier light. They never stayed one shade or color, like a living kaleidoscope. He had two large horns retreating backwards from his head that looked like they were made of pure, solid gold. The eyes burned like red hot coals coursing through lava. The dragon sat on its hind legs with its wings tucked in, the tops of them barely touching the ceiling. As Darvell and Argenti walked in, the dragon smiled, revealing his razor white teeth.

"Darvell, it is nice to see you again."

"Darrous, you know the Old Flame?" Aurum marveled.

"He was the one who saved me from my doom at Zlo's eternal and deathly grasp," Scales said as he raised his eyebrows, hinting to agree. "Isn't that right Darvell?"

Darvell slowly nodded as Scales smiled.

"Well it seems my grandson has made quite a name for himself. Tell me Old Flame, are you here to bless the wedding of my grandson?" Ignis declared.

"That is why I came here in the first place: the wedding must be canceled for the child is ineligible to be an heir," Scales explained as he looked towards Aurum.

Ignis furrowed his brows as Aurum approached him.

"I had wanted this to stay between us Ignis, but now that Argenti and Darrous are here I might as well explain the situation. The Old Flame has explained to me that the child Darrous would produce would still be considered the child of a divine being so he would still not be eligible to be on the Council."

"I refuse!" Ignis roared, startling everyone in the room. "My lineage cannot die like this when my only heir is literally the savior of the world!"

"Ignis, please calm down," Argenti interjected.

"I will not calm down! I have nothing while everyone in the Council has heirs to spare!"

"Mind your tongue Ignis, do not speak to her like that," Frio said as he stomped through the door with Hector by his side.

Darvell looked at Hector's new armor in admiration, throwing up a thumbs-up. Hector lifted up his visor and smiled.

"Stay out of this Frio," Ignis snapped. "It looks like you got yourself a new heir just now."

"Ignis, this is not like you," Nimh said as she walked into the room.

"How did you even know we were here?" Ignis demanded.

"I called everyone here," Nimh said as she flew in with Chantal and Theia on her back. She landed and morphed into her human form. "I could hear your fit all the way from my abode. I suggest we switch to a less endangering form before we start throwing insults and talons at each other."

The rest of the dragons morphed into human form. Aurum was surprisingly in simple clothing. He wore a black cassock with a golden stole around his neck. His golden skin contrasted with his furrowed dark grey eyes. Scales shrunk down and became more humanoid, yet he still retained his dragon head.

"This is better," Nimh said as she looked around. "I suggest we get to business now that this matter has been brought up again. Since our very god has come down to interject, we have nothing but proof to deny Darvell from creating an heir for the Council. Ignis, there is nothing we can do since Darvell has angelic blood in him."

Ignis scratched his beard in quiet contemplation. He turned to Scales with a harsh look in his eyes. Scales looked at him and gulped quietly.

"I do not want to offend you Old Flame," Ignis growled. "But your word here holds little to no value to me."

"Why is that?" Scales responded coldly, nervousness in his voice.

"I lost everything to Zlo, a being who should have been dealt with by any of you gods. Yet nothing was done and I lost my family and almost my entire race. You were not here with me and you decide to come here now to ruin my one chance of regaining something out of my loss? I think not, and I shall stand here as a testament to my words."

Scales looked at him with eyes full of anger and remorse. Rubrum was biting his lip as Aurum prayed heavily. Frio and

Argenti were standing behind Hector and Darvell, Frio clenching his fists while Argenti breathed heavily, causing a light cover of frost to build up on Darvell's wings before melting away. Scales sighed and looked at Darvell, a look of regret in his eyes. Darvell shook his head slowly as Scales looked back at Ignis.

"Then let it be," Scales declared. "The position you are in is my fault, who would I be to deny you? The child shall be recognized by me as an heir to Ignis."

The others shifted uncomfortably as they watched Scales sigh heavily. Suddenly, Darvell growled in disgust as he turned around to see a woman dressed in brass-colored clothing. Her dress stopped at her ankles and shone under the torchlights, an intricate set of lines resembling connected wings. Her long hair was intertwined into a large braid. She had a long complex tattoo across her eyes, as if a fire was burning across her face. She quietly walked in and bowed. Her brown tanned skin was almost perfect. On her wrists were two bracers embossed with a snake intertwining with itself.

"It seems that the wedding will continue. I am overjoyed to hear it," the woman said gleefully.

"I would like all of you to meet Eris, my chosen person for Darvell," Ignis said as he walked over to her. "She is one of the brass dragons that survived Zlo's onslaught."

Darvell growled quietly, observing Eris from afar. She turned her head slightly and gave him a wink. Darvell went for his guns but Scales gave him a look. He looked back and saw Scales shake his head.

Don't even think about it, Darvell.

Darvell moved his hand away and bit his tongue.

"If it's not too much to ask for, I would like to spend some time with Darvell to get to know him better," Eris asked.

"Of course!" Ignis boasted. "He would be happy to, right Darvell?"

Darvell was inching towards the door as he turned around

and stuck out his tongue. Eris laughed and walked towards him, hooking his arm with hers.

"I'll take good care of him, Ignis. Are you ready to have a wonderful day, Darvell?"

Darvell growled, baring his teeth as he tried to unhook his arm. Eris laughed and walked him out of the room. Hector stood amongst the rest of the Council along with Scales.

"Hector, how about you gather your friends and send the rest of the Council here?" Frio asked.

"You got it," Hector said.

Before he left, Frio grabbed him by the armor and whispered in his ear, "Keep an eye on those two."

Hector nodded and left the room.

"Will you be staying for the wedding, Old Flame?" Aurum asked. "It would be an honor to have our deity bless us with his presence."

"I'm afraid I will not be able to stay. I have business with the other gods so I must return. May you all have a wonderful evening," Scales declared as he left the room.

I wasn't able to do anything! Scales thought to himself. *It's up to them.*

Eris and Darvell walked out of the Citadel along the streets of Drakon. They stopped at a large fountain, near a crossroads of the city. The fountain had a large marble hydra with ten heads spewing out water from their mouths. The eyes of each hydra had a unique pair of gemstones that glistened under the giant globules of light that floated above. Eris took a seat on the ridge as she forced Darvell down with her. Dragons walked around them, conversing with each other in the harsh tongue they had used since the beginning. However, Darvell could somehow understand them this time. Yet, he didn't care, paying no mind and slowly moving himself away from Eris.

"Isn't this nice Darvell?" Eris asked sweetly. "You and I, taking the time to get to know each other under such a marvelous statue."

Darvell didn't respond, looking away. Eris huffed and moved closer to Darvell.

"I know you can't speak, Darvell. You were hit in the head by that awful woman. I know you are in pain my sweet Darvell," Eris said as she got closer to him. "You could at least look at me."

Darvell rolled his eyes and looked at Eris. Her eyes shined with a sentimental look, a feeling of longing. Darvell furrowed his eyes and looked away, growling under his breath. Eris smiled and laid her head on his arm, not being able to reach his shoulder because of his height. Darvell shifted uncomfortably, moving his weight to distance himself.

"I guess you know it's me then. I'd like to let you know I'm not the same Lilith you remember from back then. I've learned how to control myself and I came back to be with you."

Darvell snarled and pulled out a cigar. He lifted up his hand to light it and found that Eris's hand was wrapped in his. He looked at her and watched her lean in closer and kiss him. She had her eyes closed while Darvell had his open. All he could think of at that moment was where Jade was. She leaned back and smiled, still holding on to his hand.

"I've missed you Darvell. You were always the hero for my heart. What you're doing is not just good for me, but for your grandfather," Lilith whispered. "We should head back to plan the wedding. I'll let you invite your friends if it makes you happy."

Darvell looked at her, his anger slowly dwindling. He closed his eyes and sighed as he looked back at the Citadel.

"I suppose you're right," Darvell said, his defeated will traveling with his words. "We should get going then."

CHAPTER 23

"So this marriage is going to be an actual thing, Hector?" Theia asked as she strapped her bow on her back and walked with Hector and Chantal.

"I guess, Darvell isn't too happy about it and I can feel that the other Council members aren't liking it either," Hector worried as he looked for Darvell. "We have to find the others and get Darvell out of here before the wedding is even planned."

As they walked down the hall, they ran into Aurelina, Jade, and Aeris. They were frantically looking through the halls.

"What are you guys doing?" Theia questioned.

"We're looking for Darvell; he's still in an unstable condition," Aeris explained. "Have you seen him?"

"Who the hell let him out?" Hector asked.

"That was me," Jade glumly admitted. "He sort of fell asleep and I went to sleep with him."

"You slept with him?" Theia asked. "I thought you said you didn't like him."

"Not like that! Listen, he is somewhere in the Citadel or in the city alone—"

"Or with that girl Ignis chose," Hector interrupted.

Jade darted her eyes to Hector, who took a step backward

with a flinch. Aeris sucked her teeth as Theia and Chantal looked towards Aurelina for clarification.

"Who? What girl?" Jade demanded, grabbing Hector by the shoulders.

Suddenly, a large explosion sounded out from a far corner of the Citadel. Guards flew over the group in the direction of the explosion, carrying iron spears and shields with them.

"We'll talk about it later!" Hector yelled, grateful for the excuse. "I suggest we head over there to make sure it isn't Darvell."

Cutthroat flew through the air past Olius, smacking into a bookshelf of ancient scrolls and books. Inpulsa had reverted back into her human form, a violent and sporadic surge of blue lightning traveling across her arms like a violent wave. Her glasses were shattered and the ends of her hair stood up. She panted slowly as her crazed face stared at him. Cutthroat got up and wobbled, cackling to himself.

"This was a pretty shitty comeback," Cutthroat declared as he cracked his bones. "I could've sworn I was a lot stronger than this."

"Listen, I want that book!" Inpulsa raged as she curled her fingers slowly.

"You aren't getting it!" Olius yelled as he clutched his staff.

"Then you and I are going to fight for it!" Inpulsa threatened. "A good old-fashioned magic duel will decide the owner of the book."

"What about me?" Cutthroat said as he cocked his flintlock.

Inpulsa laughed to herself and snapped her electrified fingers. The floor in front of her began to rumble as the stone turned to a putty of stone-colored liquid. It rose from the ground and formed a golem. Once it solidified, its eyes glowed a dark blue as it stood there menacingly.

"To keep you busy, pirate. Go forth golem, take care of him!"

The stone golem charged towards Cutthroat, knocking back with a full force punch that Cutthroat tried to block. As the fight between them took place in the background, Olius stared at Inpulsa with anger in his eyes. Inpulsa had a crazed smile on her face as she moved her hands, finishing the elegant movements by extending her hands outward. A shepherd's staff of pure opal manifested from her palms. Inside the curve of the staff was a glowing orb that changed colors periodically. Inpulsa twirled the staff. A fading trail of colorful light blazed behind the movements, blocking Olius's view of her. As the light faded away, Inpulsa was dressed in a flowing blue silk robe with intricate runes moving around on the cloth, changing colors and flashing brightly.

Olius gulped, glancing at his knobby wooden staff and ragged wizard clothing. He shook his head and bit his lip, causing a trickle of blood to pour out. He directed his hand forward with a forceful thrust. A rune on the palm of his hand flashed, three squares overlapping each other.

"Ter Vi!"

Three individual bursts of white energy blasted out of his hand, flying at sonic speeds towards Inpulsa. They spiraled around each other, curving towards her. She scoffed at them and tightened her hand into a fist.

"Saepem Coici."

The electricity traveling across her body sprung forth and encircled her, rising upwards, forming a barricade of energy. As the blasts reached her, they collided with the barricade, forcing it to fizzle in and out. Inpulsa looked surprised and smiled, swirling the electricity back into herself.

"It seems that you multiplied each blast by three as well," Inpulsa said, her sarcastic voice biting Olius in the heart. "You caught me off guard only once, wizard. Now it's my turn, Concursores Fluctus!"

As she boldly spoke her spell, the electricity coursing through her blasted upwards and exploded, creating reverberations in the air that sped towards Olius at incredible speeds. Instinctually, Olius bent downwards and put his hand on the ground, his palm touching the floor. He closed his eyes and a circle was emblazoned on the ground.

"Ut lapis ferro clypeus!" Olius shouted.

The ground around Olius shifted from mossy stone to a gleaming iron shield. As the reverberation reached the shield, it glided off it, leaving Olius unharmed as he opened the shield. He was sweating, beads falling from his blonde hair. His breath was heavy as he watched Inpulsa cackle.

"Alchemy magic? You must be well informed then. All the more reason to get that book," Inpulsa provoked as she widened her eyes.

Olius breathed heavily and raised his staff. A projection of a triangle sprung forth and shattered, sprinkling itself on Olius.

"Fel Ingens Mutatio!" Olius gasped.

The dust on him began to glow white as a flash of light blinded Inpulsa. She hissed as she covered her eyes and looked away.

"A simple flash spell isn't going to make me back down wizard," Inpulsa insulted as she regained her vision. "Show me some real magic!"

She turned to face him and saw before her eyes a giant black cobra baring its fangs. The flaps on its head were detailed like the night sky. Individual bright shining scales resembled stars sparkling in space. The eyes of the cobra were red rubies, endlessly shifting forward and backward. Inpulsa chuckled, grasping her staff as she took a defensive stance.

"Illusory magic?" Inpulsa scoffed. "Are you running out of things to pull out of your sleeve? Show yourself!"

"I'm still here, Inpulsa," the snake hissed loudly.

The cobra lunged forward as Inpulsa dodged out of the way, barely colliding with the fangs of the cobra. She looked at the immensity of the snake in fear, not seeing the smack of the whipping tail that sent her backwards. She skidded across the floor until she hit the wall. She got up promptly to see Olius coiling himself once again for another strike. She tapped her staff against the floor and smiled creepily.

"Obrigescunt."

A bright beam of black energy shot forth from the opal staff and dashed towards Olius, a horrible humming sound piercing his ears as it got closer. As the beam made its way towards him, Olius ducked down, watching it whiz above him as his transformation shattered into glass around him.

That petrification beam would have had a better chance of hitting me in that form, Olius thought, his aching body demanding rest. *Wait...why is she still smiling?*

He looked quickly at Inpulsa, who was still smiling and still holding her staff tightly. She then began to move it towards her, as if she was guiding something. Olius darted his eyes back as he watched the black beam of light curve back towards him, only a few feet away from him. The palpitations in Olius's heart went from the violent bashing of drums to a slow, heavy one. All he could see was the black beam staring him down, a beam of pure nothingness stealing the light from his eyes as he watched it inch closer. The world around Olius slowed as he could see the dust from the room float around, Cutthroat blocking punches from the stone golem, the falling of books and scrolls unraveling on their way to the floor. Olius looked back at Cutthroat and could see Regibus instead, standing there, taking the pain alongside him.

Olius's heart began to beat faster once more as he put out his hand towards the beam of energy. Starting from the tips of his fingers, he began to shift to a royal blue hue with coal black fingertips. The hue shift moved across his body, eventually reaching his face, turning it a similar color. Crystal black eyes formed without a drop of white in them. His hair began to alter itself as well, turning each blonde strand blacker than tar. His extended hand revealed small lines of intricate symbols and runes that glowed a dirty white.

The black beam entered his body as he turned to face Inpulsa, who stood there trembling with fear as she stared at Olius. She could see a pair of horns, the same design she had on her head. As Olius spoke, she could see two fangs protrude from his mouth as he said in a deep, fiendish voice that rattled her soul:

"Speculum Amicus."

The black energy coursed through his fingertips and into the staff. The staff exploded in his hand, firing off a darker beam of black energy towards her. Inpulsa put her staff in front of her, a shield of pure white energy forming in front of her. The black energy divided itself against the shield, crashing into the wall behind her, causing it to shatter and explode outwards. A cloud of dust swirled around the room, escaping through the newly created hole. Inpulsa huffed heavily, scared and hurt as she stared at Olius, who was barely able to keep himself on his legs. His black eyes stared at Inpulsa, causing hundreds of repressed memories to painfully crawl back to the surface.

No wonder he has the book, he left it with him.

Inpulsa could hear the flapping of soldiers' wings coming down from the hall. She watched as Olius fell, collapsing onto the floor. She hurried over and moved her hand over him, altering his appearance to what he looked like before. As the dust settled, she could see her stone golem's head being crushed by Cutthroat. He was too busy turning her creation into gravel to notice what she had done. The guards flew in from the floor opening while Aurelina led the others through an alternate entrance to the room.

"What happened, Council Leader?" one of the soldiers asked.

"The wizard and I were practicing magic until a rogue spell brought a golem to life."

"Like hell it did!" Cutthroat began to say as he switched to Regibus. "She was trying to steal Olius's book from him."

"What do you mean steal?" Hector said as he gripped his spear.

"Listen, this is no time for accusations," Inpulsa pleaded. "Olius needs medical attention and—"

"He needs to be tried!" Ignis demanded as he led the rest of the Council from the same alternate entrance. "The harming of a Council member is forbidden."

"Ignis there is no need," Inpulsa beseeched. "Please don't put him on trial."

"He will be put on trial Inpulsa, I am the leader of the courts and the law. I don't see why you want him to walk if he has hurt you."

Inpulsa had a distressed look on her as she held her tongue. Soon after, Darvell and Eris walked through and watched the discourse happen. Ignis turned to the two and smiled as he walked over to them.

"It seems that the wedding will have to take place after this trial. I'm sorry Darvell, but your friend Olius will have to be tried."

"Jail, for how long?" Darvell asked, the others quickly turning in shock at hearing him speak.

"Actually, his harming of Inpulsa is a death sentence," Ignis declared.

"What! No, there has to be another way. Isn't Sca—I mean the Old Flame here, can't he pardon him?" Darvell pleaded.

"He could but he is no longer here. He had to leave to deal with something he couldn't express to us," Aurum announced.

"Isn't there another way?" Darvell begged. "There has to be another way."

"No there isn't Darvell; the law does not make accommodations here."

"Not true Ignis," Aeris butted in. "Remember when you fought to save Zuur from execution? When he had bitten me, the law demanded that he be put to death but you fought in his place and won."

"What do you mean 'fought?' A death sentence only has one outcome," Jade said as she tried her best to not burn a hole into Eris, who was standing a little too close to Darvell.

"A death sentence here, child, is a fight to the death with a creature designed to kill dragons. If the accused can overcome the beast then they are deemed innocent of the crime, for the guiding hand that is the Old Flame will help the innocent and punish the guilty," Ignis said reluctantly. "But I will not have my grandson fight, he is getting married."

"I'll do it," Darvell said as he stepped forward.

"You will not! I forbid you!" Ignis said as smoke fumes billowed out the sides of his mouth.

"I'm going to do it. You can't stop me," Darvell said as he turned to him, his voice projecting confidence and defiance.

"Darvell, listen to him please," Eris pleaded.

"No, I'd like to see him stop me." Darvell growled without looking away from the furious Ignis.

Ignis stared down at Darvell. Ignis was grinding his jaws against each other as he stared at his grandson, standing confidently as he clutched his greatsword. Ignis could feel something crawling at the back of his head that refused to sit still.

"Marius, I forbid you from leaving! You will not leave!" Ignis said as he stepped out from the entrance of a large cave.

The winter snow melted around his presence as icicles dripped on to him, sizzling across his heated back. Another dragon, who was a lot smaller in comparison, stood out facing the mountain ranges before him.

"I know that the others in the village don't want me there. I can feel it in your voice that you don't want me either. You just think your obligation as the herd leader is to keep everyone safe."

"No! You are my son and I don't want anything bad to happen to you. I'll find a way to help you fit in—"

"Well I don't want to. I'm going to leave..."

"And there is nothing you can say to change my mind," Darvell said sternly.

Ignis's furious stare softened into a face of remorse. His heavy breathing quieted as he closed his eyes as he sighed. Aeris looked at him and smiled faintly.

"Prepare the arena then," Ignis choked. "Darvell will fight to free his friend Olius."

The room was silent with awe as all eyes redirected themselves from Ignis to Darvell. Ignis slowly walked out, shuffling his feet down the hall. The guards looked at each other and walked towards Darvell.

"We are going to have to take you to the prison chambers. The law prohibits the fighter from any interactions post decision."

"I see, lead the way."

"Darvell, are you sure you want to do this?" Jade said as she stepped in front of him.

Darvell didn't look at her. He walked past her and out of the room. The group was stunned, while the Council had concerned and worried faces. Inpulsa was especially worried, for the guilt was building up in her. Regibus helped Olius up from the floor. Olius was completely knocked out and barely breathing as Regibus held him in his arms. Regibus walked over to Inpulsa and scowled.

"You just had to try to take it from him. Not only did you almost kill him, now you have Darvell's life on the line."

"He won't die, he has a chance," Inpulsa said, her voice shattering upon speaking. "Even if they did let Olius rest up for the fight, he would surely die. Even you would have succumbed to its monstrous ferocity."

Olius groaned as he shifted his head slowly, alerting Aeris as she walked over to him and examined him.

"Jade and Aurelina, could you please accompany me? I might need some help in making sure Olius isn't too hurt. Zuur, could you help take Olius to the infirmary as well?"

Jade and Aurelina nodded while Zuur, who was hidden away in a corner of the room, poked his head out and nodded. As the room dispersed, Aes walked over to the large hole in the wall and sighed.

"This is going to take a big chunk out of the budget."

Zuur carried Olius in his arms as Aeris led everyone back to the medical center of the Citadel. Jade and Aurelina had never seen Zuur in human form before, up until now. He was dressed in an elegant white shirt paired with sleek and shining black pants. He walked with a grace that was almost unseen by the ladies, only ever seeing Olius walk so. Zuur carried with him a long sturdy cane with a black dragon's head at one head. His skin was dark, bringing out the green eyes he had that stared ahead. He had a long black cape hanging from two golden straps on his shoulders. The cape itself was decorated with two green scimitars flowing with every jostle of the cape. Zuur's hair was combed backwards, a shade darker than his skin, almost perfectly, ending in a couple of braids at the back of the head.

"Aeris and Zuur make a good couple, don't they Jade?" Aurelina whispered.

Jade didn't respond, staring blankly forward as she walked. Aurelina stretched out her wing and brought Jade closer for an embrace, one that Jade quickly accepted.

"I know you're worried but you out of all of us should know that Darvell can handle himself in a fight," Aurelina consoled.

"It's not that," Jade responded, her voice beginning to choke. "Even if he manages to kill whatever they planned for him, he still has to marry that...that..."

"So you're jealous?" Aurelina said smugly.

Jade didn't respond, blushing slightly as they continued to walk.

They turned the corner and entered the room, laying Olius down on the medical bed. Aeris touched his head and then his body. She got up and began to gather ingredients into a bowl. Zuur took a seat in a chair and nervously tapped his foot on the floor. Jade leaned against the door as Aurelina went over and moved her hands around Olius. Her face expressed concern as she turned to Aeris.

"He hardly has any magic in him. He isn't dying but he is in a lot of pain," Aurelina said as her hands began to glow.

"It's best that he's in that coma, he'd be groaning in pain if he had to feel it," Aeris said as she placed the ingredients on the table. "He'll be fine; he doesn't need to be stabilized. Aurelina, would you mind fixing this medicine for me? I'd like to talk to Zuur outside for a moment."

Zuur looked up worriedly. He got up from the chair and grabbed his cane as he made his way out the door. As Aurelina worked on the medicine, Jade looked off into space as she contemplated. Aurelina glanced at her and sighed.

"He'll be fine; I don't know why you're so worried. We all know that he can kick anyone's ass."

"I know that but what about after that? He'll have to marry her and—"

"You aren't too fond of that are you?" Aurelina smirked.

"I know he doesn't want it. I've spent a lot of time with him and I know he's a free spirit."

"Yeah, your free spirit. Listen Jade, you're going to have to tell him some time soon," Aurelina suggested. "You'll breathe a lot easier."

"Tell him what?" Jade said as she blushed.

"If I have to tell you then I might puke a little."

Jade laughed a little as she stared into a lit candle on the table. It flickered back and forth on the burning black wick. Jade looked deep into the fire, its bright light imprinted onto her eyes. Suddenly, the door opened as Aeris and Zuur walked back in. They were holding hands as they both walked up to Jade with toothy smiles on their faces. Just as the door was about to close, Inpulsa walked in clutching her staff by her side.

"Haven't you caused enough trouble Inpulsa?" Aeris sneered. "You pushed the boy too far and look at what happened to him."

"I know," Inpulsa said quietly.

"But you don't care do you? You just...you know?"

"I have come here to atone for my mistake. I would first like to say sorry to the wiz—I mean Olius. Mostly, I came here to help the dragon boy as well."

"How so?" Jade interjected.

"The trials here have always been a bit extreme in my opinion. But the reason why Ignis was reluctant to let Darvell do this is because the monster he will have to face nearly killed Ignis, who, mind you, was at his strongest when this happened," Inpulsa explained. "You remember the creature Zuur."

"It was a hellish abomination." Zuur shuddered. "I suggest we let Inpulsa help, her magic can come in handy."

"I just want to know why you had a sudden change of heart," Aurelina prodded. "What made you crawl all the way here?"

Inpulsa stared at the rising body of Olius. Moving slowly, it was as if she could see through him to another looking up at her, a distant memory of a face stinging her eyes. The others looked at each other as she approached Olius, pulling out the box they tried to open and her staff, laying them right next to him.

I'm doing it for the boy and him.

Darvell sat down in his cell, the same one where he had first woken up. They had fixed the wall while he was gone; he could see the fresh new bricks contrasting the old ones. He felt his body heat up despite taking his clothing off. He had taken off his chainmail, the shoulder armor and the white shirt he had on. He threw them on the floor and watched as his once human skin turned more dragon-like. The patches of scales glistened in the light of the fire as he scratched himself, feeling the toughness of his claws on his iron skin. He pulled out a cigar and lit it by pressing one end into his palm. He took a deep puff in and let out a long stream of thick smoke. His stomach rumbled as he searched his pockets for some food, ultimately not finding a single crumb. He walked to the bars of his cell to see no one around to get him something to eat.

They probably wouldn't have given me anything anyway.

Darvell backed away from the bars and walked back to his sitting place. He sat back down, his stomach rumbling a little louder. He sighed, trying to think of something he could do to distract himself from his hunger. He glanced over towards his chainmail and remembered something from long ago. Darvell had stopped at a few bars that had a couple of dragon hunters who told stories of dragons eating their hoards of treasure.

He looked at his chainmail some more and reached for it. He

sniffed at it and gagged since it smelled like a few days of sweat and dried blood. His stomach rumbled harder, reminding him that this was his best option. He took a bite out of one of the links and chewed on it. It felt strange biting on it, as if he were actually eating jerky. He could only taste the strong iron flavor in the link but he didn't mind it. He took another bite out of the link and continued to eat his chainmail. As he finished the last link, Darvell realized he had eaten his only armor, armor that covered most of his body.

"Well shit." Darvell groaned as he patted his stomach.

As he sat down on the floor, he heard the footsteps of two guards walking over to his cell. They were two black dragons in cone helmets, carrying large spears with them.

"Okay, it's time to head out. Belmor, get the handcuffs," one of the dragons ordered.

"Thurmir, how about you do it?"

"Why?"

"I have no idea what the hell he'll do to me!" Belmor quivered as he looked down at Darvell.

"I'm right here," Darvell chimed in.

"Fine, I'll do it."

The dragon walked over and saw that Darvell was no longer wearing his armor. He also noticed that his chainmail was nowhere in sight.

"Didn't you have chainmail with you?"

"Yeah but I ate it," Darvell stated as he picked his teeth. "I was hungry and no one was around."

The two dragons looked at him in shock. They looked at each other and one left the hall to vomit.

"You do know you just ate the equivalent of eating raw meat?" Belmor pointed out.

"What!" Darvell yelled as he got to his feet. "I thought you guys just ate it like that and that's it!"

"Gems! You can eat gems like that! You aren't supposed to

eat—how the hell did you eat the metal?" Thurmir explained frantically. "By the Old Flame, how do you feel?"

"I don't feel sick or anything," Darvell worried as he rubbed his stomach. "Just a bit less hungry."

The dragon looked at him cautiously. He threw the cuffs in the cell and pointed at them.

"Put them on."

Darvell put on his shirt and shoulder armor then reached for the cuffs. As he walked out, the two dragons put more cuffs on his wings just to be sure. They exited the building and headed down into a deeper part of the cavern.

The bountiful buildings of the city under the stalactite building grew scarcer as they walked deeper into the cavern. They eventually entered a barren stone area, with toppled and crumbled pillars of marble and granite. Along the stone wall before them was a large wooden door, larger than any door Darvell had ever seen. It was branded with a large three-fingered dragon's claw, clutching a balanced scale. Darvell gulped silently as the two guards pushed open the door to reveal a dark open area, filled with other dragons and weapons. The dragons around the other rooms were possibly a mix of prisoners up for trial and guards keeping watch. Along the walls were weapons and shields, banners with the same insignia as the door, and faded paintings of a landscape of a forest and mountains consumed by an eternal sunset.

He walked across the dusty floors, guided by the soldiers to a caged off area of the large room. They guided Darvell into the cage and closed the iron bar door. Darvell observed the floor of the cage, littered with bones, splatters of dried blood, and broken weapons. Darvell also noticed that the cage had a large part missing, like a cube absent an entire face. He walked towards the missing iron bars and inspected them.

"Hey, what happened to the iron bars here?"

"Oh they were ripped off by what you're going to fight," Thurmir said.

"I see...What am I fighting exactly?"

"Can I tell him?" Belmor whispered towards Thurmir.

"Go ahead, I know how much you love telling them about it," Thurmir confirmed, chuckling to himself afterwards.

"Great! Okay, the thing you are going to fight is possibly the most dangerous beast ever created by the gods. Maybe it even wasn't created by them; it could have been a horrible mistake. It's bigger than Council Leader Rubrum and he is the biggest dragon in the Council. It has two horrible eyes, which are able to paralyze whatever unlucky soul lays its eyes on them. It has two pincers made from iron that can rip the wings off a dragon in a second flat. On its back is a thick hide covered in puss and bleeding holes that spurt out black ooze. Its claws are covered in spines with hooks for fingers. It used to lurk in the caverns until it came across Zuur and almost killed him. He had to capture it since we could not kill it with any of our weapons or any magic without putting anyone in serious danger. The prisoners around here have given it a name. They call it 'the Cavern Lurker.'"

Darvell looked off in the distance, a quiet gulp going down his throat.

"How did I do this time?" Belmor asked.

"You've been practicing have you? Quite well if you ask me."

Darvell looked at the two with a short perplexed stare. He shook his head and returned to looking at the missing iron bars. Suddenly, the wall he was facing began to open outwards, revealing a large pit of sand with large black torches lining the white, circular wall before him. He walked outside and could see that possibly almost every dragon in the city was attending this trial. There, quite a ways from his origin of entrance, was a large marble podium with a carved symbol of a similar dragon's claw and scales. There was Ignis himself overlooking the arena, wearing a large black cape and clutching a black ribbon in his talons. He had a look on him, not angry disapproval nor that of an indifferent judge. Darvell could see that he had the face of a broken man, having to judge the last thing he would want to see in the pit.

As the fluttering of wings diminished, Darvell walked out some more, to the center of the pit. He could see that the other Council members had taken the seats closest to the podium. Darvell looked for his friends and saw them sitting alongside Aeris and Zuur. Before he could have a moment to think to himself a little more, a large black ceramic pot ignited in a colorful fire above the podium. The rustling that was still in the stadium seats had finally grown quiet. Ignis wrapped the ribbon over his old and weary eyes and addressed the crowd in the native dragon tongue. As he spoke, the harsh sounds of the raspy language suddenly did not sound like a foreign language to Darvell anymore. He could somehow understand every word Ignis spoke.

"The laws that have guided us have now called me again to this podium to enact judgment on Darvell Letholdus. He is the son of the outcast Marius Letholdus and as you all know they are both my descendants. Do not let that cloud your judgment of me, for it will not cloud mine. We are a race that has lived on this earth for generations. We have remained here because of our strength, virtue, and wisdom. This trial will determine if Darvell's friend may walk free or be killed for harming a Council member of the Citadel. With that, I will now address the fighter."

Ignis bowed his head downwards towards Darvell. He stared at him through the black and ragged cloth. He could see him stand in the sand, clutching the chains that bound him. Ignis could not help but see Marius stand there in his place, something that made his words even harder to force out.

"Darvell, do you truly accept this?"

There was a murmur in the crowds. Aurum leaned over to Rubrum, who was watching the ordeal happen with a pensive look.

"He's never asked that before. He's always sentenced them to the duel and that's it," Aurum stated.

"Aurum, you forget one crucial thing: justice may be blind but Ignis is not justice itself. We can never fully be what we practice, no matter how much we try. We did not ask Ignis to put his grandson on trial, he believed this was his duty and he did it. However, he still feels the inner desire to get him out of there. So he is asking him to do it for him."

They both stared down at Darvell, who was gripping his chains tighter. He slowly looked around, observing the crowd before he smiled.

"I'll fight to my last breath," Darvell roared proudly.

The dragons around him burst into an uproar, the sound of so many distinct roars melting into a harmonious sound. They beat their wings and created the sound of drums to show their approval. Ignis raised his claw and silenced all of them. He looked down at Darvell and sighed.

"Very well then."

Ignis raised his hand outward and stuck out one, slender brass finger. He made a motion that looked like a thumbs down, a signal to the guards opposite of him. They began to pull chains and levers as the wall behind him closed. Darvell ripped his chains off with one swell yank, looking back at the two guards who had escorted him.

"You're telling me he could have..."

"Then he could have killed us at any time he wanted to."

They both looked at each other and gulped.

"I need a new job."

Darvell reached for his greatsword as he looked around for the opening that would release the beast. Then, below the podium where Ignis sat, a large door began to slowly open. Two red eyes glowed against the dark shadows of the room containing the beast. Darvell ignited the blade of his greatsword and pointed at the doorway.

"Come get it you son of a bitch!" Darvell roared.

CHAPTER 24

Darvell stood there on the sand, and looked into the deep void of the dark room in front of him. Suddenly, a sound came out that Darvell had never heard before. It was like the buzzing of a beetle but on the sound scale of a whale. It was an unholy droning sound that, as it got louder, became more painful for Darvell's bones to withstand. The beast put out its two arms, both covered in alternating spines combed backwards. The spines were hooked with bits of flesh hanging off, possibly from its most recent meal. At the ends of its giant forearms were two large white pincers stained red at the tips.

The beast then walked out a bit further, revealing its insectoid head that drooled white spittle, merging with the sand as it fell onto the ground. On both sides of its head, two bulging eyes stared blankly at Darvell, their complicated hexagonal pattern reflecting his image like a million mirrors. On the front of its forehead, two wine-colored eyes shaped like beads stood out against the moldy wall of yellow flesh. The black mandibles near its mouth clacked against each other like two iron swords, the clinging and clanging creating an irritating chime that did not sit well with the droning sound that came out of the monster's mouth.

It crawled out some more, revealing its hunched body. A

single row of spikes trailed across its back as the monster's elephant-shaped feet left heavy imprints in the bloodstained sand. As it stood up, towering over Darvell, it just surpassed the stone wall where the other dragons sat and roared with enthusiasm.

The monster looked down and buzzed wildly as Darvell took a few moments to take in his enemy. He gripped his greatsword and ran towards the monster, roaring madly, before a burst of purple fire sent him flying backwards. The dragons inside the stadium roared in fear as the monster bowed to its knees, the once red wine eyes morphing into a deep purple.

Walking out of the fire was an armored man, who was a bit taller than Darvell. He had a thick scar over one of his eyes and a gaping hole that never closed. His armor seemed to eat at the light around it, like a shadow that wanted to see the sun shrivel up and cease to shine. He carried no weapons on him, but his scarred hands let off the occasional flicker of dark, purple fire. His lower jaw was made out of the same iron of his armor and flexed as he smiled. Darvell opened his eyes and felt his body ache as a memory he never had banged against his head. He saw the vile face of the man, his smug smile and mocking aura emanating from him as the fire burned behind him.

"Hello Darvell," Zlo said, his voice chilling his bones. "It's good to finally meet you."

"Why are you here?" Darvell roared, showing off his sharp teeth. "How the hell did you find me?"

"Magic is a wonderful tool isn't it? Those who are smart enough, and wield it, can see the infinite potential all at their fingertips," Zlo mocked as he curled his fingers, the burning purple flames dancing around his hand. "However, I did not come here to talk about magic. I came here to tell you that your path given by the gods is futile. Your quest to end my life will only be the end of yours."

"Your threats don't scare me!" Darvell barked as he got up. "I will kill you!"

Zlo stared at Darvell as he put his hand down. Darvell gulped as he looked into Zlo's remaining eye, the vacant and cold stare making him feel insignificant.

"Then so be it," Zlo declared as he stepped forward. "Your life ends now."

Zlo put out his hand as a thin pillar of black energy swirled upwards, black smoke drifting off it until it suddenly condensed into a thin pole. There was no extravagant design to the pole, no runes of mystical origin or etchings to recount past battles. It was only a thin pole of black magic. Zlo grabbed it and walked over to Darvell.

"What are you going to do?" Darvell jeered. "A big stick isn't going to do much against—"

Zlo swung the pole towards Darvell as the black energy around the end morphed into the head of a warhammer. The attack found purchase against Darvell's ribcage, sending out a stream of blood from his mouth. Zlo pulled the hammer back and everyone, paralyzed with fear, saw the warhammer head shift again as it took the form of a greataxe. Darvell, groaning in pain, caught a glimpse of the shift and quickly put up his greatsword to block the attack. Zlo smirked as he quickly stepped backward, causing Darvell to waste the block. Zlo grabbed the handle and twisted his hands as the greataxe shifted once more, taking the shape of a barbed spear. He thrust it forward as the screams of dragons roared through Darvell's head.

Suddenly, he heard Zlo scowl as he saw the spearhead pierce through the shimmering body of Eris, her clothing turning to dust to reveal the battered body of Lilith. He could see that she was in the same armor he had seen her wearing before, but much more tattered and broken. On her back were two wing stumps and between them was the head of the spear Zlo was wielding. Lilith's eyes were covered by a black silk ribbon stitched into her face.

"So you went to him to protect him?" Zlo growled. "Even after he cast you away?"

"I'd like to think of myself as a guardian angel," Lilith whispered, coughs of blood dripping between her words.

Zlo and Darvell watched as she faded away, crumpling into sand that fell to the floor. The black silk ribbon drifted to the ground, Zlo scowling as he recalled his spear.

"This is what I get for making a show out of this," Zlo said as he looked around. He looked to see his arm flicker in and out. "You have wasted my time so I won't be able to kill you with my own hands. The Cavern Lurker will kill you and everyone else."

Darvell looked up and saw Zlo snap his fingers, disappearing as the monster let out the same droning sound as it twitched wildly. It opened its mouth as a swarm of giant flies flew from it. The flies flew around, screeching and attacking the dragons in the stadium. Inpulsa raised her claw as a barrier of blue light crystalized above the arena ground. They watched as a large cloud of flies that had escaped flew towards the Citadel. Rubrum reared up and turned to the guards behind him.

"Make sure these creatures do not harm those in the city. Have a group bring the Council to safety and we can—"

"No Rubrum," Ignis interjected. "My grandson is down there. I will not leave him behind."

"You won't be able to fight that thing again, Ignis," Aeris pleaded angrily. "We need someone else to stop it."

"Then allow us," Theia offered as the rest of the group approached them. "Darvell is just as important to us as he is to you."

Ignis ground his teeth as he saw the cloud of shadow creatures bang against the blue barrier. He looked towards Rubrum and the other Council members and sighed.

"Put them in there Inpulsa," Ignis commanded as he turned to face Theia. "Please save my grandson."

They all nodded as Inpulsa put her hand around them and

closed her fist, a puff of blue smoke causing them to disappear into the sand pit. Ignis turned to the rest of the Council and narrowed his gaze.

"Come, while they fight this beast let us go to the Citadel. We will not lose our homes again."

The group appeared as a cloud of blue smoke dispersed around them. All about them, the creatures of shadow darted with such chaotic movements that trying to focus on one was impossible. Some tried to dive-bomb them and attack, but the aura of holy light that Aurelina let off turned them into dust once they got too close. They looked around for Darvell or the monster.

Suddenly, a burst of fire exploded as a horrible buzz filled the air. They dashed towards the source and saw Darvell dodging the claws of the monster. Every strike it took, it plunged its pincers into the sand. Darvell looked back and dashed towards them as he pulled out his revolvers. He fired a shot into the flesh of the monster, watching it pass through and hit the barrier and the shadow creatures.

"Am I glad to see all of you," Darvell praised as he fired another shot.

"Likewise," Olius remarked as he pulled out his book. "Okay everyone, focus on the big thing and we'll worry about the things flying around us later."

As the others went to fight the creature, Olius curled his fingers and summoned his new staff. The beautiful design of the shepherd's staff and the floating opal put a grin on his face as he fired a bright blue beam of energy at the monster. As it hit, a dent formed in its flesh as a dark purple bruise formed. The monster let out a gurgle of pain as Regibus pulled out his flintlock from thin air. He fired one shot, aiming for the gut of the creature. The shot richoted off the insect-like armor of the creature, and into the shadow creatures flying above. He cursed and put away his flintlock, instead forming his cutlass from thin air as well. He ran towards the creature as Theia and Jade, from opposite sides of the monster, fired their arrows and bullets. Theia widened her magic eye and looked for the soft spots in the creature's armor while Jade fired off bullets to create cracks.

Chantal and Hector both flanked from the left as they attacked one of its legs. Hector slashed and stabbed with his spear, feeling his lighter armor let him keep up with Chantal. Chantal summoned her brother's axe and wielded it with both hands. She took one large swipe across the Achilles' heel of the monster, forcing it to buckle down as the ethereal edge of the axe slashed through the thick hide of the foot. The creature roared and smacked the pincers on its mouth together before it took both of its claws and dragged them through the sand, trying to hit one of them.

The claws moved the sand as Regibus dove forward, trying not to get dragged under and get crushed. He reached the right foot of the monster and jabbed his cutlass into it. As he did, a stream of water began to wrap around him, enveloping him completely as Cutthroat appeared, his skeletal grin showing off golden teeth. He dragged the cutlass downwards, cutting through the hide as the monster groaned in pain. The monster raised its left foot and stomped it, sending Chantal and Hector a few feet back as it raised its right foot and flung Cutthroat through the air.

Meanwhile, Aurelina fired off beams of light at the shadowy creatures that tried to attack the others as she soared above the pit. As she saw the monster stomp its foot and send Hector and Chantal back, she thrust her hand towards the monster as an arc of holy fire flew through the air, scorching its face. Darvell took flight and moved through the fire, taking his greatsword and slashing it across the giant right eye. White puss burst forth as the monster swiped at Darvell, knocking him back to the ground.

Infuriated, the monster moved its claw towards Aurelina and tried to snap her wing. She tried to dodge, but wasn't able to escape its clutches. Hector gasped and raised his shotgun towards the eye of the monster. He fired and watched as the bullets lodged themselves into the eyes, creating smaller streams of white puss and successfully preventing the creature from snipping off Aurelina's wing. Unfortunately, it was able to cripple her, sending her into a downward spiral to the ground. Olius quickly looked up and thrust his staff upwards as a thin cloud formed below Aurelina, slowing down her descent as she passed through the cloud, causing it to poof out of existence.

Cutthroat, as he flew through the air, threw his arm forth as a tendril of murky seawater burst forth from his fingertips and wrapped around the claw of the monster. He held on for dear life as he swung back to the ground, taking his flintlock and firing into the creature. The monster let out a feverish buzzing sound, disorganized and chaotic, causing everyone to cover their ears in pain and agony. The monster reared up and slammed its claws in the sand, sending a shockwave through the ground that sent those on the ground falling on their backs.

As they fell over, Jade ended up staring directly at the monster's two beady purple eyes. The sound of the buzzing began to hurt and stiffen her body. She felt cold and unable to move as she became paralyzed with fear. The monster raised both of its claws and slammed them both onto Jade, crushing her beneath the sand as her final breath left her mouth.

Darvell, recovering from the droning sound, watched the monster crush Jade. His eyes widened as the grip on his greatsword tightened. His wings stretched outward and the fire that flew off his wings began to turn white as it flickered violently in the air. Darvell leaped up, taking flight near the head of the beast and raised his greatsword, igniting it with a blinding flash of similar white fire. Darvell roared once more, twirling his blade before sinking it into the monster's head. Darvell's strike, guided by his blind wrath, caused him to continue downwards with no resistance, slicing the entire creature even farther until he reached the ground and slammed into it with an earthshaking thud. The sensation of shattered bones rippled across Darvell, starting from his legs and into the arms that refused to let go of the blade. The creature let out one last gurgle of pain as it slowly separated, strings of dark green flesh and sinew coming undone as the two pieces of the monster hit the sandy arena, sending a small cloud of sand across the pit.

Darvell roared once more, letting out a jet of white fire that flew upwards and caused the shadowy creatures flying around to wilt in the light. The sand around Darvell had turned into smoky glass while the blade of his sword shattered in two, the sound breaking the silence. Darvell collapsed immediately, blood trickling from the sides of his mouth as sweat drenched his beard and hair. The ring on his finger was still there, glittering in the torchlight as Darvell's body lay lifeless.

Cutthroat disappeared as Regibus dashed towards where Jade was slain. The others congregated towards Darvell, slowly and reluctantly as they stepped around the smoldering glass. Regibus looked through the sand and unexpectedly found no blood or any sign of Jade's corpse. He sifted through the sand, crying and bawling as he hoped to find something. Suddenly, the sand in front of him began to accumulate as Jade's face appeared, followed by her body. Once the sand stopped moving, Jade breathed in and coughed. Regibus, shocked and stunned, picked her up and hugged her.

"Hold...hold on," Jade wheezed. "Give me a minute to recuperate."

"I thought I lost you!" Regibus cried. "Don't scare me like that!"

"I'm fine," Jade consoled weakly as she coughed out some sand. "See how important it is to know if we're okay?"

"I'm still not telling you what the deal was," Regibus said as he clutched her.

"Fair enough," Jade groaned. "Where's Darvell?"

Regibus bit his lip as Jade looked at him. She then directed her attention to the group behind them. She got up slowly. As she walked over Regibus slowly followed behind. She walked through the group as they parted to let her see Darvell. She saw his cold body laid across the glass ground he had created. Jade shuffled closer, falling to her knees as the glass beneath them cracked a little bit. Her body shook as tears slowly dripped from her eyes. Hector held Aurelina, who was quietly crying while Theia and Chantal looked away, Theia helping Chantal conceal her tears. Olius gulped quietly as he took off his hat while Regibus did his best to hold back his sadness. They all stood there as the barrier shattered above them, the particles of magic dust falling downwards, like artificial snow, as the sound of wings filled the air.

CHAPTER 25

The medical bay was cold and dark. None of the beds were occupied, all except for one. A single light emanated from a large brass-colored candle that sat on a chamberstick. It was placed on a dark bedside table along with some jerky in a small brown bag, a glass of water on a white doily, and Darvell's revolvers laid one on top of the other. Darvell rested on the bed, stripped of his regular attire and wearing a white linen shirt and pants. On the other side of the bed was his sword, broken in twain from the violent heat it endured, and a small floating orb that glowed at the pace of a slow heartbeat, occasionally letting out a rhythmic hum. A large blanket had been placed over him to keep him warm and ward off the cold temperatures of the medical bay.

Aeris walked over to his body and placed the back of her hand on his forehead. She shivered slightly at the frigid temperature he emitted. She inspected the candle and saw that the small runes inscribed in it had melted away. She took out another candle and lit it, the runes on it glowing a dim red. The heat around the room increased and she left with the melted candle in her hand. She walked out into the hall and made her way through the dark corridors, the sound of her steps echoing softly in the still air.

She opened a door to her room where Jade and Ignis were seated around a table of black tea and lemon bar cakes. Jade's eyes were puffy from crying while Ignis looked like he had not slept in a few days. Although he was still breathing, albeit slowly, Darvell had shown no signs of movement or life in the two months after the battle. Aeris sat down between them and picked up her tea.

"He's been doing a bit better. The cold that he was suffering from is settling down a little bit. I'm surprised he didn't go into shock during that stunt he pulled."

"He has a strong will," Ignis said, trying to convince himself. "He knew what he was doing."

"He didn't know," Jade said abruptly. "Nor did he care. I just can't believe he would do something so suicidal for me."

"You're right, Jade," Aeris said before she sipped her tea. "I'm sure he had a bunch of pent-up anger in him and it just let loose seeing you supposedly meet your demise."

"I thought he could have handled it," Jade quietly stated. "But he believed I really died and he..."

"Let us talk about something else, dear child. I feel, nay, know that Darvell will get better. We just need to have a bit more hope in him and the gods that watch over us," Ignis replied with weaker stoicism in his voice.

Aeris nodded in agreement while Jade sighed deeply, expressing her worried acceptance of the situation at hand.

"I believe that it's time to talk about something that may have been on your mind for a while, Ignis."

Ignis looked up at Aeris with confusion on his face. He put down his cup and listened intently.

"As we know, you still don't have an heir to the throne. There were also a bunch of marriage festivities ordered under our noses before any of us came to an agreement."

"Argenti always did have a fondness for parties..." Ignis chuckled.

"We still have the groom but no bride. We can't leave this event out in the open and you still need an heir."

"Where are you going with this Aeris?"

"You'll know what I'm talking about. We'll settle this when Darvell wakes up. For now I suggest that we all get some sleep, staying up late won't bring him out of his coma."

Ignis and Jade got up and thanked Aeris for the tea. They left the room and stood by the doorway. Neither Jade nor Ignis moved away from the door, awkwardly looking at each other.

"Are you going to..." Ignis softly stated.

"Going to do what?" Jade asked sheepishly.

"Are you going to go see how he is?"

Jade looked down at her feet and nodded her head. Ignis smiled awkwardly and looked away.

"You want to come with me?" Jade asked.

"I would like to."

A shining light began to glow over Darvell's eyes. He covered his eyes in defiance and groaned.

"Ugh...five more minutes at least."

"There's no time to sleep when you're on an adventure, son," Marius said as Darvell was shaken awake.

Darvell opened his eyes and propped himself up to see the Oracle, Scales, and his father surrounding him. He got up from the cold hard floor and saw that he was back in the *Realm of the Ancients*. He rubbed his eyes and saw that he was also still in his corporeal form.

"I guess you noticed you're still alive," Scales said. "That's good..."

He promptly slapped Darvell across the face with all of his force, knocking Darvell back to the ground.

"Ow! What the hell was that for?"

"You almost died!" Scales roared. "You're lucky that ring saved you from nearly bursting into a ball of fire but don't push it!"

"Old Flame, please, relax. Allow me to talk to my child," Marius asked.

Scales gestured to go ahead and Marius turned towards and also slapped Darvell cleanly across the face.

"Are you trying to kill your grandpa?! You've been giving him heart attack after heart attack! I'm dead and somehow I've been having irregular heartbeats!"

"Again, ow!" Darvell yelled.

"You two have no control," Oracle reprimanded. "Let me explain what happened Darv—"

Darvell was slapped for one last time by the Oracle as she tried to lunge at him, being held back by Marius and Scales.

"You let my daughter die!" the Oracle screamed. "Not directly, but you could have saved her!"

"God damn it, can someone tell me what happened!" Darvell yelled as he rubbed his cheeks from the slaps.

The Oracle dusted herself off and sighed as Marius and Scales let her go.

"You almost died Darvell. You used up so much of your magic in one sitting that when you stopped using it, you went into some sort of relapse and fell unconscious. You have been stuck in bed for almost two months now."

"I...I died!"

"No, unconscious," Scales said. "You somehow accessed a type of fire that was first created when the world was brought into existence, a flame of pure white energy."

"White fire?" Darvell asked as he softly pounded his chest.

"You could have died!" Marius angrily stated. "No one should even exist after using all of that magic."

"Anyway," Scales continued to explain, "we had to prevent

your friends from using any magic to heal you right away since it wouldn't give you the proper time to heal your body. We didn't want you walking around fighting anything with broken arms. Actually, you pretty much broke everything; you really did a number on yourself."

"So can I go back now?"

"Before you do, can you tell Ignis that I forgave him?" Marius asked. "I haven't been able to visit him at all."

Darvell nodded as the Oracle approached him. Darvell prepared for another slap to the face, but watched as the Oracle placed her forefinger on his forehead and her thumb on the bridge of his nose.

"Please don't do this ever again."

Jade pulled up a wooden stool and sat next to Darvell. She could see that he was growing a thick and unkempt beard. She sighed and laid her head across his chest. She could hear his heart beat slowly and quietly, barely making its presence through his thick scaly skin. Jade tried to keep her eyes open, but found it hard as the soft sound of the halls swayed her to sleep. Ignis watched her fall asleep and sighed as he went over to another bed and reached for a blanket. He placed it over her and left them alone. He walked back to the main hall and found himself with Aeris again, who was standing outside her room.

"So, what do you think of her?" Aeris asked.

"I'll tell you this much, you really do know how to pick them."

"So does Darvell."

Ignis stopped in his tracks and chuckled slightly.

"I feel that it's time I open up the bloodline."

He left Aeris as he walked towards his room, the cold air of the medical hall following him like a ghost. Jade rested her head on Darvell's chest, breathing deeply as she waited for any response from him. She lifted her head and stared at his face. During the two months, he had grown a full beard that was thick and unruly. She took out a brush from one of her cloak pockets and began to groom it, loosening the tangled hairs.

"I hope you wake up soon Darvell, it's been awfully lonely without you," Jade mumbled as she listened to his slow breaths. "Since I don't have you around, I don't feel all that welcome in the group. Regibus tries to get me into the conversations but I...I'd rather have you here instead."

She finished combing his beard and put away the brush. She glared at his now smooth beard and felt the urge to add some flair. She summoned two small knobs of brass and began to braid two strands of beard hair, closing off the ends with the knobs. Jade wrapped the blanket tighter around her body to shield herself from the cold. The rhythmic beating of the orb gently danced into her ears. She waited patiently for Darvell to wake, biding her time cleaning her gun, pacing around the room, trying to fix the shattered sword as she watched for any signs of life from Darvell. She walked over to Darvell and looked at the floating crystal. She could feel in her heart that he wasn't going to wake up anytime soon. She leaned over and gave him a soft kiss on the lips and started to leave. As she stepped out into the hall, a nostalgic voice spoke behind her.

"Holy shit, I have beard braids," Darvell groaned.

Jade stopped in her tracks and she slowly turned around to see Darvell playing with his beard braids. Jade began to cry as she ran up to him, jumping onto the bed and hugging him close.

"It looks like someone missed me," Darvell joked through his mumbling. "Have I been—"

"Don't do that ever again! Don't scare me like that!" Jade sobbed as she hugged him tighter.

Darvell gulped quietly as he slowly returned the hug. He quietly played with her hair until he whispered in her ear.

"Can I get up now?" Darvell asked.

"Just a few more minutes please."

"I have to go use the bathroom."

Jade opened her eyes and abruptly moved away, chuckling quietly.

"Sorry."

She got off the bed and Darvell slowly moved towards the edge. He wobbled off the bed and touched the floor, stumbling to keep himself up. The feeling of the cold floor made him shiver as he turned to Jade.

"Do you need help?" Jade said as she helped him stand up straight.

"No, no. I'm good," Darvell replied as he made his way towards the hall.

He took a few steps before he stumbled and fell to the floor. A small spot started to form around his pants. He lifted his head towards Jade, who was trying not to laugh.

"Is that offer for help still available?"

Jade helped Darvell with a change of pants and guided him towards the others. She propped him onto her shoulder as he weighed down on her. He weighed so much Jade had to make her legs iron so they wouldn't buckle. They made it to the common hall where everyone was eating a late meal. They walked through the door and everyone lifted their heads and saw Darvell walk in with Jade, a big goofy smile on his face.

"You're alive!" Hector said as he stumbled out of his chair to hug him.

"Someone owes me five gold pieces," Theia jokingly said as she and Chantal walked towards them.

The others got up from the table and greeted him with open arms. Before they could talk anymore, the entire Council walked into the room. They walked in their human forms as they confronted Darvell and the others.

"It looks like our hero has woken up," Rubrum stated

cheerfully. "After the incident, we have deliberated and decided that Darvell still has to marry."

"Didn't he just save all of you?" Olius asked. "Can't you give him a break?"

"I still need an heir, wizard," Ignis stated. "But I have decided to let the decision be more inclusive. So we decided to ask all of you to join in the decision."

"Really!" Darvell cheered.

"Well, the problem is you can't be in the decision. It would violate a lot of the other laws we have, not to mention we are breaking some right now," Frio replied.

"Oh," Darvell ended with confusion in his voice.

"So if you could all come with us we would like to solidify this as soon as possible," Argenti beamed. "We already have the marriage planned out and most of the festivities have been ordered."

Everyone looked at each other and followed the Council. Jade guided Darvell to the table and sat him down in front of a plate of prepared steak and soup. She kissed him again and made her way towards the others. Darvell looked down at the plate and began to eat slowly, trying to ignore the silence of the room.

A few hours had passed and Darvell had finished off a few plates of food and regained some of his strength. He got up and decided to head back to the wagon to get a change of clothes. As he boarded the wagon, he walked around and saw that Olius, Hector, and Regibus were sitting around the firepit drinking beers. Regibus had red and stuffy eyes as he reached for his drink, trembling as he made his way.

"Where's everyone else?" Darvell asked.

"Aurelina wanted them all to stay and help with the

decorations," Hector replied as he put down his drink. "We decided that we wanted to give you one last day of being a bachelor."

"What's that mean?"

"It means being single, but you won't be having the title for long." Olius chuckled.

"I suggest we get started, what do you want to do first, Darvell?"

Darvell thought hard on what he wanted to do but nothing was clicking. He shrugged and took a seat next to Regibus, who was staring intently into the fire. Olius furrowed his brows and sighed.

"You just want to drink beer?" Olius sassed as he crossed his arms.

"Pretty much," Darvell explained. "I don't really know what I'd like to do."

"I could have stayed and helped with the decorations but I stayed out of the kindness of my heart for you, and all you want to do is drink beer?"

"Yeah," Darvell said as he sipped his drink.

"I'm going to go help the girls with the decorations," Olius said as he finished his beer and left the room.

"What about you two?" Darvell asked as he waved his drink at Hector and Regibus.

"I'd rather sit here and drink," Hector answered.

"Same here," Regibus glumly responded.

Darvell stared at Regibus suspiciously, wondering why he was so sad. Despite trying to come up with a reason, he couldn't figure one out. He gave up and continued to drink his beer before going to take a bath. An hour passed and Darvell walked out of the washroom and towards his room. As he walked in, he could see, sprawled out on his bed, a set of fancy clothing. He could see that there was a long brass robe laid across the bedclothes. The cuffs of the sleeves were embroidered with silver lines and simple designs of snapdragon flowers rising across the sleeves. Darvell picked up the cloak and turned it around, seeing a dragon's talon embroidered onto it. Inside the palm of the dragon claw was an upright lavender flower. Across the rest of the bed was a much nicer white linen shirt, a black pair of pants, and a belt with a golden buckle and rubies cast into the rim.

"I'm liking the new clothes but this cloak is too elaborate for my taste," Darvell remarked.

"It's a shame, I used the same one when I got married," Ignis said as he walked into the room. "It's good to see that you're doing fine."

"It's good to see you are not so angry," Darvell joked as he put down the robe.

"I suppose it is a nice change of pace." Ignis chuckled. "May I ask you something, Darvell?"

"Shoot."

"Why are you on this journey? I know you are destined to kill Zlo and save us all but why are you doing it?"

Darvell sat down on the bed and scratched his chin.

"At first it was solely out of vengeance. It still is; he killed my dad after all. Although, after living with my friends for so long, getting to know them and them getting to know me, I feel that I should do this for everyone."

"You are a lot nobler than you let on, you know." Ignis smiled as he nodded his head in agreement. "Speaking of Marius, did you ever meet him?"

"Physically? I didn't get the chance to. I did meet him as a ghost though."

"So he has passed," Ignis said glumly.

"He sends his regards by the way. He also wants you to stop being so hard on yourself."

Ignis looked up wide-eyed and smiled, a single tear trailing down his face. He rubbed his eyes and laughed quietly.

"I guess he has forgiven me. Darvell, I'd like to give you something for your marriage. A gift of some sort."

Ignis opened his palm and turned it downwards to the floor. A bright flash of fire burst forth and a sword slowly began to fall out. Darvell watched in amazement as Ignis handed him a new greatsword. The handle was black with a brass pommel spike on the end. Unlike his old sword, which had hooks and was rather broad and flat, the greatsword was long, sleek, and had a glowing shine. Written across the entire length of the blade was a script that Darvell couldn't read. He traced his finger across the engravings and the sword began to light on fire.

"This sword was given to me a long time ago, before dragons even lived in communities like the one right now or those of long ago. I had met a kind and old blacksmith who was born with arcane magic in his blood. He was a skilled sorcerer who could bend the elements to his will, yet he decided that he wanted to work with swords and armor. I met him on one of my journeys across the Four Kingdoms, living on the outskirts of an old town in a snowy forest. I was able to take refuge in his home and he had given me the best hospitality. We were the best of friends and he decided to give me this sword as a gift."

"What happened to him?"

"Oh nothing, he's fine. Like I said, he has arcane blood in him so he's living a pretty long life."

"Huh."

"Anyway, this sword was forged to withstand any flame and to always remain sharp. I would like to pass this down to you. If Marius were still here, he would have had it and passed it down to you."

Darvell raised the sword and held it in the air. A quiet, metallic hum could be heard coming from it. He twirled it around and felt like he was holding nothing at all as he cut through the air.

"Thank you so much. Now I have two swords!"

"About that..." Ignis winced.

Darvell turned towards Ignis with a concerned look on his face.

"Your old sword broke and we tried to fix it but Frio wouldn't let us do it. He said it was a relic of the best dragon he had the honor to meet. He now has it in his weapons museum."

"Okay then," Darvell sighed. "I'm back to one sword again."

"It seems so. I'll leave you be for now Darvell. I suggest you start getting ready, the wedding is tomorrow."

Ignis left the room and left Darvell alone in his room. He looked back at the cloak and picked it up again. He shrugged and began to put it on.

CHAPTER 26

The halls of the Citadel were full of life as the day of the wedding came around. All sorts of dragons decorated the walls with colorful banners and replaced the old flowers with fresh new ones. Chefs raced down the halls with trays of food, carts packed with desserts and pitchers and jugs full of drinks, all towards a grand dining room. The roof of the room had two large golden chandeliers with diamond pendeloques hanging and dangling whimsically in the air. The servers began to set up the large table, affixing the white tablecloth, lighting the numerous candles set on silver candelabras, placing plates and utensils evenly between each other and extensive plates of food all across the table. The small musical group on the stage consisted of one large wooden harp with golden flowers imprinted onto the broad part, a couple of lutes and dulcimers, a small section of fiddlers and two expert lyre players. They were practicing a smooth and quiet song as a small green dragon conducted the musical ensemble. Among the towering dragons, Olius examined the tables and saw that they were dragon sized.

"Something wrong, Olius?" Argenti asked as she walked up to him.

"Yeah, how are we going to eat if everything is so big?"

"No worries, we'll be dining in human form. In fact, for most of the wedding we'll be in human form since our two newlyweds can't turn into full dragons."

"I see. You seem very excited planning all of this."

"I'm overjoyed!" Argenti trilled. "I've always dreamed of planning a wedding of this proportion."

"I feel like I've seen this arrangement before," Olius remarked, smirking as he looked back at Argenti.

"You have?" Argenti asked, her voice rising as she spoke.

"I remember this from a book I read called *A Marriage Beneath a Hundred Suns.*"

"You read it too!" Argenti squealed. "Oh it was such a wonderful book!"

"Wasn't it?" Olius smiled. "I felt that it captured the beauty of the desert wedding wonderfully."

"Would you like to help me set up? I could use more input to make this wedding memorable."

"Of course I'll help, I've always wanted to help plan a wedding as well."

As Olius joined Argenti in the wedding planning, the rest of the room continued to set up. All around the halls, an atmosphere of joy could be felt. The glittering of the golden streamers reflected the bright candlelight and the smell of traveling confectionaries enticed everyone's noses. As the hours passed, the time for the wedding was arriving. A few gold dragons went around the halls and dimmed the candlelight, moving their claws over the candles. Dragons from all over the Citadel flocked towards a ginormous room towards the top of the building, the sound of flapping wings filling everyone's ears.

Two large wooden doors opened up to a room full of marble columns, each engraved with images of dragons. The ten columns held up the roof of the room, where an expanding painting of three major dragon gods hung above. The painting portrayed three different dragons circling around the map of the world. The first dragon was painted with its wings extended outwards over the world. The flaps of the dragon were sprinkled with glistening gems against a black background. The scales on the dragon magically changed every few seconds, cycling through different colors. The eyes stared down stoically on the world below, changing between different colors for dawn and dusk. To the left of the world was a female dragon, with rows of platinum scales adorning her body. She carried in her right claw a leather tome and with her left claw she held up one portion of the world. The other dragon had five chromatic heads. The heads were intertwined with each other and the dragon held a spear in her left claw and with her right she held up the other half of the world.

As the dragons entered the room, they transformed their bodies into human shapes and walked towards the pews. Although they all wore expensive clothing, each outfit was unique to its wearer. Elegant dresses sewn with jewels and diamonds of expansive colors walked alongside graceful robes detailed with crests of family shields, each one tailored to their wearer as they floated around the pews. The playing of an organ could be heard from above the doors. The pipes shone against the floating lights in the room. A single greying, red-skinned man played the organ. A quiet harmony rang through the warm air as he gingerly moved his fingers across the keys. Aurum, in his human form, walked over and smiled as he listened to the music.

"You always played beautiful music, Father Satyrus."

"Well you know, the old ship sails on the scarabs' dung to swallow the snake and the sound is the sound we hear on the morning star."

Aurum patted him on the shoulder and laughed.

"Of course it does, of course."

As he continued to play the organ, the last remaining dragons sat down in the pews. The rustling of wings and tails quieted and the ringing of three bells, one followed by the other, completely silenced the room. As the ringing of bells rang through the air,

Aurum walked along the middle of the pews, carrying a sword made of pure gold. Its handle was made of white marble with a thin silk ribbon wrapped around the blade. As Aurum walked through the pews, the organ played a somber melody that floated gently through the air. The rising of the music slipped into the hearts of its listeners and slowly faded as Aurum reached a black altar along the back wall of the room. A large red banner hung above the altar, a single black sword painted onto it. Aurum raised the sword and jabbed it into the socket of the table. The hilt burst into a rainbow fire, burning brightly as the silk ribbon was slowly consumed by the fire, not burning away at the touch of the flame.

"Today marks the continuation of a bloodline of brass, our brothers and sisters of judgment and strength. We have found rejoicing in the eternal fire that the three prime dragons have provided, for they watch over this wedding to ensure that the bloodline of brass shall continue. The time for the bond has come and may we all wish luck to the two who will be wed."

"Long live the Old Flame, the Wise Flame, and the War Flame," responded the dragons in the pews.

"But first, a few words from the holy scriptures recited by Father Balbutire."

Small groans could be heard in the crowd as a small green dragon walked to a stone pulpit and opened a dusty book. He set aside his knobbly cane and smiled.

"Good...good...good morn....good morning every..."

The groans grew louder as the priest continued to read from the book. As the procession went on, Darvell was in another room not far off. He was sitting in a chair absentmindedly listening to Olius as he tried to explain the wedding process. As Olius explained, all Darvell could hear was the muffled sounds of talking behind him.

"—and finally you take the ring, put the ring on her finger, and you're married," Olius concluded." Got it Darvell?"

"Huh?" Darvell mumbled. "Oh yeah of course, no problem."

Olius looked at Darvell angrily and crossed his arms.

"Trust me! I know what I'm doing," Darvell said with a smug face.

"Okay then, where's the ring?"

Darvell stopped smiling and gulped. He reached for his pockets and searched them.

"Where did I put it? It has to be here somewhere," Darvell mumbled frantically.

Olius put out his hand and showed Darvell a golden ring in his palm. On the inside of the ring was a small inscription that read *Sanctum Vinculum.* Darvell looked at the ring and chuckled as he reached for it.

"Please keep it safe. You aren't getting another one," Olius reminded him.

"Understood, when are we going to start by the way?" Darvell asked as he tapped his foot. "I'm getting antsy."

Olius walked over to the hallway and listened to the reading.

"An...and the...and the drag...the dragon fell from...from the sky."

"It might be awhile before you get out there so there's no problem. Hector and Regibus should be here right now," Olius mentioned as he looked around.

"Hey, Olius? I have a question," Darvell hedged.

"Yeah, what is it?"

"While I was knocked out, Scales told me that if I got married, my mission wouldn't be able to be continued," Darvell explained as Olius rubbed his chin. "Is this marriage going to do anything to stop that?"

"Well I've read my fair share of history books where adventurers had to stop since they now had family to take care of. However, that problem won't affect us." Olius chuckled.

"What? Why?"

"Just wait and see."

Suddenly, Hector and Regibus walked through the door. Regibus was stumbling as Hector helped him walk.

"Where have you two been?" Olius asked sternly.

"Drinking," Regibus coldly said as he took a seat.

"You don't look wasted," Darvell pointed out. "What about you Hector?"

"I found him drinking at the bar in the recession room."

"We don't have time for this," Olius groaned. "I'll just make a tonic and—"

The ringing of bells sounded through the air as Aurum's voice rang out.

"Thank you Father. Now, the wedding will commence!"

Olius swore under his breath and turned to everyone else.

"Okay, here is what we're going to do. Darvell, go out and stand by the door. For the rest of us, let's put on the attire and meet him there."

They all nodded and quickly readied themselves. The music out in the room began to play as Aurum was preparing a drink on the table. He broke open a pomegranate and poured the seeds and juice into a chalice. He recited a prayer in the native dragon tongue and poured a clear wine into the chalice. As the music switched from a blaring sonata to a quiet and harmonious serenade, Aurum lifted the cup in the air and began to speak.

"We signify this matrimony with the blood from the heart of the Old Flame, whose love for all dragonkind forged what became the strongest bond that we aspire to emulate. May the marriage of these two aim to do the same."

Suddenly, Darvell was pushed slightly forward as he was followed by Hector, Olius, and Regibus. He could see a little glowing spot in front of the table and he walked towards it. His feet suddenly froze and he couldn't move.

Darvell don't panic, Scales's voice urged as it nestled into Darvell's mind. *Just don't move from there and it'll all be okay.*

Darvell nodded subtly and felt the magic release from his legs.

"Do you, Darvell Letholdus, accept this marriage as your own?" Aurum asked as he handed him the chalice.

"Yes," Darvell responded.

"Then drink from the chalice and seal your bond to the tree of the universe."

Darvell drank from the chalice and tried to drink all of it. Aurum yanked it from his hands before he could finish. As he wiped the rim, four people began to walk out from the other side. Theia, Chantal, and Aurelina were following a lady in a sparkling white dress. The bottom brim of the dress was lined with rows of dark green jewels spiraling around the puffy skirt. The bodice was decorated with flowing lines of gold that made their way to the back of the dress and neatly tied themselves into a silk bow. The face of the bride was covered by a wall of thick silk. The candlelight reflected off the jewels and mesmerized Darvell as he stood there, admiring the beauty. As she stood in front of him, the other girls went down to the pews and sat next to the guys.

"Aren't you excited Hector?" Aurelina gleefully asked as she hooked arms with him.

"I feel kind of giddy," Hector bubbled. "This is the second time I've been surrounded by fancy people and stuff."

"Can you two be quiet?" Theia interjected without looking at them. "I want to see this."

As Aurum handed the woman the cup, she lifted the veil. Darvell's face lit up as the corners of his mouth jolted upward. He watched as she smiled back at him innocently, her eyes twinkling like the green jewels on her dress.

"Do you, Jade Oshiano, accept this marriage as your own?" Aurum asked.

"I—"

Darvell swooped in and embraced her tightly. The people in the pews stood up and cheered loudly as Darvell put her back down, tears rolling down his blushing face. Jade let out one tear and put the cup to her face and drank from it.

"I do."

"Then may the gods guide your love for each other. Give each other the ring and you can live happily ever after."

Darvell pulled out the ring and kneeled as Jade put out her hand. Darvell looked at the hand, nervously trying to figure out which finger he was supposed to put the ring on.

"This one Darvell," Jade whispered as she wiggled her index finger.

Darvell chuckled as he slipped the ring on the finger and stood up. Jade pulled out a glossy black ring and slipped it onto Darvell's hand. He looked at it and saw that the ring was made out of a black granite rock smoothed around the edges to make a ring. Darvell looked at Jade and pointed at the ring.

"We couldn't find anything that wouldn't melt except for this."

"It's okay."

Jade walked closer to Darvell and kissed him. The room exploded in merriment as they kissed in front of the altar. Everyone stood up, clapping and hollering for the newlyweds as Darvell swept Jade off her feet and carried her down the pews. As the two walked out the doors, Darvell took a hard right. The clapping and cheering subsided as they watched them make their way down the hall.

"Isn't the reception hall the other way?" Hector asked.

The music of the reception hall glided into everyone's ears and made their way to their feet as people danced on the floor. Along the table, food was passed around and drinks were poured as conversations ranging from long awaited hellos to intense debates on the proper way to skin a minotaur. Darvell and Jade sat next to each other, calmly eating the food as they were bombarded with compliments from all sides of the table. Right across from them was a happy and intoxicated Ignis sloppily pouring more wine onto the table than into his cup. He switched from speaking human to speaking dragon on different occasions as he told stories from when he was younger. Olius and the other girls talked about how beautiful the ring was and the success of the reception while Darvell led the men along with Chantal into a combination of arm wrestling and intense drinking.

As Darvell and Chantal conceded to a tie after a long battle between spilled beer and wobbling hands, Regibus stumbled towards the music stage and pulled out his guitar. The other musicians quietly played as they listened to his drunken yet equally entertaining plan of playing something more upbeat. After the current song stopped playing, everyone at the table began to murmur and question the lack of music. Suddenly Regibus announced that he would be playing the next song with the accompaniment of the band. Then the sound of a Southern Kingdom song filled everyone's hearts as they felt magically compelled to dance along to the rhythm, tapping their feet before a few got up and found partners to dance with.

As more food was served, more people rose from their plush chairs to dance. Darvell and Jade found themselves dancing together in the middle of the floor as everyone danced around them. Although they were surrounded by everyone at the party, they felt like they were the only people dancing on the floor, unwatched by anyone but the candlelight around them. However, they couldn't help but snicker together as they occasionally saw Hector lead Aurelina in the dance, who somehow forgot to show her radiance on the dance floor. They turned their attention to Ignis who continued to drink heavily with Rubrum and Aurum, who sang the lyrics to the song in their slurred dragon tongue. The two laughed as they watched Zuur and Aeris dance elegantly, almost as if they guided the music with their dance, while Frio and Argenti awkwardly danced together trying to convince everyone else that they'd danced before.

Darvell and Jade returned to being enveloped in each other and continued to dance swiftly along the floor. Their feet floated along the decorated stonework like whispering clouds on a calm beach day. Their embrace was warm like a crackling yule log, which could have mostly been Darvell's doing. The two danced away as the music hung around them, guiding each step of the dance until they found themselves guided by the music outside of the reception hall. They danced out and found themselves alone on a balcony overlooking the city below. They watched time slowly drift before them as the braziers of fire burned away below them. Their hands met on the stone rail and their eyes followed suit. Although Darvell stood a good foot above Jade, he lowered himself onto one knee and embraced her once more.

"I love you Jade," Darvell said

"I...I love you too Darvell." Jade sobbed through Darvell's beard, trying to hide her face from him.

"Oh gods! My head hurts!" Darvell groaned as he lay on the couch.

"Darvell, can you please not speak so loudly, all of our heads are hurting," Jade slurred as she brought over two cups of lemon water.

She sat down next to him and handed him a glass. Darvell took it and downed it in one gulp. He fell back onto the couch and rubbed his temples.

"I have no idea why I have a hangover, I've drank alcohol in larger quantities before."

"They could have served us some liquor meant for dragons. I'm glad it wasn't strong enough to knock us out completely."

"Whatever it was, I'm glad it's out of my system. I never want to drink again."

Jade turned her head and stared at Darvell with her eyebrow raised at his remark.

"Ha ha! I'm just pulling your chain," Darvell laughed. "I was thinking of drinking again."

"Can it be something light? I'd still like to join you but I don't want my head to start pounding again."

"You want to drink and open gifts?" Darvell asked as he walked over for some oranges and champagne.

"I guess it would help us pass the time since no one else is up right now."

After a few minutes of drinking and opening gifts, Darvell and Jade found themselves with a table full of gold coins, small and expensive chalices, gems and jewels of various sizes and colors. The two sat there and drank as they stared at the treasure.

"I'm getting kind of bored with all this gold. We have nothing to spend it on." Darvell sighed as he picked up a coin to flip it around.

"It's still a nice gesture from everyone. We still have some more gifts to open, I saved the best for last," Jade said as she pulled out a small chest and handed it to Darvell.

As he received the chest, Darvell could see that it was made completely out of a dark wood with two brass bands traveling across the lid. He opened the chest and saw a beautifully woven white ribbon folded neatly inside. Darvell took out the ribbon and pulled it out, unfolding it until it extended fully outward. Painted on the white background was a serene black painting of mountains and forests with a dragon flying around the landscape. At the bottom of the chest was a note made out to Darvell.

Dear Darvell,

Take this ribbon to replace your old one. The Council all agreed that to truly bring you in as one of us, an important relic should be given. The background is the story of the first dragon to grace the world and how his indomitable strength inspired warriors to become the best they could be. Keep it as a memento to keep you inspired that you can brave through anything if you keep your spirits high.

Sincerely,
Ignis

"This is a nice gift," Darvell remarked as he tied the ribbon to his sword. "What did you get, Jade?"

Darvell looked around and saw that Jade was no longer sitting with him. He looked around the room and tried to find her. He stood in the middle of the foyer and scratched his chin in confusion. As he looked around, he felt a small tap on his head followed by a small gust of wind. He quickly turned around and grabbed at the air and restrained something.

"Stop! It's me!" Jade said as she revealed herself in Darvell's grasp.

Darvell let go of his grasp on Jade and she fell to the floor. All he could see was her head floating in the air.

"What happened to your body? Who did this?!"

"No, don't worry Darvell. It's just my gift that I got from Aeris."

Jade's body came into view as she let go of a green amulet hanging around her neck by a silver chain. Darvell looked at the ribbon he got and slumped back in his chair, throwing his hands up in the air.

"You got an amulet that makes you invisible! What the hell, all I got was a ribbon!"

"Don't worry; we can go get you some cool stuff later at the bazaar in the city."

"I guess we could do that. When do you think we should start heading out?"

"Maybe after breakfast, I heard that they serve amazing jerky here," Jade explained as she hugged Darvell closely.

"I'm glad I married you. Now let's go get some of that jerky!" Darvell yelled as he jumped off the sofa, running out the door as Jade followed him.

CHAPTER 27

The night sky loomed over a desolate castle that extended its grasp over a broken and tarnished land. The surrounding grass and trees lived in a state of eternal death, constantly rotting but never enjoying the end that comes after. Corpses of animals and people roamed between the scattered boulders and grey murky rivers. The moon shone down on this abandoned piece of earth with a silvery glow, floating permanently above the black stone castle. Tattered purple banners flew around the castle, the foreboding skull of a lion painted on them. Skeletons shuffled aimlessly along the walls of the castle, carrying crossbows and blades. Deep within the halls of the castle, bloodstained rugs decorated the cold dark oak floors as melted candles were smashed onto the walls. Obsidian chandeliers hung from the marble ceilings while carved drawings of dying corpses falling from cliffs decorated every inch of the roof.

Walking down the halls, the sound of quiet footsteps barely filled the emptiness as Ronson made his way towards a grand velvet red door. He grabbed the bronze ring on the lion skull doorknob and banged it against the door. He waited for the doors to open, picking at his putrid black teeth and wiping the gunk against his yellow bones. The creaking of the doors signaled their opening as Ronson walked through them, entering the low lit throne room.

Along the floor was a rug made of blackened skin unfurled towards a throne of solid iron bones where Zlo himself sat, eating an uncooked steak. The juice flowed out of the steak with every incision from Zlo's knife. Upon his throne, Zlo's hellish face did not look up at Ronson as he chewed on his food. He wore his armor on his body, now refined and shined after years of use. Ronson stood there a little bit longer, getting more anxious as Zlo finally finished his meal. Zlo looked up, the hole where his eye would have been looking straight at Ronson's face.

"You could have talked while I was eating, I could have listened to you and enjoyed my meal," Zlo said as he wiped his mouth.

"Oh, I'm sorry. I came to ask about your orders to barricade the fourteenth sea."

"Tell your subordinates to keep an eye out for any ships that aren't theirs," Zlo explained as he waved his hand over the plate in front of him, causing it to disappear. "If they spot one, shoot it down."

"There are also questions about the limited rations you supplied them."

"They are out at sea; they are in the most bountiful ocean that has graced this earth."

"But hunting in an ocean guarded by gods is—"

"The gods are nothing to us!" stormed Zlo, his veins bulging out in frustration.

Ronson swallowed quietly as he stepped back slightly. Zlo breathed in heavily and composed himself. He wiped the sweat on his head, stood from his throne, and walked towards Ronson, laying a grey lifeless hand on his shoulder.

"My anger towards them has gotten the best of me from time to time. Please forgive my sudden outburst, Ronson," Zlo apologized.

"Of course," Ronson stammered.

"Anyway, I would also like to speak to you," Zlo added. "I'm sure you can get my message to your sailors in no time. Do you have some time to spare?"

"I have some to spare."

"Then follow me."

Zlo, followed by Ronson, walked out of the throne room and they made their way through the winding halls. Skeletal servants roamed the corridors, cleaning and tidying up portraits, tables, lanterns throughout the halls.

"Tell me Ronson, do you know why you joined me?" Zlo asked without looking back at him. "Was there a reason you shed your mortal flesh to be among my ranks?"

Ronson stayed quiet as he continued to walk alongside Zlo. They stopped as Zlo stood by a table that was being dusted by a skeleton. He traced his finger against the table and found no dust lingering on his fingertip. Zlo smiled and patted the skeleton as he turned to face Ronson.

"You have no idea do you?" Zlo concluded. "Then let me come up with a reason that may suit you."

They began to walk again, stopping before a large staircase that led towards an open balcony. As they ascended the steps, Zlo continued to speak, his voice echoing through the room.

"What brought you here was nothing more than mere chance. I heard of your talents only because my underlings spoke of you. I didn't search for you and you didn't search for me. You were content pillaging seaports with your crew before one of my underlings introduced you to me. Now here you are, a leading general of my entire sea fleet only through mere chance and through your strength that let you stay here," Zlo summarized as he walked up the staircase, his heavy footfalls breaking the eerie atmosphere.

"Where are you going with this Zlo?"

"Simply put Ronson, humanity and all mortal creatures

are the playthings of gods, especially to the Oracle. They have worked together to undermine the power of individuals like us. I have heard the lie that the gods are immortal and stronger than us, but for countless years I have been able to see them cower at the thought of my power. They are not immortal; simply no one has tried to kill them."

Ronson bit his tongue as Zlo observed him, chuckling to himself as he could see him shake. He motioned to follow him further and Ronson obliged despite his apprehensiveness. Zlo kept quiet as he guided Ronson through the halls, his glowing white grin piercing through the castle's darkness. As they reached the top of a flight of stairs and entered the balcony, Ronson could see the desolate woods and fields that made up Zlo's domain. He peered through the fog of death and saw that in the fields were smattered corpses of angels, devils, and other mythical creatures strewn about the land. Some floated in the rivers while others were impaled on the branches of the dead black trees. As he continued to watch, unable to bear the madness in front of his eyes, he made out the sight of skeletons ripping apart and sewing together different pieces of the corpses.

Ronson breathed heavily, his scattered breathing alerting Zlo. He laughed loudly into the empty air and grabbed Ronson by both of his shoulders. He turned Ronson around to face him and greeted his horrified skull face with a demonic grin, his sharp jaws grinning into whatever remaining soul Ronson had left. The black void that was the hole on the left side of Zlo's face sucked in the light around it, forming a small white slit right down the middle.

"My purpose Ronson, the goal I have given myself is to kill all the gods. Every single one of them!"

TO BE CONTINUED

ABOUT THE AUTHOR

Daniel Cano is a Sophomore at Providence College, studying for a bachelors in Literature and Creative Writing. When he isn't busy making sure his work is handed in, he occupies his time reading books ranging from the ancient to Renaissance era, planning Dungeons & Dragons campaigns and raising his black cat Sabbath.

www.ingramcontent.com/pod-product-compliance
Lightning Source LLC
Chambersburg PA
CBHW052017020726
47501CB00004B/1106